GOD, THE GHETTOS AND A PRETTY FACE

Barbara King

MINERVA PRESS
LONDON
ATLANTA MONTREUX SYDNEY

GOD, THE GHETTOS AND A PRETTY FACE

ISBN 0 75410 338 2

First Published 1998 by
MINERVA PRESS
195 Knightsbridge
London SW7 1RE

Printed in Great Britain for Minerva Press

GOD, THE GHETTOS AND A PRETTY FACE

Chapter One

Around five feet ten inches tall and weighing ten stone, Elliott had vulnerably boyish good looks, was broad shouldered and narrow hipped. His grey blue eyes held a mischievous glint and his hair, cut regulation service length, was thick and dark brown – almost black – with a natural unruly kink. The RAF uniform which he wore suited him, the tailored tunic emphasising his slim athletic build. He had only recently celebrated his twenty-second birthday, and guessed, as he surveyed the group of young men in whose company he found himself, that that made him one of the youngest members. They all wore services uniform, not confined to the British Services, and their ages ranged up to about twenty-five years.

Elliott was the last to board the plane, apart from the two civilians who supervised them and for whom the first two seats were reserved. There was one vacant aisle seat; he slid into it and fastened the seat belt. Loosening his tie he pulled it off and shoved it into his pocket, then unfastened the top button of his shirt. There was a subdued murmur of conversation, introductions being made. The young man in the window seat, wearing an army officer's uniform, glanced at Elliott. He looked away quickly as Elliott noticed him and stared out across the tarmac towards the buildings of the small airport. Elliott studied the profile, and figured that his neighbour was maybe a little older than himself and around the same height, but almost too slimly built. His light to medium brown hair, like his own, was cut to regulation short back and sides, and he had sharp, well-defined features. Elliott noted the stripes and emblems of Captain on the sleeve of this commissioned officer's tunic. The young man looked a little nervous. Elliott's eyes moved on and roved over his other near neighbours. He grinned at the marine on the aisle seat opposite his own, a friendly faced lad of around twenty-five.

'Tommy Purnell,' said the marine introducing himself with an obvious accent, and extending a large hand.

'Chris Elliott,' he responded. 'Scottish?'

'Yeah, it shows, uh?'

'What part?'

'All of me.' His grin widened. 'Inverary. Londoner yourself?'

'Tower Hamlets.'

The engines revved and drowned out the conversation. The plane began to move, edged towards the runway and lined up for the sprint. Elliott's eyes returned to his neighbour who still stared out of the window.

Jan Zader, an army captain in the bomb disposal division, was only a couple of weeks from his twenty-third birthday. He felt a little out of place. The majority of his new colleagues, he thought, came from the uncommissioned ranks and he felt a little apprehensive. There had been little socialising between the commissioned and uncommissioned ranks and he was unsure how to make an approach. Nobody had attempted to make conversation with him, and he was, by nature, reserved. His upbringing had been sheltered, confined to his 'own class'. He was not a snob, and did not usually think in terms of class, simply because he usually worked and socialised within his own. It was not easy to try and break the ice when there appeared to be no common ground.

Elliott weighed up Zader obliquely. Probably he was public school educated and with family traditions to maintain. No doubt he had been to Sandhurst and earned his stripes in exclusive tutorials, bomb disposal was no cushy number, took guts and not a little know-how. Elliott's eyes moved on to the window, he was more accustomed to driving than to being chauffeured. He watched the tarmac and distant buildings flash past as the plane hurtled along the runway and became airborne.

On glancing around at the other passengers, Elliott supposed that, like himself, his new colleagues had been 'killed off', and their previous identities and careers dispensed with. His own 'death' had hardly seemed necessary as he had no one to miss him – a flying accident, naturally; his test plane had exploded as there had been a continued fuel leakage – and he was grateful that he had not been in it! He had had his new identity for only a couple of days, and it seemed strange to use the name Elliott, not McKiery. No doubt he would become accustomed to it.

The overhead instruction lights went out. He unclipped his seat belt, looked at Zader and grinned.

'Not used to being in the passenger seat.'

'No, I suppose not.' Zader looked towards him, his eyes lingering momentarily on the wings on the uniform.

'Chris Elliott,' he said as he offered his hand.

'Jan – Jan Zader,' he spoke hesitantly, his new name almost slipping his memory. 'You're a test pilot?'

'Yeah – least I was.' Elliott shrugged lightly and mused, 'Wonder what we're going to be now?'

Zader shook his head.

'Bomb disposal?'

'Yes.'

'Hope you haven't brought any of your work with you!'

'No,' Zader conceded, half smiling as he began to relax a little. He released his seat belt. 'Will you miss your family?'

'No, I don't have any.'

'I'm sorry.'

'S'okay, I can't miss what I don't have, can I? There was just me and my mam, and she died when I was seventeen, just after I joined up. I can miss my mates in the RAF; maybe they'll even miss me for a while.' He grinned. 'I'll make new mates.' He looked at Zader and offered, 'You want to be the first?'

Zader was unsure that he was serious.

'Don't suppose we've got much in common. Could be interesting.' Elliott sank down in his seat.

'Is that a cockney accent?'

'I wasn't exactly born inside the range of Bow Bells, but I guess it was pretty close.' He paused, then asked, 'You want I should tell you about myself?'

Zader decided it was something to take his mind off his own thoughts, from the homesickness which was already beginning to raise its head. He nodded, grateful that Elliott did not ignore him.

Zader's own 'death' had been engineered as a road traffic accident on a particularly hazardous stretch of road near to his army camp. He supposed that his empty coffin would be buried with full military honours in the grounds of the little chapel near his home. It was the realisation that he would never again be with his parents, his family and friends which was newly dawning on him and which was beginning to tear at his guts. Momentarily he envied Elliott before recognising that Elliott had probably never had the experience of enjoying the warmth of a close family.

'You feeling a bit low?' Elliott offered him a cigarette.

Zader nodded. 'I don't have any to give you back.'

'That's okay, maybe I'll give up.'

He took one and leaned across for a light. 'Thanks.' He rarely smoked.

'Close family you come from?'

'Yes, very close.'

'Makes it hard I suppose.'

'You have no family at all?'

'Guess there might be somebody knocking around some place. I wouldn't go looking for them; they never came looking for me,' he added as he drew on his cigarette. 'My mam was a prostitute, I must have been an accident,' he shrugged dismissively, 'I don't know why she kept me instead of having an abortion or dumping me. She was only sixteen, maybe she thought I was a doll or something. She lost interest in me when I was about two, walking and talking. She slept most of the day and worked all night, that didn't leave too much time for me.' He grinned. 'I was okay, I was a good little scavenger. Used to go down to the markets, knee high to a bleedin' grasshopper I was. Knew my way around all the markets; I was the costers' mascot. They used to feed me on bacon sandwiches, chips and fruit off the stalls, all washed down with tea strong enough to rot the guts.' He drew again on the cigarette. 'My mam usually remembered to let me in before she went off street-walking. Sometimes I didn't get back to the tenement before she'd gone out and I'd kip down in the little cupboard where the meters were. The milkman would find me when he came round with the deliveries, and on a good day he'd give me a bottle of orange juice.' He glanced at Zader. 'She was all right, my mam. Head full of cotton wool. She lived in a fantasy world where some knight in shining armour was going to come along on his white charger and carry her off into the sunset. He never turned up. You bored?'

'No,' Zader answered truthfully.

'She was a romantic, my mam. She used to tell me that my dad was a gypsy – true Romany – tall, dark and mysterious, you know.' He half laughed. 'More likely she got raped by her bleedin' pimp and I was the result.'

'Did nobody report her for neglecting you?'

'No, I was okay. I didn't get battered or anything. I got fed, sometimes I even got washed. The market lads would take me into Mollie's kitchen and scrub me in the sink when the washing-up was done, and I'd come out shining of grease from the plates.'

'What about school?'

'My mam never sent me; she didn't need to. I couldn't get there fast enough. I tried to go when I was two – followed the other kids. The teachers wouldn't have it though, they wouldn't let me in until I was four and a half. I must have been the only kid in the area who liked going to school: I cried during holidays.'

Zader smiled, and wondered whether he should believe Elliott. Was Elliott telling the truth or did he think that Zader was gullible, a bit of a sop?

'On my first day at school I was given milk at morning break and food at dinner. I thought it was because I'd been a good boy. It was about two months before I found out that it was usual and by then I was liking learning. I didn't have to work at it, see.

'How did you come to join the RAF?'

'I don't know,' Elliott mused, looking at him. 'My mates were all joining the criminal statistics. I reckoned I wanted something with full board and lodging, and the Scrubs didn't appeal to me. I'd been on a school trip to Heathrow once and I liked the planes; I knew that the only way I was going to get on one was if I flew it myself, and I couldn't afford flying lessons. RAF pilot training seemed to be the answer so I signed up. I was seventeen then; I'd just completed my 'A' levels.' He stubbed the cigarette out. 'The RAF agreed to take me on, my exam results turned out okay, they put me through university, and assigned me to pilot training.' For a moment he was silent, a little distant. 'I'd hardly got into uniform and my mam was dead. She was thirty-three. She'd OD'd on phenyl barbitone and washed it down with a bottle of whisky.' He looked at Zader and smiled wryly. 'It was probably the most fun she'd had in years.'

It sounded a little flippant, callous even: this was his way of dealing with it. As he had grown older his mother had become more like a sister and a younger sister, at that. She had been pretty, cherubic featured with a mop of curly brown hair and a childlike innocence.

'I did university part-time, tied in with pilot training. I got my degree in maths and physics and I got my pilot's licence. Did another degree after that – law – just for the hell of it. So how about you? Does Zader reflect your previous identity?'

Zader nodded. 'My parents are... were Hungarian. Exiled with their parents they fled to Western Europe and chose to settle in England. I was born over here, in Warwickshire.'

'Prince or pauper?' Elliott asked.

'We weren't paupers,' Zader admitted, sounding a little apologetic. 'In Hungary the family were aristocracy.' He hesitated. 'We have...' he faltered momentarily. 'That is, my parents have,' he amended, 'a country house. The housekeeper and her husband live in a cottage in the grounds. I went to a local prep school as a day-boy until I was seven, when I was sent as a boarder to a small public school.' He paused. 'I don't suppose that you're really interested in...'

'I'm interested, honest. I like knowing about people; plain nosy I guess. I always was the type who never stopped asking questions. If you don't want to tell me about yourself, that's okay, you can tell me to sod off, mind my own business.'

Zader shook his head and said, 'I don't have much to tell.' He felt self-conscious of his somewhat privileged upbringing. 'My life story isn't very colourful. I wanted to be an accountant but my family had a long military tradition in Hungary and my father was a colonel in the British army. My name had been put down for Sandhurst and I was brought up to honour my parents.'

'You got a girlfriend?'

'Yes, a fiancée.'

'You can't have been too keen on the idea of getting married.'

Zader looked at him.

'This lark wasn't compulsory. If she was all that important to you, you wouldn't be here, would you?'

There was a pause.

'I suppose not,' Zader admitted. 'She was a nice girl. Katyana, her name was. She was very attractive.' He didn't want Elliott to think that she might not have been. 'We were supposed to be getting married next month. I liked her but I wasn't in love with her.'

'And you were going to marry her?'

He nodded. 'She was my second cousin. We'd known each other since we were babies. Our parents had agreed that we would marry, and I suppose that we were just going along with it. She wasn't in love with me any more than I was in love with her.'

'Honouring your parents?'

'It would probably have worked out,' Zader conceded. 'To like each other isn't a bad basis. Maybe it's more practical than being hopelessly in love and we would have done what our parents wanted.' He stopped and smiled a little wistfully. 'We already had a house, a Georgian style mews in Chelmsford. I don't know what Katyana thought about arranged marriage, we never really discussed it, just accepted it.' He glanced at Elliott. 'I pictured myself in uniform, in the army until I could comfortably retire. Katyana would hold coffee mornings and be a member of the Women's Institute. We would have the average two children, James and Georgina, two cars, and take our annual summer vacation in Marbella and a winter break in Gstaad.' He hesitated then asked, 'Did you have a girlfriend?'

'Had a few, wasn't committing myself. There was nothing serious. I didn't like the idea of getting hitched, one girl for the rest of my life. It didn't seem right I should be standing in the church or register office trying to subdue my natural inclination to screw the chief bridesmaid.' He grinned. 'I've got this thing about conformity – I don't want to spend the rest of my life in a straitjacket.'

'It seems strange that you should have joined the forces, the regimentation of service life.'

'You reckon? With my background I was odds on to join the dole queue in between doing stir. That was the first thing I didn't conform to – as a conscious decision.'

The flight had taken around an hour. The plane circled and landed on a small airfield in a remote and rugged area of Scotland. There was a coach waiting, and the thirty young members of the intake were shepherded aboard by the two supervisors for the final leg of the journey. It was late, almost one in the morning, and the youths were quiet – excitement, homesickness and unfamiliarity had all taken their toll. It was pitch black, the roads were unlit and the only light to break the monotony was that of an occasional farmhouse.

In the distance a thick black silhouette rose up, the high wall which surrounded the training centre. Someone muttered, 'Colditz' and there was a nervous ripple of laughter. Massive solid steel gates were the only legitimate access to the fortress-like camp. The coach rolled through and the gates sealed immediately behind it. There was a large quadrangle, and on three sides there were single storey buildings, brightly lit despite the late hour. The coach came to a halt outside the main entrance to the buildings and the doors opened. The young men retrieved their baggage, one item of personal hand luggage each, from the overhead racks and made their way out on to the asphalt.

One of the supervisors took a roll call, and then they were led into the reception area. There was a low murmur of conversation as the sleepy, travel weary youngsters still had adrenaline pumping. Their futures were unknown, they had been plucked from their chosen careers, and the reality was beginning to sink in.

Zader stayed close to Elliott, the only introduction he had had, a friend in an ocean of strangers. They surveyed their immediate surroundings. These were a little desolate – blank painted walls, the only break being an unadorned noticeboard. In each wall there was a door, and to both front and rear there were double entrance/exit doors. To the left and right there was access to other parts of the buildings.

'Quieten down, gentlemen, please,' said one of the supervisors calling their attention.

The youths fell silent and looked to the front. Here was a small, gaunt-looking man in his forties.

'Welcome to Central Training Centre; this will be your home for the next six months. Your time here is designed to prepare you for your future careers. The training will be intensive and exhausting but you have all been selected on the basis of your service records in your careers to date. You have been selected as being the elite, the cream, as having the intelligence and stamina and the instinct to survive. You're tired, gentlemen, we will not at this late hour delay you longer than necessary. I refer you to Mr Tyler, our senior instructor.'

He moved aside and the other supervisor surveyed them.

'Gentlemen, we aim to bring you to the peak of your mental and physical fitness. Your programme will include cross-country exercises, ground manoeuvres and simulated assignments. There will be intensive courses in self-defence, marksmanship and tactical planning. There will be subtle torture,' he smiled, 'designed to assess how much pressure you can take.' He surveyed the youthful faces. 'My name is Dom Tyler, I'll know your names soon enough. You're going to be my family for the next six months. You will address me as "sir". That's S.O.B., sir.' He looked towards his colleague. 'I would like to introduce you to Doctor Laverne.'

The youths looked towards the first speaker.

'Doctor Laverne is a psycho-analyst and will be monitoring your progress during your time here.' He again surveyed the youths. 'The dormitories are located in the south wing, that is, through the door on your right and follow the corridor to its termination. There will be five doors, on each door there will be a list of six names. Those six people will occupy that dormitory. At the end of each dormitory there is a shower area. You will each remove your uniforms and deposit them in the bin at the entry to the shower area. You will shower and then retire for the night. Your names are written above the beds, you have each been allocated a wardrobe which contains underclothing, various items of casual dress and one suit, one shirt and one tie. You, gentlemen, are civilians now and you will dress in your choice of the civilian clothing at your disposal. Tomorrow, this morning, there will be no reveille. Breakfast will be served between eight and ten. At eleven you will report to medical, north wing. In the afternoon at fifteen hundred hours approximately, you will report to room fifteen for physical instruction. In future, reveille will take place at four forty-five hours, breakfast at five hundred hours, first educational period at six hundred hours. As from twenty hundred hours each evening your rota for the next day will be displayed on the noticeboard.' Tyler hesitated. 'Locate your dormitories, strip, shower, bed. Goodnight, gentlemen. Dismiss.'

Elliott and Zader had been allocated to the same dormitory with neighbouring beds. They shared with Tommy Purnell, the marine, Dave Feiney, a paratrooper, Clem Jesson, a Canadian Commando and Darrell Goodwin of the Australian police. There was approximately an eight foot space between beds, three on either side of the room, a cabinet, wardrobe and drawer fitment between each. The central aisle was around six feet wide; there was no individual privacy.

It had been a long day, and they were sticky with nervous perspiration and travel. The showers in the dormitory were communal, nothing new to the dormitory mates – Zader apart. He hesitated unsurely.

Elliott looked at him. 'Maybe your blood's a different colour but the rest of you's the same – no room for modesty.' He began to strip off, throwing his clothing into the bin. Zader followed suit, self-consciously, and stepped into the showers. The warm water melted away the tensions and the stickiness.

Towelled down they made their way to their allotted beds. A couple of minutes and the lights went out; the dorm was dark and silent.

'Anybody still awake?' Purnell asked.

'No,' Feiney responded.

'Come on, lads, let's get to know each other, uh?'

'How well did you have in mind?' Elliott asked.

'Not that well,' Purnell responded quickly. 'You guys wanna play "truth consequences"?'

'Sod off,' Goodwin muttered.

'Ask any of us any question you want and we've got to answer. We don't answer or the others don't think we're telling the truth, we do a forfeit.'

'Shut up and go to sleep,' Feiney snapped.

'I'm not tired now,' Purnell complained. 'Come on, you miserable lot, just for a little while, uh? We won't do any forfeits, just ask questions.'

'Not going to get any bleedin' peace if we don't, are we?' There was a hint of amusement in Elliott's tone. 'Okay, I'll play. How about you, Zader?'

'I suppose so,' Zader agreed reluctantly.

There was a murmur of grudging assent from the others.

'Shall I ask the first question?' Purnell asked.

'It's your bloody game,' Jesson hissed.

'Okay. This one's for Feiney. What's your favourite fantasy?'

For a few moments there was no response.

'Finding myself marooned on a desert island with fifty nymphomaniacs. Yeah, that'd suit me fine. Probably I'd die young but I'd have enjoyed myself, go happy.' He paused, then said, 'It's my turn to ask a question now, uh? I'll ask Zader. You went to public school, didn't you, Zader? Is it right they're full of raging homosexuals? And what direction do your preferences lie in?'

'That's about three bleedin' questions,' Elliott responded, 'And what sort of bleedin' questions are they anyway?'

'Ones I want answering,' Feiney snapped, 'I want to know whether I'm safe in my bed or whether I need to be on my guard for sleep-walking poufters.'

'If that's the best answer you're going to give me,' Elliott retorted, 'I'm more suspicious of your preferences than his.'

'There's a lot of stories about public school boys.'

'Yeah, they must have passed me over,' Elliott muttered. 'What service were you in, Feiney?'

'Paratroops.'

'Explains a lot. Maybe your brain got blown out by the rush of air when you jumped.'

'Why don't you let Zader answer for himself? You sweet on him or something?'

'You want my fist down your bleedin' throat?' Elliott started out of bed.

'Look, if he just wants to know whether I'm homosexual or not, I'll answer him,' Zader offered.

'Why the hell should you?'

'Because I don't have anything to hide. I'm not a homosexual and I don't think I've come across any more homosexuals in my life than the average bloke in the street has. I don't think it's an upper class disease.'

'Does that answer your question, Feiney? You got any other prejudices or do you want to tell us what direction your preferences lie in? Maybe we should just work on the assumption that you're a class bigot, uh?'

There was no response.

'Did I tell you about last year?' Purnell broke the silence.

'No, but I guess you're going to,' Elliott responded.

'Yeah. We'd stopped off at Hong Kong, seven hours shore leave. There were about fifteen of us went to this club on the waterfront...'

'Let's all settle down,' Jesson murmured, 'Purnell's going to tell us all a bedtime story.'

'Hey lads, listen,' Purnell continued, 'It was a real sleazy joint. Upstairs you could watch live sex shows, whatever turned you on – girls, fellas, both.'

'What was your turn on?' Feiney yawned.

Purnell ignored him and continued, 'Some of the girls were really pretty. For a few quid you could have an hour with whichever one you wanted, do what the hell you wanted with them. They didn't say no to anything. I picked this girl out and she took me up to the second floor where there were these – like cubicles, you know. It just had this sort of low bed, no sheets or anything. All she was wearing was this short robe thing. She undressed me and massaged me all over with some sweet smelling oil. Sounds a bit messy but it was a real turn on.'

'Is there some point to this?' Jesson asked.

'Yeah, listen. She took off this robe and I rubbed her with this oil and I was like, buzzing. We got down to business. I went to get on top of her and she damned near shot into the next cubicle.'

There was no round of applause, somebody snored, there was the sound of rhythmic breathing.

Purnell sighed, 'Suit yourselves.' He rolled on to his side and pulled the bedclothes over his head.

Morning came round fast, and at ten fifty-five the young men filed silently through the admission block escorted by Tyler. He led them through to the medical unit and the long corridor outside the examination cubicles.

'All right lads, strip down to your shorts and let's have you ready for the medics.'

There were no changing areas, and there was a buzz of activity as they stripped off and folded their clothing, setting it on a shelf affixed to the long wall of the corridor. It was a little chilly, and for those towards the end of the queue there would be a long, cold wait before they were examined.

Tyler walked along; his eyes roved over them. He stopped at the head of the line.

'A pretty manky shower, aren't you? I've seen more muscle on a sardine than the lot of you put together.'

He walked slowly back along the line, and stopped in front of Purnell. His fingers shot into Purnell's stomach. Purnell half doubled.

'If that was muscle you wouldn't have felt anything,' Tyler growled. 'Straighten up, lad, pull that gut in, tighten up.'

Purnell was a solidly built young man, no fat on him, and had a pretty well honed physique. Tyler's jab had not been a gentle prod, as his muscles were still in spasm.

'I thought the marines were tough, Purnell. You're a disgrace, a bloody disgrace.'

Tyler moved on and stopped in front of Elliott.

'Now here's a pretty one.' He glanced along the corridor as the front five were taken through to the small curtain fronted cubicles, Purnell amongst them. He turned his attention back to Elliott.

'A right little Shirley Temple, aren't we?'

Elliott said nothing.

'The lads in your dorm had better not sleep on their stomachs, had they?'

'Why would that be, sir?' Elliott asked innocently.

Tyler smiled malevolently and said, 'Name?'

'Elliott.'

'Elliott, sir!' Tyler snapped. 'I'll be watching you, Elliott.'

'Look forward to it, sir.'

Tyler's expression darkened. 'I'll make your life hell.'

'Whatever turns you on, sir.'

'Cocky little bastard,' sneered Tyler, looking him over slowly. 'By the time I'm through with you, you'll wish you'd never been born.'

'That's okay, sir, I'm used to bloody minded bastards trying to put me down.'

'Is that right, Elliott? I'll have you boy, I'll destroy you.'

Tyler moved towards the cubicles.

'Pleasant character,' Zader whispered.

'Yeah, most places have one – the resident nice guy.' Elliott grinned. 'I won't lose any sleep over him.'

Zader hesitated and said, 'I hate medicals.'

'Not my favourite hobby either.' Elliott glanced along the line. 'They ask you a pile of stupid questions, stick needles in you and tell you a whole load of things you either already knew or you didn't want to know in the first place.'

Purnell watched as the doctor fastened the inflatable strap of the blood pressure meter around his arm and inflated it, then slid the stethoscope into position. Apparently satisfied he removed the strap, moved on to sound out Purnell's chest.

'Do you smoke?'

'About fifteen a day.'

The doctor shot him a disapproving look, then asked, 'Have you got or do you suspect that you might have contracted VD?'

'No, sir.'

'Have you ever contracted any venereal disease?'

'Yes, sir, last year.'

'Treated?'

'Yes, sir. It's cleared up okay.'

'Have you got or do you suspect you may have contracted AIDS?'

'No, sir.'

'Have you been tested?'

'Yes, sir, last year while I was having treatment after our tour of the Middle East.'

'Any recent homosexual relationships?'

'None, sir, I don't have any tendencies.'

The doctor marked his records, reached for a sterile wrapped syringe and tore off the cover, then swabbed Purnell's inner elbow.

'We'll just find out what colour your blood is,' he said as he lined up a row of syringe barrels in a holder.

Purnell looked away as the doctor inserted the needle into a vein and proceeded to draw blood. He replaced the barrel four times before withdrawing the needle and discarding it into the sharps bin. He placed a cotton wool pad over the perforation.

'Stand against the measure please.'

The doctor motioned vaguely towards the side wall of the cubicle, then noted the details of height and weight.

'Shorts off and lie down on the couch.'

Purnell walked across to the couch, removed his shorts and lay down. The curtain part opened and Tyler stepped inside.

'Everything all right, doctor?'

Tyler's eyes rested on Purnell.

'Fine.'

Tyler's eyes did not deviate.

'We'll soon be through with them; I'm sure they're a healthy bunch.'

'Good.'

It was a few seconds before Tyler retreated. Purnell had had no liking for the way in which Tyler had looked at him. No sweat, maybe he was jealous. Purnell grinned to himself. Tyler didn't look to be a particularly big boy – if he could be seen in his shorts it would probably be good for a laugh.

The doctor completed his examination. Purnell pulled on his shorts and escaped gratefully out into the corridor. About fifteen of the lads were still waiting to go through, others were in various stages of dressing. He began to dress. There was no sign of Tyler. Perhaps he was in some other cubicle getting himself a cheap thrill from admiring someone else's equipment.

Elliott emerged from a cubicle, retrieved his jeans from the shelf and pulled them on.

'Not so bleedin' warm. Reckon it's all part of the torture?'

'Probably,' Purnell agreed, 'What do you think of Tyler?'

'Not much,' Elliott reached for his tee shirt.

'Did he come in to view your assets?'

Elliott shook his head and said, 'Maybe he doesn't reckon I've got any.'

Zader joined them, rubbing his arm and complained, 'Taken about three pints, or at least it feels like it.'

'Not too often they get blue blood to play with,' Elliott grinned and observed. 'Doesn't seem to be much doing until about half two. If you two get a move on we can get in a couple of frames before lunch.'

Chapter Two

The afternoon was to be occupied with a physical education session. In good spirits, but not particularly enthusiastic about the forthcoming rigours, the intake made their way to the gymnasium. They had been introduced to the numerous instructors at a brief meeting just after lunch – too many people, too much information for most of them to take in in one go. Bob Mulcahy, their instructor, was an American with a good deal of Irish blood in him. He was a big bloke, a good six feet in height, broad shouldered and built like an ox. Probably he was in his mid forties; with his craggy, lived-in face it was hard to tell. His dark hair was greying a little but he had a humorous glint in his eyes. He watched as the intake shuffled into the gymnasium. They were, in the main, casually dressed in jeans and tee shirts, the most casual items in their wardrobes. They lined up and regarded him expectantly.

'Well, it's a sorry looking bunch we've got here,' Mulcahy commented in a soft Irish lilt. His eyes ran over his students and he shook his head. 'It's going to be an uphill struggle knocking you lot into shape – any sort of shape.' He paused, half smiled and said. 'You're here because you're potential WIA agents or operatives. Jesus Christ, I've seen livelier looking stiffs!' He walked along the front row as he spoke. 'Physical fitness. In this game if you're not fit, fast and alert you're dead.' He moved on to the second row, stopped in front of Elliott and demanded, 'Name?'

'Elliott, sir.'

Mulcahy nodded, consulted his list and looked back at him. 'Am I the first to tell you that you're a pretty little bastard?'

There was no malice.

'No, sir, I've been a pretty little bastard all my life.'

'I expect you have,' Mulcahy acknowledged and smiled. 'Never mind, son, we'll soon change that, rearrange your face for you, rough you up a bit.' He brushed at the small scar beneath Elliott's left eye and observed, 'I see you've already made a start.'

'I've been trying, sir.'

Mulcahy nodded, and added, 'And no doubt you'll continue to be very trying. You're not my type, Elliott, but I don't make the same guarantees for all of the staff. Watch your rear guard.'

'Sir.'

Mulcahy returned to the front, surveyed them momentarily and sighed. 'Has anybody here brought an excuse note signed by their ma?' he asked as he looked around. 'No? Good. Let's get on with it then. We don't wear PE kit around here...'

There was a buzz of conversation.

'Don't get excited boys, we're not going to play in the raw.'

There was a round of catcalls.

'All right, quieten down, it isn't playtime. When we let you out on the streets and you're chasing some bastard or there's some bastard chasing you, you're not going to have the opportunity to slip into something more comfortable, are you?' He hesitated, smiled, then continued. 'So we aren't going to make things easy for you now. You can take your jackets and ties off, those of you who're wearing them and that's as far as the strip show goes. If you want to see more of each other you'll have to pay attention in the showers.' He had an easy rapport. 'All right, six teams of five, get a move on. By the time I'm through with you lot you'll be running up and down Ben Nevis as an appetiser for breakfast.'

'Yeah, but who's going to be waiting at the top to serve it?' Elliott whispered loudly to Zader.

'If you've got the breath to spare, Elliott, we'll let you run back down and fetch it. Save your energy for the exercise, lad.'

'Sir.'

Mulcahy moved towards the set out apparatus. 'Pay attention,' he instructed curtly.

'Up the rope, across the catwalk, down the tube, over the netting and drop. And when you've done that, you do it again in reverse and I don't mean arse first. First team home gets most breathing space before the next exercise.'

Some of the intake discarded jackets and ties in an untidy heap in the corner of the room, and they all lined up.

'We'll soon know which of you smoke – go!'

For two hours Mulcahy put them through their paces, climbing, sprinting, vaulting and somersaulting. No rest – he kept them in perpetual motion. Bruised, battered, perspiring, their muscles protesting, shins and knees black and blue, they reassembled into their teams.

'Okay boys, take five.' Mulcahy watched as they collapsed on to the matting and sprawled across it. He grinned. 'Knackered already, and another two hours before I'm through with you.'

This news was greeted with a unanimous groan.

'Sir?' Elliott raised himself into a sitting position.

'Elliott?'

'How often are we going to find ourselves chasing some bastard around an adventure playground for two hours?'

'Let us hope never, Elliott, but if you ever do you'll be ready for it,' he retorted and smiled broadly. 'And since you've still got the energy to ask questions, you can be the volunteer for part two of this afternoon's lesson. Jump to it, lad.'

Elliott rose to his feet amidst cheers and whistles from his colleagues, relieved that they had not been chosen.

'Thanks, fans,' Elliott acknowledged and took a bow.

'Your turn will come,' Mulcahy warned the rest of the class good-naturedly. 'Self-defence, a practical demonstration.' He hesitated then clarified, 'Let us suppose that Elliott is the assailant. Armed with a knife he makes his approach from the front – Elliott?' He motioned him forward. 'All right, you should all have done this as part of your basic training with the various forces. Sit up and pay attention. You're going to talk me through it.' He waited whilst they rearranged themselves. 'Can everybody see?'

There was a murmur of confirmation.

'Good. Now – come at me, Elliott.'

Elliott moved towards him, right hand clenched around an imaginary knife, his arm raised.

'Grab his arm, sir,' a voice advised Mulcahy from somewhere at the back of the audience.

Mulcahy obeyed.

'Kick him in the balls, sir,' Purnell suggested enthusiastically.

'Love you too,' Elliott responded dryly.

Mulcahy twisted round and unbalanced Elliott, and threw him over his right shoulder. Still holding Elliott's right wrist he placed his foot on Elliott's throat as Elliott lay sprawled across the mat.

'It should now be…'

Elliott's left hand darted out, curled around Mulcahy's right ankle and pulled his leg from under him. Mulcahy landed flat out across the matting. The class cheered as

Elliott scrambled across and pinned him down, the imaginary knife to his throat.

'Think you should have knackered him like I said, sir,' Purnell advised.

The intake members breathed a sigh of relief as Mulcahy dismissed them at eighteen thirty, class over for the day. He had worked them hard, every one of them perspiration-saturated and aching. Evening and night classes would come, tests of endurance but not yet, they were being broken in gently.

'Look forward to seeing you tomorrow, boys, you'll know every muscle in your bodies by then,' Mulcahy called after them cheerfully.

The prospect of showers and a change of clothing was enticing. They headed wearily towards the accommodation quarters and their dormitories. Dinner was not until nineteen hundred hours.

'Jesus, I'm dead beat,' Feiney complained as he emerged from the showers rubbing his hair with a towel.

'Think how you're going to feel after twelve weeks without a break,' Purnell jibed and grinned.

'I'm not going to last that long, I'll have faded away inside a fortnight. When those gates shut behind us I was thinking how was I going to manage for six months without a bird. If there was a page three girl in my bed right now I'd be too damned knackered to do anything with her.

'Anybody wants to put one in my bed, I'll work up the enthusiasm,' Elliott commented as he pulled on a clean pair of jeans.

'It's what keeps him so bloody fit,' Purnell countered, 'Been making it since you were ten, haven't you, Elliott?'

'Fourteen.'

'Come off it.' Feiney was disbelieving.

'Honest. She was seventeen and just starting out on the streets. She strayed on to my mam's patch and my mam brought her home...'

'Your mam's patch? Your mam was a prostitute?' Purnell interrupted.

'Yeah. This girl was green, naïve; I mean, she wasn't a virgin but she'd always known the blokes she'd made it with.' Elliott paused. 'She was a nice kid, not a born hustler. It must have been around three in the morning. I was asleep and somebody switched on the light. I heard this girl say something like "He's only a kid", then my mam said, "He's old enough, his balls have dropped".'

There was an audience of his room-mates now gathered.

'Your mam wanted this girl to make it with you?' Jesson was incredulous. 'So what happened?'

'I was at that age where I was noticing that girls were different but wasn't realising how different. I was still more interested in playing football.' Elliott paused, then continued, 'So this girl, she stripped off and got in bed with me. She'd got more arms than a bleedin' octopus and they were bleedin' cold. She didn't have a gentle touch either. She had nails on her like a bleedin' eagles and boobs like water melons. She got on top of me – I was blue by the time I got to the surface for air. Nothing else, she was pretty enthusiastic; she damned near killed me.'

'It wasn't a good experience then?' Jesson asked.

'Well – not at first,' Elliott admitted as he pulled on his tee shirt. 'But I was getting the hang of it after around a quarter of an hour. My mam was a good trainer.'

'Bloody hell,' Purnell muttered, 'You didn't make it with your mam, did you?'

'My name's not Oedipus. My mam might have been a prostitute but she'd got some moral standards. No, I didn't make it with my mam, I was probably the only bloke over twelve within a five mile radius of Tower Hamlets who hadn't.' He shrugged. 'She was good at her job, she knew every position there was to know and she liked her customers to be satisfied. She was teaching this girl and she wanted her to get it right. I was handy for practising on. I picked up a few tips myself.'

'She watched while some tart raped you?' Jesson asked.

'Suppose you could say that.'

'Lucky bastard,' Purnell muttered.

'Whole heap of bloody bullshit if you ask me,' Feiney jibed as he moved towards his bed. 'Reckon he's all bloody talk.' He pulled open his wardrobe noisily and took out a shirt, looked across as Zader emerged from the shower room and asked, 'What about you, Zader? You ever slept with a girl or have you been too busy playing with the boys? Maybe you're a virgin, uh?'

Zader coloured noticeably and glanced at his room-mates uncertainly. 'No, I...' he tailed off, 'I had a girlfriend, a fiancée.'

'Oh, he had a fiancée,' Feiney mocked.

'Yeah, but what did he have on the side?' Elliott breached the potential silence, 'It's the quiet ones you've got to watch – and you're a bleedin' stirrer, Feiney.'

Zader shot Elliott a grateful half smile as he passed, and moved across to his wardrobe fitment. It was not a set up with which he was familiar and he was not practised in scathing repartee. He selected a shirt, pulled it on and fastened it. Being public school educated with an upper class background made him the odd one out in the intake. It was not a fact which he could ignore – apparently Feiney was not about to let him. He was obviously the cause of friction between Elliott and Feiney, and he wished that he could fall into the easy camaraderie which the others seemed to adopt. It was in his nature to be reserved; the glib responses which the others had mastered were alien to him.

'I think I'll take a look at what they've got lined up for us tomorrow,' Elliott said as he headed for the door. 'Better not be late for dinner,' he warned, 'In this place you probably get sent to bed without dessert.'

He left the dormitory and walked up the corridor to the reception area where the rota was pinned up on the noticeboard – a two hour lecture on the WIA followed by three hours' firearms training with Tyler, an hour for lunch, a two hour lecture on communications, then another two hours with Mulcahy to finish off.

Most of the intake had gone through to the refectory. Zader hesitated and made his way across to where Elliott stood studying the noticeboard.

'Mach?'

Elliott turned to see Zader, there was no one else around. 'Mach?' he inquired as he looked at Zader.

'Air speed,' Zader explained a little uncertainly, 'You don't like nicknames? We all...' he foundered. Was it a quirk of his class?

'Yeah, fine. I like it.'

'I... I just wanted to say thanks.'

'For what?'

'For helping me out.'

There was a pause.

'Maybe the company's a bit different to what you're used to. You'll be fast enough with the answers once you get into it.'

'I don't have the experience everyone else seems to have had; I've never played the field.'

'So make it up, they'll buy it.'

'But you're all talking from experience.'

'Yeah? How do you know?' He grinned. 'All you've got to do is tell them your eccentric uncle bought you a blow-up doll for your tenth birthday and you screwed the kitchen maid on your twelfth birthday.'

'We didn't have a kitchen maid and I've never seen a blow-up doll. They wouldn't believe...'

'They'll believe anything you tell them if you keep your face straight.'

'Do you think so?'

'I know so. They've all read *Lady Chatterley's Lover*, and they think all the aristocrats are having it off with the rough.'

'And that we're all homosexuals.'

'No. Those of us who don't have blue blood, all we know about the aristocracy's what we read in the scandal rags. Not interested in Lord Peter screwing his wife, are we? Lord Peter screwing the stable lad's more interesting. Couldn't care less about Lady Jane's coffee mornings but if she's sharing her Jacuzzi with the gardener... We think the entire landed gentry's running a production line of bastard kids and screaming poufters.'

'You don't think that.'

'No, I'm just telling you that there are preconceived ideas. I'm suggesting that you tell them what they want to hear.'

'I've never made love to...'

'We're not talking about making love,' Elliott corrected as he took his cigarettes from his pocket, lit one, and leaned back against the wall. 'That's something else altogether. We're talking about sex, screwing, getting your rocks off. Loving doesn't have anything to do with that. Sex, you don't even have to know the girls, you just do it.' He hesitated. 'Look, if you're a virgin...'

'I'm not a virgin,' Zader cut in, maybe a little quickly.

Elliott looked him over. 'Katyana's the only girl...?'

Zader nodded.

'That's nice.'

Zader wasn't sure that he meant it.

'Just tell them to mind their own bleedin' business.'

'I want to be one of the crowd.'

'So lie, everyone else does,' he said as he straightened up.

'You don't.'

Elliott took a long draw on his cigarette, then said, 'Welcome to my life – doesn't come to much, does it?'

There was a silence. Elliott snuffed the cigarette between his fingers, dropped the stub to the floor, and asked, 'Have you never read a sexy book or watched a steamy film?'

Zader nodded.

'There's your material, change he to I or tell them what was happening on screen just as if you were doing it.'

'What if they've read the book or seen the film?'

Elliott grinned and suggested, 'Ask if it's the same one they're talking about.'

Zader followed him through to the refectory and across to the service bar. 'I suppose you think I'm pretty wet.'

'I've got no room to criticise anybody else's values, and I'd never accuse anybody with the guts to be in the bomb squad of being wet. I couldn't care less who you have or haven't laid.' His grin broadened as he added, 'So long as it isn't me!'

'Look, I'm not a homosexual, really.'

'I know. Wouldn't worry me if you were.' Their empty plates filled rapidly as they moved along the line. 'Just be yourself. If some people don't like you, that's tough, why should you care? You can't go around pretending to be what you think other people want you to be – if that worked I'd try keeping my bleedin' mouth shut, wouldn't I?'

He led across to the table which they shared with their room-mates.

'You two love-birds finished whispering sweet nothings?' Feiney inquired snidely.

'Yeah.' Elliott placed his plate on the table, pulled back a chair and looked at Feiney as he sat down. 'You want to make something of it?' he asked belligerently.

The others looked towards Feiney expectantly. Suddenly he seemed to find his dinner of great interest, and the possibility of a confrontation passed.

'You know,' Goodwin said in his Australian accent to Elliott. 'This isn't a bad restaurant. If nothing else, they're feeding us well.'

'They need to,' Elliott responded. 'If we're going to work out with Mulcahy on a daily basis we need all the protein we can get. We're not going to put weight on in this place, that's for sure.' He reached for the coffee pot. 'There's nothing else to do but work and sleep.'

'There's the bar,' Purnell chipped in, 'It opens for an hour every night, seven thirty to eight thirty. We're limited to two single measures of spirits or two pints – not a lot of chance of going on a bender. We all have to be tucked up in bed by nine.'

'It's no problem,' conceded Goodwin, salting his meal liberally, 'Four hours with Mulcahy's enough to knacker anybody.'

Chapter Three

The morning opened with a two hour lecture on the role of the WIA. This was delivered by the Deputy Chief Superintendent Administrator, Takis Omaru, of oriental origin, and with a pronounced accent. An interesting talker, he held the rapt attention of the students. The thirty young men were, initially, potential agent line, and Omaru was in the business of shattering illusions. They were training for a job in which tomorrow may not exist – agents were lost to death or injury on a regular basis – there was a high mortality rate. Omaru wanted them to have no romantic notions about their futures; he was talking about sweat and blood, sheer hard work, pain and no ecstasy; a good result was usually coupled with exhaustion and not celebration. Agents could find themselves caught up in the worlds of drug traffickers, intrigue and espionage. Many agents lost their lives as a result of their own negligence – a brief drop of their guard, from either complacency or sheer exhaustion. It was not a nine 'til five job; there was nothing unusual in working around the clock for days and even weeks.

'So I could have been a junior casualty houseman,' Jesson muttered.

Any man expecting to find himself leaping into bed with beautiful female counteragents was likely to be disappointed – the WIA was world-wide and not a secular Organisation as were MI5, the CIA or the KGB. If beautiful counteragents existed, and Omaru had never come across one, then it was not usually WIA agents upon whom they sought to bestow their favours. What could be expected were long hours, appalling conditions, the ever present threat of being discovered, and an inability to trust anyone.

Omaru illustrated his points with videos recorded by the Recovery Teams whose task it was to clean up in the aftermath. Some agents had been eliminated swiftly and cleanly – they were the lucky ones. In the main, those whose investigations had been discovered had been savagely dealt with, and had suffered slow and tortuous deaths or barbaric mutilation.

Omaru himself was confined to a wheelchair, his back broken. He was not bitter for he had left the training centre under no illusions and had spent four years on agent line – a good innings.

This was not a lecture in which it was necessary to make notes. The young audience listened in fascinated and occasionally disbelieving silence as Omaru recounted tales of agents past and present, and his own experiences. It was being made abundantly clear that they were on no picnic – it was going to be hard graft.

The WIA was an organisation incomparable to the better known Government agencies. Its activities were far more varied and it was not restricted by national or political persuasions. A special calibre of men made agent line – proficient and adaptable, able to take the initiative, and confident in their own abilities. They worked in teams of two, their partners selected to complement their own temperaments and talents. Traditionally they were ranked by number – with over one thousand agents world-wide, to be one of the top one hundred was to be amongst the elite.

It was unlikely that more than five members of this intake would make the grade. This gave the young men plenty to think about. Perhaps another ten would qualify in Observation or Recovery. As for the rest – deprocessing, fabricated histories and a return to the real world with no recollection of their true past and their time at the training centre was their expectation.

Clearly Omaru was in awe of one man – Lester James Marlborough, founder and Chief Superintendent Administrator of the WIA. A difficult man to deal with, he had an aura which defied dissent, his manner terse and uncompromising. He demanded and received one hundred per cent loyalty and commitment. His own career had begun with a special assignment division of MI5. When moves had been made to disband it he had sought and finally, through sheer persistence, obtained dispensation to continue it as a private enterprise.

The background and CV of every potential WIA operative had been stringently investigated, the final decision on their suitability having been taken by Marlborough. Initially, would-be recruits had been recommended by their commanding officers but only one in eight recommendations were actioned as Marlborough had high standards. The WIA held detailed information as to the backgrounds, family history, education and service records of the recruits. It could well be that the WIA knew more about the thirty young men than they knew about themselves.

Omaru's videos were, in the first instance, inoffensive. They showed WIA facilities, the administrative work which kept the wheels in motion. None of the intake was prepared for the final film, a series of on-site illustrations, the aftermath when Recovery had moved in on an assignment gone wrong. The dead and the dying were apparently little older than themselves. There were scenes to churn the stomach of even those with cast iron constitutions. Two of the young men passed out cold; several made hurried departures to throw up.

Purnell was amongst the latter whose guts had balked at the scenes which Omaru had shown. Consequently he found himself referred to, and temporarily detained in medical. He supposed that it was now on record that he had a weak stomach. Still, he had at least made it to medical himself, he had not been carried there comatose.

Recovered, he decided to return to the lecture theatre. Probably the proceedings had progressed beyond the sickeningly gory.

'Sir.' He knocked on the door of the MO's office. It was slightly ajar and he poked his head round. 'I feel okay now, sir, I'll go back to the briefing.'

'All right, Purnell,' the medic agreed, barely glancing up from his reports, 'If you feel up to it.'

'I feel fine, sir, I shouldn't have had the fried breakfast.'

He left medical and walked back along the corridor towards administration reception.

'Took bad, did you, Purnell?'

Purnell stopped and looked back as Tyler emerged from one of the side rooms.

'I'm okay now,' he confirmed, and moved on.

Tyler fell into step with him. 'It's nothing to worry about, some of our best agents flaked out watching those videos. A stiff drink and you'll be as right as rain.'

'I've got a long wait, sir, the bar doesn't open until seven thirty.'

'I think we can find a way around that. If you're a true Scotsman a good whisky should sort you out.'

'I can't say I'm averse to the wee dram, sir,' Purnell confirmed a little uncertainly, 'But I'll be getting back to the lecture theatre.'

'There's no hurry, you still look a little peaky. I think if you were to have a quick nip of the amber nectar before you went back you'd be fixed up for the day.'

There was a pause.

'I really think I should be getting back.'

'It's an order, Purnell.'

'Sir?'

'No brownie points for the lecture,' Tyler said, smiling thinly.

Tyler led into the accommodation block and along the corridor past the dormitories to the staff block. He took a key from his pocket, unlocked the door to his room and pushed it open. Purnell followed him inside hesitantly – he did not trust Tyler's apparent concern.

'Nice room you've got, sir.'

It was around six yards square, with a single divan bed in one corner, a couple of armchairs, a coffee table, TV and video, a cabinet and a wardrobe.

'Sit down.' Tyler indicated towards the chairs as he moved across to the cabinet.

Purnell sat down, his eyes roving around the room.

'I... I think I ought to get back to the briefing,' he said as he felt strangely uneasy.

'You aren't missing much. The lecture's just an introduction, nothing vital to your training. Your dormitory mates will fill you in on the more interesting bits, the blood and gore.'

Tyler carried a large measure of whisky across and handed it to Purnell. 'You get that inside you and you'll be ready for anything,' he instructed as he returned to the cabinet.

'Do you get along all right with your dormitory mates?' he asked, as he poured himself a drink and lowered himself into the other chair.

'Yeah, they seem to be a pretty good bunch.'

Purnell took a sip of his drink; it tasted strong and a little sweet.

'None of them have tried anything?'

'Sir?' Purnell looked at him.

'What about the public school lad, Zader?' Tyler asked, taking a drink.

'Jan? He's okay, straight.'

'And what about the pretty faced little bastard, Elliott?'

'He's a laugh.' Purnell took another drink. 'I haven't tasted a whisky like this before.

'You don't like it?'

'It's good.' Purnell hesitated. 'A bit powerful.'

Tyler nodded and coaxed, 'It's a special blend, liqueur based. As you're a Scotsman I thought you might appreciate its quality.'

Purnell nodded; he felt a little light-headed. He was still a bit groggy, he supposed. His eyes were feeling heavy.

★

Purnell did not make an appearance at lunch time. His room-mates supposed that he still felt rough and had remained in medical. There were a couple of others still absent, the film apparently stronger than their guts. Elliott and Zader felt fine. Elliott had seen active service, and Zader had been called upon to defuse bombs after others had gone off and had seen sights similar to those shown on film firsthand.

The rota had the afternoon marked down for firearms training and their instructor as Dom Tyler. In the event the first hour was supervised by another instructor and Tyler materialised finally, with the excuse that he had been dealing with administrative paperwork.

Elliott fell foul of him, and was put on a report for insubordination for no better reason than that Tyler took exception to his looks – and perhaps the fact that he was an excellent marksman.

Purnell did not make an appearance during the course of the afternoon although all of the others who had taken ill returned. Nor was he in the dormitory when his five roommates returned to shower before dinner.

'I thought the marines had cast iron guts,' Feiney barbed as he sank on to the edge of his bed and lit a cigarette.

'Perhaps he was already feeling off colour,' Zader suggested.

'Or maybe the marines aren't as tough as they like to make out,' Feiney sniped.

'Today hasn't been too bad,' Goodwin said, changing the subject, 'Except those videos; I thought snuff movies were illegal. At least I've got some energy left tonight – I could cope with a nice blonde piece with curves in the right places.'

'Only bird you'll find within fifty miles of this place is a bloody grouse. Stand more chance of sighting a wild haggis,' Feiney commented in a sarcastic tone.

'If you don't want to contribute why don't you keep it buttoned?' Goodwin snapped.

Dinner over, Elliott did not join the others in the recreation area for a couple of games of pool before the bar opened. Instead, he returned to the dormitory; he had it in mind to collect his jacket and take a look around, explore his surroundings. Maybe he would run across Purnell – surely he was out of medical by now. He let himself into the dormitory and his eyes roved over the beds. In the half light he could make out that they were all empty.

It was a little chilly outside. Elliott hesitated and surveyed the quadrangle; it was deserted. He walked along the line of buildings and around the back to the sports fields and the woodland beyond. It was slippery underfoot as he crossed the open space. He walked slowly along the perimeter of the woodland.

'Mach?'

He stopped and peered into the gloom.

'Tommy?' he asked, 'Where are you?'

He scanned the shadows. There was only silence.

Elliott moved a little way into the undergrowth and towards from where he thought the call had come. Purnell sat hunched beneath a tall oak tree, his knees drawn up to his chest. He seemed to draw more tightly into himself as Elliott approached.

'Tommy?' Elliott looked down at him and asked, 'What the hell are you doing out here?'

'Nothing.'

Elliott sank to his haunches, reached out and touched him. Purnell flinched. His skin was cold beneath Elliott's fingers.

'How long have you been out here, you're frozen.'

'I'm okay.' There was a tremor in Purnell's voice. 'Go on back to the others, I don't need any company.'

'Hey, come on. You weren't the only one turned green watching that film.' It was more than that but Elliott could not begin to guess at what. 'There's only me here if you want to talk.' He lowered himself on to the ground beside him. 'You might feel better if you talk it out.'

'I don't want to talk.'

'If you've got a problem, Tommy, tell me about it.'

'Will you just fuck off and leave me alone!'

'No,' Elliott looked at him and said, 'I'm not leaving you out here on your own.' He paused. 'You trust me, don't you? I'm just asking you to tell me, I won't tell anybody else – not if you don't want me to.'

Purnell looked at him finally. 'You won't tell anybody?' he asked uncertainly.

'I won't tell anybody.'

'Swear it?'

'I swear it.'

A brief silence.

'Swear it on something.'

'My mother's grave, my own life – take your pick.'

Another silence.

'Come on, Tommy, something's happened. A gyp stomach isn't going to get you like this. You're not doing yourself any favours keeping it bottled up. I can't help you, Tommy, not if you won't trust me. There's only you and me here, nobody else is going to hear.'

Purnell buried his face against his arms. 'Will you talk to me, Mach?' he asked, stifling a sob. 'I need somebody to talk to me.'

Elliott hesitated, then agreed, 'Okay. You talk when you're ready, uh?'

Elliott talked – about his flying experiences, girls, a few jokes, anything to try and relax Purnell a little.

'I want to go home.'

Elliott looked at him.

'I just want to go home – get out of this place.'

'What's happened?'

'My guts hurt.' Purnell brushed at his eyes. 'Make them send me home. Please Mach, I… I hurt, I don't want to stay here.'

Even in the muted moonlight which filtered through the trees the tears were visible in Purnell's eyes.

'Did something happen this morning? In medical? Come on, Tommy, you can talk to me about it. Did one of the medics do something?'

Purnell shook his head.

'If all I'm going to get out of you are a few half clues, it could take a week for me to put together what's happened. There'll be a search party out for us before then. You need help now; talk to me, for Christ's sake.'

'You can't do anything.'

'I can listen.'

'And you won't tell?'

'I won't tell – swear on my life.'

A pause.

'My stomach settled down pretty fast, I wasn't in medical too long.' His voice was barely a whisper. 'I decided I'd go back to the briefing. I told the MO I was feeling okay. I was on my way back...' He fell silent.

Elliott didn't push it, didn't prompt.

'I ran into Tyler.' His voice was unsteady. 'He asked me how I was feeling, said a glass of scotch would set me up for the rest of the day. I told him that I was okay. I said I was going back to the lecture... but he was pretty insistent, said it was an order. He took me down to his room...'

Another pause, longer. Elliott cottoned on fast; was in front of Purnell's halting narrative.

'I don't want to talk about it.'

'Take your time.'

They sat for a while in silence.

'He poured me a drink and we sat and talked. He was asking things like was I settling in okay, did I get along with the rest of the lads. It was a pretty large whisky he gave me, at least a double. He didn't offer water or soda with it. I thought it tasted a bit strange, sort of sweet and with a real bite to it. He said it was a special blend, a liqueur base. I started feeling a bit strange, light-headed...'

'You passed out?'

He nodded. Elliott took his cigarettes from his pocket, lit two and passed one across.

'When I came round...' He drew on the cigarette as he explained, 'I was on the bed, stripped, and that bastard...' He stopped, choked up.

'He raped you?'

Purnell nodded. 'I... I couldn't... I knew what was happening but I couldn't... It was like I was... paralysed and he was...' His voice broke and he sobbed.

Elliott gave him a couple of minutes. 'You bleeding or anything?'

Purnell shook his head and said, 'Not now.'

'You need to see a medic.'

'No.'

'You need to get yourself checked out and make sure…'

'No!'

'You can't let Tyler get away with it, he needs stopping, Tommy. He can't do that to you and no comebacks. You've got to report him.'

'I don't have to do anything.'

'You want me to report him?'

'You say nothing to anybody. You swore.'

'Okay, but you need to see a medic.'

'I don't want to see a medic, I just want to get out of this place.'

'You hurt?'

'What do you think?'

'I think you should tell somebody, Tommy, somebody who can do something. How about Mulcahy?'

'I'm not telling anybody, I shouldn't have told you.'

'I won't tell anybody. I promised and I don't break promises.' Elliott looked at him and said. 'You can't stop here all night, let's go back inside.'

'You go back inside.'

'I'm not going without you.' Elliott looked at his watch. 'The lads'll still be in recreation; if we go back now and you go to bed you won't need to face them tonight; no questions.'

A pause.

'Come on, Tommy, if the lads bug you I'll take care of them. You need to get to bed, thaw yourself out and get some rest.' He rose to his feet. 'You were just taken bad; I'll sort the lads.'

With a little more persuasion, Purnell reluctantly agreed to return to the accommodation block. Elliott was right – the dormitory was deserted as their room-mates were still in the recreation area.

'I'm scared Tyler's going to come looking for me.'

'Don't worry about him.'

'I don't want to be on my own with...'

'I'm not going any place, I'll be right here.'

A pause.

'Will you swap beds with me?'

'Sure, no problem.'

Purnell undressed quickly and slipped between the sheets of Elliott's bed. 'Appreciate it, Mach. You listening I feel better for talking.'

'Any time,' said Elliott as he climbed into Purnell's bed, 'Try and get some sleep.'

It was still early, half an hour to the close of the recreation period. The dormitory was in darkness, and silent. There was a low creak of hinges as the door opened slowly and a shadowy figure stepped inside.

'Not joining your mates, Purnell?' Tyler moved to the bedside, and sneered, 'Still feeling rough? It'll pass. Just relax son, you'll get used to it. You might even get to enjoy it.' He hesitated. 'You're just the way I like them, young, athletic, good build, hetero. God, you bled.'

Elliott could feel the malevolent smile.

'You be good to me, Purnell, and I'll be good to you. You know what I'm saying. I can rig your marks.'

There was no response.

'Don't take too long thinking it over. There'll be others ready to sacrifice their ass for the easy option – special privileges and graduation guaranteed – less than half the intake make it through. At the three month assessment you could find yourself turned out on the streets, no history, no friends or family. Deprocessing's no picnic. I'm offering you a future on a plate.'

'It's a tempting offer, Tyler, but if it's all the same to you I'll keep my ass my own and take my chances on my own abilities.'

There was a stunned silence.

'What the hell are you doing in Purnell's bed, Elliott?'

'Not planning on sharing it with him, that's for sure. Get the hell out of here, Tyler.'

'I...'

'I said get out – before I throw you out.'

'Are you threatening me, Elliott?'

'Threatening you, sir?' Elliott asked sarcastically. 'No, sir – I'm giving you the option. You'd better go now while you've got the chance. I won't bother opening the door before I put you through it.'

'I'll have you, Elliott, I'll make your life hell. I'll see you in the bloody gutter.'

The door slammed as he left.

Elliott hesitated, then whispered loudly, 'Tommy?'

There was no reply. With a little luck Purnell was asleep and had missed Tyler's visit.

*

The following day Purnell was quiet and withdrawn. His room-mates put it down to his still feeling off colour and kept quiet about it, all except Feiney who had done some jibing and who had been silenced by Elliott. Purnell's blooded clothing had been discreetly disposed of; Elliott made sure that no one would find out what had happened by finding them.

The first three hours were scheduled to be a tortuous session with Mulcahy, and Purnell supposed that he could cope with that. He toyed with his breakfast, had no appetite. The nausea and disgust had still not begun to subside, and his guts still hurt. Elliott had told nobody, would not tell anybody, Purnell was sure about that. He still wanted to go home.

The intake filed into the gymnasium. Mulcahy was not present. There was no apparatus set out as there had been on their first day, so apparently they were not to be running an assault course. The vaulting box was out, a springboard in front of it, and the mats were set out around it. The general hubbub of conversation subsided as Tyler entered.

'All right you mangy bunch of little bastards,' he sniped, surveying them. 'Mulcahy's been delayed by bad weather and so you have the privilege of my company.' He looked them over with disdain. 'Springboard exercises; one springboard, one vaulting box and thirty dubious specimens I'm supposed to believe are the cream of our youth. God help the lot of us,' he finished scathingly. 'Elliott, Feiney, catchers either side of the box; we wouldn't want there to be any accidents, would we?'

Elliott and Feiney moved to their positions on either side of the box.

'All right, the rest of you line up behind the mark. One at a time and take a run up, off the springboard and somersault over the box. Let's see what sort of shape you're in.'

The remaining twenty-eight members of the intake shuffled towards the back of the gymnasium and assembled.

'Go for it,' Tyler instructed, taking up his position a couple of feet in front of the springboard.

Sixteen of the intake had completed the routine. Purnell now moved up the line.

'Come on, Purnell, we don't have all day,' Tyler bellowed.

He nudged the springboard as Purnell made the approach, and the deviation threw Purnell wide of the box and awkwardly off the side. Elliott reacted quickly, sprinted forwards and caught Purnell, twisting him upwards and outwards so that only his shin, rather than his head or neck, made contact with the wooden frame. Purnell landed feet first as he went over Elliott's shoulder. He slithered to the floor, and was clearly shaken although his leg was only slightly bruised.

'Get up and do it again, Purnell,' Tyler snapped, 'And get it right this time.'

Purnell hauled himself shakily to his feet.

'You'll do it again and as many times as it takes to get it right!' Tyler yelled. 'Come on, move yourself. You're useless, Purnell, call yourself a marine? You wouldn't qualify for the boy scouts. You're a useless bloody wretch! Now come on, let's see what sort of a bloody mess you can make of it this time.'

Purnell hesitated, affected by the tirade. The rest of the intake looked a little stunned.

'Come on,' Tyler shouted impatiently.

Slowly Purnell walked back. He limped a little as his shin was throbbing. He did not want to be there, did not want to be in Tyler's company. The sight of the bloke nauseated him. Other things had happened about which he had not told Elliott. Tyler had raped him but that had not been the end of it – the bastard had forced him into oral sex and had come in his throat. Whatever had been in the whisky had rendered him only immobile but not unaware. It was clear now that Tyler had got the message that his advances were not to be taken up and that, as a consequence, he intended to ensure that Purnell would fail.

Elliott repositioned the springboard in line with the vaulting box and straightened the mats, then returned to his position.

'All right, Purnell,' Tyler's voice goaded scathingly, 'Give us another laugh. You run like a bloody fairy; try spreading your wings.'

Purnell hesitated on the marker line. He could recall Tyler bringing him on. He looked apprehensive.

'And go!'

Tyler moved away from the springboard and turned as Purnell made the spring. He tripped him neatly. Purnell went down hard. The speed of his sprint prevented him from doing much to save himself, and he cracked his face against the springboard.

'Jesus Christ,' Tyler muttered, prodding him with his foot. 'You clumsy bastard! What the hell do you think you're doing!' His tone was venomous as he demanded, 'Get up you snivelling bloody moron!'

Purnell raised himself slowly, a little concussed. He rocked back on his heels, blood poured from his nose and mouth and there was a blinding pain in his head.

'I said get up!'

'Why don't you sod off and leave me alone!'

Purnell could not control the tremor in his voice or prevent the tears from escaping his eyes.

'I said get up!'

'I don't want to be here! I want to go home!' He tried to staunch the flow of blood as he spoke. 'I just want to go home.'

Tyler's hand flashed towards Purnell's head and he shouted, 'You're a lazy good for…'

Elliott caught Tyler's wrist before his hand connected. 'Leave him alone.'

'I'll have no whinging bastards in my class!'

Tyler wrenched himself free, pushed Elliott aside and grabbed Purnell by the hair, ordering, 'Get up, you bastard!'

Elliott caught Tyler by the collar, and Tyler's grip on Purnell loosened.

'Were you born a bleedin' moron or did you have to work at it?' Elliott asked as he swung Tyler round and slammed him against the vaulting box. 'Sir, spelt SOB,' he spat Tyler's words back at him. 'And pronounced fucking bastard! You know what I'd like to do with you, *sir*?'

'Come on, Mach, leave it,' Zader urged, trying to cool the situation. His hand folded around Elliott's wrist. 'You'll only get...'

Tyler saw the advantage and swung a punch at Elliott. Elliott saw it coming and blocked it, yanked his arm from Zader's grip and sent Tyler sprawling with a counter punch to the jaw.

There was a silence; the class awaited Tyler's reaction. Tyler raised himself a little, massaging his jaw,.

'You're on report, Elliott! Present yourself to the charging officer.'

Elliott hesitated, finally said nothing but turned and headed for the door.

'I'll have you for this!' Tyler yelled after him, 'I'll have you, you bastard!'

The door slammed shut. Tyler scrambled to his feet, and hostile eyes burned into him. He hesitated, wiped his hand across his mouth, turned on his heel and went after Elliott.

'Mach's had it now,' Goodwin murmured as Tyler left. He looked at Zader who had dropped to his haunches beside Purnell and said, 'The bastard'll have him crucified for that.'

Purnell still bled profusely. Zader took a handkerchief from his pocket and mopped up the blood.

'I'll take you down to medical. After that I'll go with you to the CO's office and you can put in a complaint against Tyler.'

'No,' Purnell muttered.

'But we all saw what...'

'I said no!'

'What about Mach?' Zader was puzzled. 'If you don't put in a complaint against Tyler...'

'I didn't ask him to get involved!' Purnell complained as he shook Zader's hand from his shoulder. 'I'm not his problem and he isn't my problem.' He hauled himself unsteadily to his feet.

'I'll find my own way to medical, just let me alone – you hear me?' He stumbled towards the door.

Zader hesitated, looked up at Goodwin and asked, 'What do you make of that?'

Goodwin shrugged and said, 'I guess he's going to tell the MO that he fell.'

Zader rose to his feet. 'That won't be a lot of help to Mach, will it?'

Elliott made no appearance at lunch, and was still absent at dinner. His bed in the dormitory remained empty. He was not at breakfast the following morning. The first tutorial was with Mulcahy, and Zader approached him before the exercises commenced.

'Sir?'

'Zader?' Mulcahy looked round from checking the layout of the apparatus.

'What's happened to Elliott, sir? Instructor Tyler put him on a charge yesterday morning.'

'That he did,' Mulcahy agreed.

'What's happened to him, sir?'

'Elliott? Forty-eight hours in solitary,' Mulcahy smiled wryly and commented, 'It won't hurt him. He's happy enough in his own company, it doesn't bother him. He'll come out smiling and Tyler will still be nursing his bruises.'

'It wasn't Elliott's fault, sir. Tyler was having a go at Purnell, taunting him. Elliott only…'

'Don't be telling tales now, son,' Mulcahy said to stop him. 'Just remember that I'm an instructor too.'

'But you're approachable, sir, we can talk to you. I just want you to know that Mach… Elliott, didn't start it. He was just standing up for Tommy. Tyler threw the first punch, I want you to know that, sir. We all saw it.' He hesitated. 'I'm not asking you to do anything about it.'

'All right, Zader, you've told me.'

'But you don't believe me.'

Mulcahy smiled thinly and said, 'I believe you, son. I think I know Mr Tyler better than you do. Leave things be; let's just wait and see what happens.'

'And let Mach be punished for...'

'Your mate Mach can look after himself, Zader. In fifteen years in the US Army and nine years here I haven't come across one quite like him. A little advice, Zader.'

Zader looked at him.

'Don't underestimate him – and don't overestimate Dominic Tyler.' He turned to the group of young men sprawled across the mats and ordered. 'All right, skivers, on your feet. Look lively now.'

*

The intake settled into the routine, and had become familiar with the constant rigours of the training centre. It was harder than forces life, a stiff regime with their leisure almost as rigidly controlled as the daily grind. They were fitter and faster than they had ever been, and had become accustomed to the feel of a hand gun rather than a rifle. They had come some way towards understanding better the conditions in which they might have to work. Dragged out of bed in the middle of the night to run around assault courses in the freezing night air, the glamour, had it ever existed, had paled. There was no leave, nor any opportunity to socialise outside the training centre. They were being geared to recognise their own failings, their weaknesses as well as their potential. Psychological testing to assess how they coped with stress gave them some indication of their limitations, their 'breaking point'.

'Jeez, I'm knackered,' Jesson muttered as he limped into the dormitory, bruised and muddied from yet another night manoeuvres exercise. 'Why the hell can't they just let us sleep?'

'Tell us about it,' Elliott sympathised as he dragged his tee shirt over his head and headed towards the showers.

'What time is it?'

'What makes you think we even know what day it is?' Elliott yawned and said, 'About half two I think.'

'Oh, God,' Jesson muttered, trudging after him, 'In another two hours we've got to get up again.'

'That's every bloody night this week,' Goodwin complained, 'My brain's gone AWOL.'

'You've got a brain? News to me,' Feiney jibed.

'Shut up, Feiney,' Elliott snapped. 'Where the hell did you get to? Saw you start, saw you finish.' He looked him over. 'How come you don't have any bruises to count?'

Feiney coloured a little. 'Maybe I'm just better than you guys.'

'Yeah, maybe.' Elliott didn't think so. 'Who's got the bleedin' soap?'

Zader passed it to him as he joined them in the showers, stating, 'Tyler's just called lights out in three minutes.'

'So I'm out of here before you all start groping each other in the dark,' Feiney sniped as he made for the door and snatched up a towel.

'Hang around, you might like it,' Elliott called after him sarcastically.

Purnell glanced across at him uneasily.

'Feiney's a bleedin' prat,' Elliott grinned. 'The girls had better be lining up when we get out of this place.'

Four weeks passed, about a seventh of the way through their training, during which time Elliott had had two further skirmishes with Tyler. It was against Elliott's nature to stand back and watch as mates were bullied and belittled, and Tyler had let up none on Purnell. He started nothing specifically with Elliott but knew that he could rely on Elliott's intervention. He played a game of indirect aggravation which left Purnell's nerves shattered.

'All right, boys,' Tyler called their attention. 'We've got a real treat lined up for you today – death alley.' He smiled a little malevolently. 'You'll like it. You're a bunch of gutless bastards, you won't know what's hit you. I'm going to enjoy this.' He paused, then said, 'This is going to blow your minds out. You're around a seventh of the way through your training; you think that you're doing okay; you've got ideas in your thick skulls that you're good enough to make WIA standards. Less than half of you are going to make it, and today we're going to illustrate that fact. We're going to show you what a hopeless bunch of amateurs you really are.' There was no mistaking his pessimistic anticipation. 'Through that door,' he directed, indicating towards the bottom end of the room, a door at each end of the wall, and specifically towards the furthermost, 'there's a passageway. On either side of it there are pop-outs. You won't be able to see where they are, it's like the black hole of Calcutta down there. Some of those pop-outs are going to do just that, at random, chosen by the computer.' He grinned and said, 'Who's going to jump out of the cupboard?' His grin broadened. 'You see green you shoot, you see red you hold your fire. We're playing good guys and bad guys. Green you go for it, you shoot him or you're a dead man. If you're too slow green shoots first, and you come out looking like you had an accident in a ketchup factory.' He looked them over. 'Check your guns, six bullets,' he ordered and waited. 'Live ammunition. There are five greens waiting for you. Don't pump the lead, you'll be dead soon enough without running out of ammo. You think you're marksmen? I'm going to watch every one of you die in there. I don't see you making it past the first two. You're the worst intake I've ever had the misfortune to come across.' He moved across to the computer panel and screen and activated them. 'Line up, single file from the door on the left of the wall.' He waved towards it and shouted, 'Move it!'

Tyler monitored their progress on screen. They entered singly, the next not admitted until the one before him had emerged blooded from the other door. There was no conferring; no warning of what those waiting might expect; each went in cold. The door slid open and Elliott entered, his gun tucked into his belt. They were not permitted to move gun in hand until the first green had been drawn on. Of the nine who had gone in before him only two had outdrawn it.

The door slid shut behind him and sealed him into the silent black tomb. He moved forward warily. A muted click and a figure sprang out. Red. He moved past it. Red, green, he drew and fired. Red, red, green, he fired, green, he fired. Red, green, he fired. Red, green he fired, green he fired. Six? Green, he dived. The blood pellet spattered against the wall. Elliott emerged back into the harsh light of the main room, seething. He knew that Tyler had done it intentionally, knew that he had overridden the computer control and thrown in the additional greens in an attempt to panic him.

Tyler said nothing, and ignored Elliott's unblooded appearance. Inside he burned with anger, despised him for having come through it, for being so damned good. Smart arse; he had made it despite the tricks which had been pulled and Tyler loathed him for it; he did not feel pride at having an excellent pupil.

Purnell was in, half-way through and going well. Tyler watched his progress on the screen and fumed silently. Another clever son of a bitch. He had harassed Purnell. In every intake he had selected one – usually one who was expected to do well, macho, his preferences not under any dispute, certainly heterosexual – and he had made his approach. If he had been denied he had abused and broken the young bastard. Purnell, a big tough marine, had been the obvious material.

In full view Tyler again activated computer override, his eyes on the monitor screen. He released two targets simultaneously. They sprang out directly opposite to each other. The scream was audible in the outer room, agonised. It ceased abruptly. Tyler smiled. The intake had frozen, the silence heavy. Elliott sprinted up to the entrance door and clawed at it, forced it from the jamb and slid through. A few yards ahead the gloom was relieved by the light which accompanied the targets. He could see Purnell clamped between the two sheet metal figures which had leapt out and formed a crude guillotine.

Purnell's body was limp, well jammed and held semi-upright by the figures. They pushed into his body, front and back, but had missed his head. Blood ran in rivers down the metal. Elliott pressed his hand against Purnell's neck; there was a pulse throb. He dropped to his knees and pushed against the edge of the right-hand target: it dug into his flesh. The left-hand target continued to extend as the other retracted until its limit was finally reached. The mechanisms were strong, but Elliott strained to keep the right-hand target moving back. His hands were cut, his own blood mingling with Purnell's.

Slowly the target moved back into the wall and released Purnell from the vice-like grip. He fell across Elliott and into a crumpled heap on the floor. Elliott checked that they were both clear, then let the target jump back and block the corridor.

Someone finally reinstated computer control and activated the emergency switch. The targets retracted and light flooded the passageway. Both of the doors slid open. Zader was first through with Jesson close behind. They joined Elliott and sank down beside Purnell. Elliott rose to his feet and made for the entrance, then pushed through the curious youths who had congregated. He strode towards Tyler who was still standing over the computer.

Tyler paled. He had not realised until the light had flooded the passageway the damage that had been done. He had not thought that Purnell had been physically injured, but had taken the agonised screams to signify that Purnell's nerve had failed him. He looked up as Elliott's shadow fell over him. A solid punch and Tyler hit the deck. Elliott followed him down, straddled him, his hands clenched around Tyler's throat. There was no moving him, the pressure was relentless. Tyler's hands clamped around Elliott's wrists but could not loosen the grip.

It took three of the staff to haul Elliott off, one of them Mulcahy who had responded to the emergency alert. Mulcahy pushed Elliott against the wall, and held him there with his hands on his shoulders.

'Easy lad, take it easy.' His soft Irish American brogue was soothing, and authoritative.

'It's all right, son.' He calmed Elliott's rage. 'Just cool down now.'

Elliott, perspiring but no longer displaying signs that he wanted to break loose, nodded. Tyler remained down, coughing hoarsely and gasping for breath whilst clutching his throat.

'What are you going to do, son?' Mulcahy asked Elliott quietly.

'Report to the charging officer?'

'Good lad,' Mulcahy confirmed with a smile. 'Voluntarily,' he released him. 'Off you go now.' His hands dropped from Elliott's shoulders.

Elliott's eyes went to Tyler and rested for a few moments. Turning away he strode towards the door, the eyes of the intake following him.

The twenty-eight young men who returned to their dormitories, training suspended for the rest of the day, were subdued. Purnell and Tyler had been taken to medical. In Elliott's dormitory the four who remained had no conversation. The same thoughts perhaps were going through their heads. Three times Elliott had been placed on charge, each time by Tyler, and each time for standing up for his mates – and they had let him, alone, not one of them willing to stand with him.

Mulcahy stepped into the dormitory; they all looked towards him.

'Tyler's all right.' He let his eyes rove over them and said, 'Purnell's poorly but stable after emergency surgery.' He lowered himself on to Purnell's bed. 'And Elliott's been put forward for court martial. Tyler's pressing for a charge of attempted murder. The Commander himself has been notified. Make no mistake boys, young Elliott's got himself big trouble.' He looked them over slowly. 'And for what? For being the only one amongst the lot of you with the guts to square up to a bully, to put his mates before himself.'

The four pairs of eyes lowered from his gaze.

'Tyler's blaming what happened on a computer fault.'

'He overrode computer control. We saw…' Jesson stopped abruptly.

'Did he, Mr Jesson? You saw that?'

'Yes – no – I…' Jesson stammered.

'I saw him,' Zader offered.

'Me too, sir,' Feiney confirmed.

'And me,' Goodwin said.

'I think most of the intake saw it,' Zader muttered as he looked at Mulcahy.

Mulcahy nodded. 'And what are you going to do about it?' he asked as he rose to his feet. 'It's my night on dormitory duty, boys,' he reminded them as he made for the door. 'Remember Elliott in your prayers.' He smiled thinly.

The door closed behind him. There was a brief silence.

'Mulcahy's right,' Goodwin said, breaking it, 'We've got to do something.'

'It's no use going to the CO,' Feiney stated, looking at him, 'Tyler's his blue-eyed boy.'

There was a murmur of agreement.

'Then we'll go to the Commander,' Zader suggested.

'How? And if we did, he wouldn't take any notice of us,' Feiney objected. 'We're just a bunch of students, he could have the lot of us thrown out and replaced.'

'We can try,' Zader decided, 'If he's the sort of bloke who won't give a fair hearing, I wouldn't want to work for him anyway. I'd rather be thrown out.'

There was a grudging assent.

'So let's get down to drafting a petition.'

'And how are you going to get it to him?' Feiney asked, 'We can't get out of this place, and we don't have access to any communications.'

There was a pause. Zader suggested, 'We'll ask Mulcahy. He'll have access; he'll know how to reach him.' Zader flicked through his notebook and found a blank page beyond his lecture notes.

'What makes you think Mulcahy's going to help us? What's he want to put himself on the line for? Only land himself in the shit,' Feiney pointed out pessimistically.

'Look, Feiney,' snapped Zader, his patience evaporating, 'You don't have to come in on this. If you can't come up with something constructive why don't you just keep your mouth shut?'

He lowered himself on to the edge of the bed. Goodwin and Jesson moved to join him.

'Just trying to be practical,' Feiney commented as he walked across, 'Didn't say that I didn't want to come in on it.'

⋆

Marlborough expected the training centre to take care of itself. He was a busy man, ultimately taking the responsibility for the movements and activities of all WIA personnel world-wide. He didn't expect to be troubled by events below operative level. The training centre was a secular institution, an isolated school with a ratio of two members of staff to each student in the intake. It was self contained, had expert staff, and it was not usual or necessary for him to have to intervene in the established disciplinary procedures or in any part of the routine.

Students were not of interest to him, his prime area of concern being in operative level. It was ludicrous that the training centre staff were apparently incapable of smoothing out their own problems. It was even more ludicrous that one young man should effectively disrupt its entire operation. He turned his attention again to the petition which had arrived on his desk at around lunch time, a request by the student intake that he should personally intervene in the affairs of the training centre. There was no such request from Chief Officer Klein, no indication that he required assistance. Perhaps it was the curiosity factor which prompted him to decide upon an unannounced visit.

Marlborough read the file which he had had prepared on Elliott as he made the final leg of the journey from the airport by chauffeur driven limousine: background, service history, training progress reports, details of the charges and numerous reports upon which Elliott had already been placed, and Tyler's statement of the events which had led to the request to instigate court martial proceedings.

Marlborough had already begun to form some preliminary opinions, not least that Klein, the chief officer, was apparently ineffectual. Disciplinary action meted out against Elliott as punishment on charges to date had been, at the very least, lenient.

Marlborough himself was around six feet in height, was in his early forties, and invariably smartly dressed. His fair brown hair showed no signs of grey. He was a handsome man with penetrating blue eyes which were shielded behind dark rimmed glasses. He was not a man with whom to trifle; there was a distinct aura of authority, a manner which brooked no argument. He had a tendency towards the terse, expected and perhaps demanded to receive absolute loyalty and obedience. Like him or loathe him there was no alternative but to respect him. His entire life revolved around the WIA, his home was WHQ London, an accommodation suite within the building. Usually he made himself available for consultation twenty-four hours a day. It was not in his nature to delegate the responsibility of WIA action – he was well aware where the buck ultimately stopped.

It was early morning as the limousine approached the training centre, its high grey walls looming ahead. Marlborough snapped the file shut and pushed it into his briefcase. Never in the history of the training centre had there been a request for court martial proceedings to be taken against a member of the intake – Elliott appeared to have achieved a number of firsts. In an exuberant bunch of young men in high spirits, incidents were to be expected. It was not unusual for some of them to find themselves on report or even on a charge for some minor misdemeanour. Elliott had the dubious distinction of having three charges to his credit – one of assault and two of insubordination – and now the attempted murder of an instructing officer.

It was four fifteen and morning was breaking slowly, only a hint of pale sky interrupting the blackness of the night. The ground shone in the lights of the limousine, the thin coating of frost not yet beginning to thaw. Out on the quadrangle sat the remaining twenty-eight members of the intake. Already they had been there for almost an hour, jacket collars pulled up against the chilly breeze, and determined to stage their protest in spite of the inclement weather conditions. They were silent, sitting in demonstration in support of Elliott.

Tyler pulled open the curtains that covered his windows and looked out across the quadrangle. His eyes rested on the neat rows of young men, and he froze momentarily. Snatching up his jacket he left his room hurriedly and headed towards the main doors, stopping only to instruct a colleague to get all members of staff out on to the quadrangle. He raced outside and across to the silent youths.

'What the hell's going on!' he demanded.

Twenty-eight pairs of eyes looked towards him but no one responded to the question.

'A silent strike is it? Who's responsible?'

The eyes did not deviate. Elliott was not available to be the scapegoat, nor Purnell.

'Who's responsible?' he demanded again as he moved between the unresponsive youths. 'I'll have you all on charge,' he threatened, 'Every last man of you. Get back to your dormitories. Do you hear me?'

No one moved. There was no reaction except that all eyes followed him.

'I'll have the lot of you on a charge of mutiny! You!' he screamed at Goodwin. 'Tell me who's responsible for this.'

Goodwin stared at him blankly.

'Gross insubordination – you're on a charge – report to the charging officer.'

Nothing. Tyler glanced around desperately, alone amongst the hostile youths. He hesitated uncertainly, regained his composure as Mulcahy strolled out of the administration buildings towards him.

'It's a grand morning, Mr Tyler,' Mulcahy greeted him, 'It's nice to see you encouraging the boys to get some fresh air.'

'Fresh air? I'll give them fresh air!' Tyler exploded. 'These men are all on a charge of gross insubordination. Take their names, Mulcahy.'

'Certainly, Mr Tyler,' Mulcahy agreed pleasantly, reaching in a leisurely fashion into his jacket pocket and drawing out his notebook and pen.

'Gross insubordination, blatant disobedience, obstruction, mutiny!' Tyler screamed, and hauled Goodwin to his feet. 'Report to the charging officer.' He pushed Goodwin towards the administration buildings but as soon as Tyler's grip loosened Goodwin retook his position on the floor.

'Get the rest of the staff out here, Mulcahy.'

Mulcahy was flicking idly through his pocketbook. He looked across and inquired. 'Should I finish taking names first, Mr Tyler?'

'You haven't even started. Get the staff out here. Do it now, man! Don't waste time asking bloody stupid questions!'

Mulcahy nodded and conceded, 'Right away, Mr Tyler.'

He snapped his pocketbook shut and returned it unhurriedly to his pocket. Slowly he strolled back towards the buildings.

Marlborough's limousine had been admitted by the gateman, otherwise his arrival had gone unnoticed in the chaos. He instructed the chauffeur to switch off the car lights and engine, and remained in the car. He watched with disbelief and rising anger as Tyler yelled and screamed in what he could only describe as a hysterical manner. It now appeared that at least one member of the staff had been allocated to each member of the intake and was making somewhat unsuccessful attempts to drag their uncooperative charges from the quadrangle. Dom Tyler was barking orders like a demented sergeant major.

'Would you like me to try and get the car up to the Administration Block, Commander?' the chauffeur asked.

'No, I think I'll walk it, thank you.'

'Sir.' The chauffeur opened the car door and climbed out, then pulled open the passenger door.

'Am I correct in identifying that screaming idiot as Chief Instructor Tyler?' he asked as he emerged.

'Yes, sir.'

'I thought so,' he muttered, and moved towards the chaos.

Still his presence, as he stood on the edge of the mêlée went unnoticed.

'Is there any sane member of staff around here?' he demanded.

Silence descended as his presence was finally noticed. The intake resumed their seated positions as the staff released them uncertainly. Everyone looked towards Marlborough. Unfamiliar to the intake his authority was almost tangible. They glanced at each other nervously.

'These men are staging a demonstration strike, Commander,' Tyler said as he turned and saluted sharply. 'I'm having them all charged...'

'Staging a demonstration strike?' Marlborough inquired, his eyes roving briefly over the youths before returning to Tyler. 'Against what?'

'Sir?'

'Against what are they staging a demonstration strike?'

'I, er...' Tyler foundered. He had not inquired. He seemed to shrink under Marlborough's steady stare.

Marlborough turned his attention back to the intake and surveyed their youthful faces.

'Do you have a spokesman?'

There was a pause whilst they exchanged glances; here was something they had omitted to discuss. They had not anticipated that they might be faced with the Commander. Uncertainly, Zader rose to his feet.

'I might have guessed,' Tyler snapped starting towards him. 'Bloody trouble-maker, public school agitator.' He grabbed Zader's collar. 'I'll have you boy! Inciting to mutiny, I'll have you...'

'Tyler!' Marlborough snapped.

'I want this bastard court martialled!' Tyler demanded.

'Do you, Mr Tyler?' Marlborough surveyed him coldly and added, 'Do you indeed?'

'All of them. All of the sodding...'

Marlborough's expression was a killer. 'Go to your quarters, Mr Tyler,' he instructed tersely.

There was a pause, then Tyler decided it would not be wise to argue. He turned on his heel and headed for the administration block.

'Name?' Marlborough turned his attention back to Zader.

'Zader, sir.'

'Well, Zader – a demonstration strike?' Marlborough inquired.

'Yes, sir,' Zader responded nervously. 'Will we be allowed the opportunity to...?'

'Incitement to mutiny, Zader!' Tyler spun round and shouted, 'You'll be allowed to tell it to the Court Martial before you're shot.'

'Thank you, Mr Tyler – have you quite finished?' Marlborough's patience was evaporating rapidly, and he spoke with ominous control. 'I have worked a sixteen hour shift, I have travelled all night and I am tired. It should not be necessary for me to come to the training centre, and I should not arrive to find that sixty trained members of staff are incapable of exercising control over thirty students.' He looked at Tyler pointedly, and Tyler retreated.

Marlborough's eyes ran over the plainly uneasy personnel who remained.

'I find it hard to believe that thirty young men accustomed to the strict regime of service life are rebelling without just cause.'

The silence was oppressive.

'All staff return to administration,' Marlborough instructed, looking back to Zader as the staff began to withdraw. 'I would be obliged if you could ask your colleagues to return quietly to their dormitories, Zader.'

'Yes, sir.' Zader found Marlborough daunting. 'Will we…?'

'I will give the elected spokesman on behalf of the intake the opportunity to state their case.'

'Thank you, sir.'

Marlborough strode towards the administration buildings and stepped inside. He headed briskly in the direction of Klein's office. Mulcahy fell into step with him.

'Could I have a word, sir?'

Marlborough stopped, then said, 'I'd appreciate it if you would, Mr Mulcahy. I appear to be here at your invitation – computer records indicate that you forwarded the petition for my attention.'

He regarded Mulcahy steadily. It could not be denied.

Mulcahy nodded and continued, 'At the risk of further jeopardising my job…'

'I doubt that that's a possibility, Mulcahy.'

'I encouraged the boys to stage their demonstration.'

'I see.'

'I hadn't anticipated that it would coincide with your visit.'

'But you anticipated that I would make a visit.' Marlborough smiled thinly.

Mulcahy nodded and said, 'We've known each other a long time, Commander.'

'We have,' Marlborough agreed.

'And never seen eye to eye, never liked each other...' Mulcahy half smiled.

'Do we dislike each other? I didn't know that.'

'I didn't say that we disliked each other, I said that we didn't like each other.'

Marlborough nodded. 'You're right, Mulcahy, there is a difference,' he conceded, looking at him quizzically.

There was a pause.

'If you're considering disciplinary action against the boys – what they did was with my knowledge.'

'Encouragement and approval?' Marlborough asked him.

'I was neither discouraging nor disapproving.'

Marlborough nodded and said, 'I take it that all this revolves around Elliott?'

'Maybe,' Mulcahy agreed. 'He's a good lad. A bit headstrong perhaps.'

Marlborough studied him for a moment. 'Enough of discussing business on the doorstep,' he said. 'I'll make my investigation...'

'You intend to investigate?'

'I take that to be the reason for the invitation – and I'll draw my own conclusions. No doubt you'll be available?'

'Yes, sir.'

*

There were magazines and writing paper in the cell, the confines of which were around three yards square. Bars were at the high window, and the walls were painted an uninspiring cream. A long narrow bed, a table and a chair were the only furnishings. Elliott had made good use of the paper to assemble a squadron of aeroplanes. He flew them idly around the limited space. Marlborough caught one deftly as he entered, and his eyes rested on the slim, long-legged young man sat on the hard floor with his back against the wall and his knees drawn towards his chest. Elliott glanced up. He guessed the identity of his visitor but showed no deference.

'You're apparently a trouble-maker, Elliott,' Marlborough accused, looking at him.

'Sir.'

He acknowledged the comment with a tone which neither accepted nor denied it, then launched another plane and watched as it circled and dropped.

'Is that all you have to say?'

'I think maybe I could improve on the aerodynamics with a few adjustments.'

Elliott amended the angle of the wings of his next model and aimed it towards the barred window. Marlborough watched it for a moment, then looked back to Elliott.

'This training centre has been established for over forty years, Elliott, originally MOD and as a WIA facility for almost ten. In all that time, never have four charges been brought against an entire intake, much less against one individual – and certainly there has never been a request for court martial.' He studied Elliott, then asked, 'What's your problem?'

'My problem?' Elliott flew a model plane across the cell, watched as it fell and swooped. 'I don't have a problem.'

Marlborough moved across to the bed and lowered himself on to it.

'Have you been warned that three charges are sufficient to warrant your dismissal?'

'No,' Elliott responded as he glanced across. 'But when you're stuck in the guardroom there isn't much else to do but read the rule book and practise origami.'

'I get the impression that you don't much care.'

There was no response.

'We have a problem, Elliott, and we need to identify it.'

Elliott launched another plane.

'Are you happy here?'

A half smile.

'Let me put it another way – are you unhappy here?'

'No, sir.'

'Do you resent being estranged from your family?'

'I don't have any family.'

'No, of course you don't,' Marlborough conceded, recalling the file. 'Stupid of me, I'm sorry.'

'Doesn't matter.'

Elliott rose to his feet and gathered up the planes.

'Your friends perhaps.'

'I make new friends.'

'Marlborough watched him thoughtfully, then asked, 'Do you want to be dismissed?'

'I'd have stopped at the third. Gone beyond that stage, haven't I?' Elliott turned and looked at him, 'You can't court martial me if I'm dismissed.'

'Will you answer the question?'

'I don't want to be dismissed – but it isn't up to me, is it?'

He sank back on to the floor, his back against the wall. He looked very young, was the youngest in the intake. His hair, grown from its regulation length was unruly. He looked very vulnerable, like a child, as he assembled his squadron of paper planes.

'Elliott?'

He looked up.

'Tell me why I shouldn't dismiss you.'

He shrugged, then suggested, 'It'd be more fun to have me shot?'

'These are serious charges,' Marlborough snapped. 'Gross insubordination, assault on an officer, further insubordination, attempted murder of an officer.'

'Then you won't dismiss me,' Elliott reasoned.

'I have a court martial request.'

Elliott nodded.

'Give me something in your defence.'

Elliott shook his head.

Marlborough studied him again, then asked, 'You can't or you won't?'

'I don't have anything to say.'

'I see.'

'I don't think so.'

Marlborough sighed. 'You have a liking for confined spaces?'

Elliott looked up.

'A liking for your own company?'

'It depends on the alternatives.'

There was a brief silence.

'Is the training centre not as you expected it to be?'

'I don't expect much. I can handle it.'

'There's some problem.'

'I don't have a problem.'

'Do I have a problem?' Marlborough asked. 'Tell me what I should know.'

Elliott shrugged.

'You aren't helping yourself, and you aren't helping me. Who the hell are you helping?'

'I'm helping someone?'

There was a silence.

'Is life here too hard, too spartan?'

'Here?' Elliott asked as he looked around the cell.

'Training centre.'

'I was brought up on the streets – isn't the easiest way of living.'

'Is bullying prevalent?'

'I can take being top of anybody's hate list. I don't get bullied.'

'We aren't getting anywhere, Elliott. Perhaps you want out?'

'No.'

'Why should I keep you?'

'How about because I'm going to be number one?' Elliott regarded him steadily, challenging him, and added, 'Best number one you ever had.'

Marlborough smiled tightly.

'If you don't believe me, that's okay. Pass up and you'll always wonder. Try me and I'll either prove it or get myself killed. You can't loose either way.'

'But I don't get any answers?'

'I don't have any answers.'

Marlborough rose to his feet and looked down at him. 'Maybe it's just that I don't have the right questions.' He smiled wryly and threatened, 'I'll find out what's going on around here.'

'Hope you do, Commander – and then you can tell me about it before you have me shot.'

'Will I have you shot when I know about it?'

'That's your decision, not mine.'

Marlborough was thoughtful as he left the detention unit. There seemed to be an exclusive secret. Elliott knew, he didn't doubt that, Mulcahy held his suspicions, and the intake had a cause – a cause which stemmed from the repercussions and not the root. Tyler, he suspected, was intrinsic; none of the other instructors appeared to have experienced any problems with Elliott. The charges had all emanated from Tyler. Purnell came into it somewhere, but how was not clear. Mulcahy admitted to aiding and abetting the petition and the demonstration. Things at the training centre were not all that they should be.

Klein leapt to his feet like a startled rabbit as Marlborough stepped into his office. He vacated his chair quickly and moved around to the opposite side of the desk. Marlborough took Klein's seat, and looked across at him.

'I want the file on Tyler.'

'Tyler, sir?' Klein repeated.

'Dominic Tyler. I want his entire service record.'

'Certainly, sir,' Klein said uncertainly. 'He is the senior...'

'I sanctioned his appointment, I'm well aware of his status. His service record, Mr Klein – you do have his service record?'

'Yes, sir.'

'Good.'

He watched as Klein made for the door.

'Sir?' Klein turned quizzically.

'Yes, Klein?'

'May I ask why, sir?'

'No, you may not.'

Klein hesitated. 'Sir,' he acknowledged as he turned back to the door.

'Klein?'

'Yes, sir,' he turned round.

'You have all of the dead files?'

'Dead files?'

'Students who failed to graduate?'

'Yes, sir.'

'Have them taken out to my car for delivery to DHQ Glasgow.

'Yes, sir,' Klein confirmed as he left looking puzzled.

Marlborough rested his elbows on the desk, his chin on his knuckles. Looking for clues, he was not sure what he hoped to find – or he hoped that he would not find. There was a cut and dried case against Elliott; three previous charges. It puzzled him that Tyler seemed to have no complaints about Elliott's work; there was no allegation that he was disruptive in class. There had to be some reason for Elliott's behaviour but his marks in all subjects were high, and Tyler maintained that he had done nothing which might be construed as provocation.

As for Elliott himself, he was an unimpressive young man, had just come over as a little arrogant. There was something about him, something which Marlborough could not define but which, oddly, gave him the feeling that he should not be in too much of a hurry to dispense with his services. Marlborough's immediate reaction was that he did not like Elliott. Usually he placed much weight on first impressions but on this occasion he was not sure that he should judge too hastily. Perhaps there was more to Elliott, and to the circumstances, than met the eye initially. Marlborough did not like Tyler, he had never liked him, but that did not detract from the fact that he was a good instructor with a proven track record. If Elliott shared that dislike it did not seem to ring true that he should provoke and physically assault Tyler for that reason alone.

Marlborough sighed; something was drastically wrong. He suspected that the situation at the training centre was not all that it should be. He could not substantiate his suspicions nor was he accustomed to relying upon what he supposed was intuition. It was too early to seek to draw conclusions; he had made a promise to the intake that he would give them a full hearing, and Purnell he had yet to see. He had also asked for Tyler's service record and the dead files. For what purpose, he was not entirely sure, but his visit to the training centre seemed unlikely to be brief.

Purnell was in the sick bay, conscious and lucid and no longer drifting in and out of sleep in the haze of post anaesthesia. His wounds had required over a hundred stitches along the length of his left side, front and back, and his blood loss had been considerable. A drip ran to his arm, and his pain was dulled to a constant ache by powerful painkillers. He was almost afraid to close his eyes as darkness brought back images of the nightmares. Perhaps now he would be discharged and allowed to go home.

The door of the room opened quietly. Purnell looked across as Marlborough stepped inside. This was an unfamiliar face, not one of the staff to whom they had been introduced.

'I'd like to talk to you, Purnell,' Marlborough said, stopping at the bedside. 'Do you feel up to talking?'

Purnell made no reply.

'Commander Lester James Marlborough.' Marlborough introduced himself. 'I can come back some other time.'

Purnell shook his head, and Marlborough pulled up a chair.

'If talking becomes too much for you I'll suspend this interview until you feel stronger,' he looked Purnell over as he sat down. 'I'm not given to time wasting, I'll get straight to the point. It seems to me that all is not as it should be. There's something going on here and Tyler, Elliott and yourself appear to be the central characters. I know that there's a connection and I want to know what it is.'

Purnell averted his eyes.

'Elliott's on a charge with a view to court martial proceedings – attempted murder of an officer – he'll spend the next fifteen years behind bars at the very least.'

'He's going to be court martialled?' Purnell whispered.

'He doesn't seem to want to give me any reason why he shouldn't be.'

'But that's not fair.'

'Not fair, Purnell? Court martial seems to be, to me, a quite reasonable action.'

Marlborough looked at him and said, 'Elliott has nothing to say in his own defence.'

'That bastard, Tyler, should be court martialled, not Mach.'

'Mach?'

'Elliott, sir.'

'Why?'

There was a silence.

'Elliott makes no allegations against instructor Tyler. He makes no claim that he was, in any way, provoked. He infers by his silence that his attack was premeditated and without just cause.'

'That's because he promised...' Purnell stopped.

Marlborough waited for a few moments; nothing more was forthcoming.

'Was that a promise made to you?'

'Yes, sir.'

'I see. Is the root of our problem a promise which Elliott won't break?'

A brief silence.

'Apparently he values a promise more than he values his future, or possibly even his life. It would seem that it's up to you, Purnell. You have to be the one to tell me, unless, of course, you don't give a damn for Elliott's future, in which case, fair or not, you'll both keep your secret, and Elliott may very well take it to an early grave. That will be on your conscience and not mine. The proposed charge is attempted murder. Elliott is well aware that the death penalty applies.'

Nothing. Purnell's eyes remained averted. Marlborough rose to his feet and made for the door.

'Sir?'

Marlborough turned.

'All Mach ever did was stand up for his mates.'

'Would you like to elaborate a little?'

There was a pause.

'Yes, sir.'

Marlborough returned to the bedside and retook his seat.

'In your own time.'

It was clear that Purnell was reluctant.

'Would you prefer me to come back later?'

'No, sir.'

A pause; Marlborough did not put pressure on him to continue.

'On my second day here...' Purnell started hesitantly, 'Tyler...' He stopped.

'Tyler?' Marlborough encouraged him.

He...'

It was difficult. Purnell had not wanted to talk about it again; he wanted just to be allowed to forget. He realised that he could not if Elliott was to be helped. But Tyler was a member of staff and he was just a student – why should he be believed? He looked at Marlborough uncertainly.

'Tyler drugged and homosexually raped me, sir,' the words came out rapidly.

Marlborough looked at him – no sign of disbelief in his expression – no sign of anything.

'That's a serious allegation, Purnell. Did you report the incident. Did you seek medical advice?'

'No, sir,' he admitted and looked away from him.

There was a pause. Marlborough did not press for him to continue further; he could wait. Probably he would have to wait as this was delicate ground.

'I... I'd been to the lecture given by DCSA Omaru. The video which he showed was too much for me and I had to go to medical,' Purnell continued finally. 'I started feeling better and I was on my way back to the lecture when Tyler stopped me.' He glanced at Marlborough but could not read his expression. 'He said that I needed a stiff drink. I said that I was okay and I was going back to the lecture theatre but he said there were no brownie points to be had. I went with him to his room as he said it was an order, and he poured me a large scotch.' He paused. 'It's like being at school, sir, you think you can trust your teachers, they're there to teach and take care of you when your parents aren't around.'

Marlborough nodded and confirmed, 'That's the way it should be. Unfortunately it isn't always the case.' Marlborough paused, then added, 'He poured you a large scotch?'

Purnell nodded and went on, 'It tasted a bit strange but he said that it was liqueur based. I drank it and I began to feel… light-headed.'

There was a lengthy silence.

'The next thing I remember I was on the bed and Tyler was undressing me. I didn't… there was nothing I could do. It was like I was paralysed. He was touching me; I could feel what was going on. I was aware but I couldn't do anything to stop him.' His composure was failing him. 'He rolled me on to my stomach and…' his voice cracked, 'And he had sex with me,' he barely whispered.

Marlborough said nothing.

'After… I don't know, it seemed like forever, he left. He'd made me do things, other things…' He was becoming emotional.

'We can leave it, I can come back.'

Purnell shook his head and recalled painfully, 'He made me give him oral sex. I couldn't move, I couldn't do anything.' Tears pricked at his eyes. He had said too much to stop now, believed or not. 'The effect of – whatever it was he'd given me – was wearing off. I got myself dressed. My guts hurt and I felt sick. I knew I couldn't face anybody so I went out into the grounds. Hours must have passed when Mach came looking for me. He persuaded me to tell him, and I made him promise not to tell. He took me back to the dorm, said he'd stay with me. I asked him to swap beds and he said okay. The rest of the lads were in rec. and we didn't have any lights on. Tyler came in, went across to my bed. He didn't know it was Mach, and he started talking to him, thinking it was me. He asked if I was feeling rough, and said not to worry about it, that I'd get used to it. He said I was how he liked them – young, athletic, good build and heterosexual – we could be useful to each other. For my ass he'd make sure I graduated. Mach then threatened to put him through the door. Tyler backed off, saying that he'd see Mach thrown out – finished.'

'As a consequence, did he pick on Elliott?'

'For a while. He was wasting his time; Mach didn't react.'

'Elliott's been on a charge three times for not reacting?'

'Tyler had it in for me, and Mach reacted to that and not being needled himself.'

Marlborough nodded. Purnell was clearly distressed and in a good deal of pain. It was unlikely that he was lying. It was unfortunate that he had not sought medical attention as there was no proof. Investigation now would only, at best, confirm a homosexual encounter. He rose to his feet.

'Perhaps we should talk a little more later. You're tired. We'll discuss the accident…'

'There was no accident, sir.'

Marlborough looked at him.

'All right, Purnell, what was it?'

'Mach had gone into the gallery before me. There were supposed to be five green targets. He was doing well, brilliant. Tyler overrode the computer, threw in two extra greens.'

'You saw that?' Marlborough asked as he retook his seat.

'Yes, sir.'

‘And what do you suppose happened when it came your turn?’

‘I think he overrode the computer and brought out two targets together. I don’t know if he intended that they should come out across from each other.’

Marlborough was thoughtful as he returned to Klein’s office. He was of the opinion that Purnell was a level-headed young man and not given to making imaginative and false allegations – certainly not of the nature which he had made. It was apparent that he was under considerable stress and was nervous. If such characteristics had previously manifested themselves then he would not have been considered for WIA training. At least it could be ascertained whether computer control of the reflex exercise had been overriden.

Tyler’s service record was waiting on Klein’s desk. Marlborough pulled it forward as he took his seat and opened it. For a couple of hours he studied it but the record appeared to be exemplary. Taking his communicator from his pocket he called DHQ Glasgow to where he had had the dead files taken for assessment. It appeared that in practically every intake since the inception of the training centre as a WIA module there was, amongst the dead files, a failed trainee who had been expected to do extremely well. Also, not one of these trainees had ever been a borderline recruit. Each of them had been medically assessed on discharge as being of a nervous disposition, a trait which they had not displayed previously.

Returning his communicator to his pocket he reached across to the desk top communicator and opened an internal line.

‘Detention?’

‘Have Elliott brought to Chief Officer Klein’s office,’ he instructed curtly.

‘Yes, sir.’

A few minutes later there was a knock at the door.

'Enter.'

He looked up as Elliott, his hands cuffed behind him, was escorted into the office.

'Why is he handcuffed?'

'Chief Officer Klein's instructions, sir. The prisoner isn't to be moved without restraint.'

Marlborough's eyes lingered momentarily on Elliott.

'Release him.'

'Doctor Laverne's preliminary report suggests that the prisoner displays temperamental instability, and Chief Officer Klein…'

'Are you questioning my authority?' Marlborough snapped.

'No, sir,' the guard conceded quickly, unlocking the handcuffs and removing them.

'That will be all,' Marlborough watched as the guard left. 'Sit down, Elliott.'

Elliott took the seat opposite.

'Temperamental instability?' Elliott inquired as he looked at Marlborough.

'I don't think so, Elliott. In my opinion you're very well in control of your faculties – in fact I'd go so far as to say that completely the opposite diagnosis would be more accurate.' He studied him for a few moments. 'Have you had the opportunity to study the allegations made against you, and also Instructor Tyler's statement in support? The case summary?'

Elliott nodded.

'Do you deny the allegations?'

'No.'

'Is the statement accurate?'

'In comparison to what?'

'This is a serious matter, Elliott. I'm not altogether sure that you realise the implications.'

'I could make better use of around fifteen years than counting flecks in the paintwork of a prison cell.' Elliott looked at him steadily, then added, 'Or under WIA statute it's a capital offence. It'd be cheaper to have me shot.'

Obviously he realised the implications.

'Would you be prepared to deliver a public apology to Instructor Tyler?'

'Not even if he withdrew the allegation.'

A silence ensued.

'You don't deny the allegation?'

Elliott shrugged.

'But you do deny the statement of events as given by Instructor Tyler?'

'I don't know what goes on in his mind.'

'What goes on in yours?'

'I've never been a liar.'

'And by implication, Tyler is?' Marlborough viewed him steadily, then asked, 'Give me your version of events.'

There was no response, nor did Elliott shrink from his gaze.

'I've spoken to Purnell,' Marlborough offered, 'He's told me the whole story, and about the promise you made to him.' He hesitated. 'You still won't break it, will you?'

There was no response.

'You can provide an explanation for your behaviour, perhaps even a reasonable explanation.'

Elliott shrugged.

'You do realise that your silence protects Tyler?'

Marlborough gave him a short time to think about it, although he did not expect to receive a reply.

Frustrating though it was, Marlborough could not help but respect Elliott's refusal to break a promise, no matter how misguided that refusal could be considered. What a strange young man! Marlborough doubted that Elliott's actions had been more emotive than calculated or that he would have stopped short of murder had no one intervened.

'I don't know what to do with you, Elliott,' he admitted, looking at him. 'Go to your dormitory and remain there.'

Elliott regarded him quizzically.

'Or would you prefer to return to detention?'

'No preference, sir.'

'Then return to your dormitory with dispensation to take meals in the refectory and attend evening recreation.'

*

News of Elliott's release from custody had reached Tyler's ears. He sought out Klein angrily, and burst into the office which Klein occupied. Klein looked up startled.

'What the hell's going on around here?' he demanded, 'That bastard Elliott's been let out.'

'On Commander Marlborough's orders.'

'You're the Chief around here; you could have...'

'I wasn't consulted.'

'You should have some bloody influence – you're too bloody gutless to exercise it. Marlborough shows up and you're licking his shoes and kissing his ass,' Tyler yelled. 'He shouldn't even be here – you should have handled it yourself. You didn't need to go running...'

'I didn't ask him to come. His arrival was as much of a surprise to me as it was to anyone else.'

'You didn't?' Tyler hesitated, then asked, 'Then what the hell is going on here?'

'We don't make regular requests for court martial hearings,' Klein pointed out reasonably.

'Laverne's report supported...'

'I can't account for the Commander's action, Tyler. If you want to know you'll have to ask him.' Klein hesitated. 'There's a young man's future, possibly even his life...'

'Sod that little bastard! It was my neck he had his fucking hands round! He was out to kill me and now he's wandering around loose…'

'And it's a matter for the Commander. I'm sure he has his reasons…'

'We don't need him here.'

'We don't have any choice in the matter. The Commander has the authority and I don't intend to question that authority,' Klein snapped, looking squarely at him. 'We have nothing to hide.'

'This whole intake's a bunch of trouble-makers.'

'The strike staged by the intake was unfortunate but the Commander's a reasonable man. He's bound to realise that the sudden isolation which these young men have had thrust upon them can have a traumatic effect.'

'I could have dealt with it; his interference undermines my authority.'

'You've over-dramatising things. These are exceptional circumstances – unprecedented actions – they merit the Commander's attention.'

'He's let that fucking murderer out!' Tyler made for the door. 'When I get a knife through my back maybe he'll see sense!'

The door slammed forcefully behind him as he left.

Chapter Four

Marlborough found Mulcahy supervising the evening leisure period. Clearly he was popular with the trainees. He had a humour which they appreciated and a relaxed attitude towards them. There was a group of ten or twelve of the intake gathered around him. Elliott was not in evidence. Mulcahy had clocked Marlborough's entrance. He excused himself from his company and moved across to join him.

'The bar's still open, Commander; can I get you a drink?'

Marlborough nodded and suggested, 'Let's find a quiet corner.'

He moved to a table away from the crowd as Mulcahy made for the bar. Pulling back a chair he lowered himself into it, and let his eyes rove over the recruits. They looked young, a bunch of boys – a sure sign of age in himself, he thought and smiled thinly. These were the cream of youth, a selection of homesick youngsters hiding their anxieties behind careless façades. Each had the potential to become top WIA agents or operatives, but only a few of them would.

Mulcahy set the drinks down on the table, a large whisky for Marlborough and a half of lager for himself. He took a seat.

'Let's talk about Elliott,' Marlborough said as he looked at Mulcahy.

'Sir?'

'What's his problem, Mulcahy? You seem to have an empathy with the boys; they confide in you.'

'Elliott doesn't confide in anyone,' Mulcahy said, taking a drink. 'And he doesn't have a problem.' He looked at Marlborough steadily. 'The problem lies in another direction. I reckon Elliott's a good lad, he's fast, he's clever and he's receptive. He'll make number one if you let him.'

'So he's already told me.'

'I'll admit that he's probably going to take some handling…'

'Is this a reference?'

'If it is, I'm making a bad job of it,' Mulcahy conceded, half smiling. 'No, I'm just trying to explain the boy but I can't profess to understand him myself. He's an enigma, a natural for agent line if you ask my opinion, but you won't.' He hesitated. 'I don't think he's ever been, or ever will be, a yes man. I doubt he'll obey orders without question, and he could be trouble to anyone who tries to keep him on a leash.'

'We appear to be amassing numerous reasons as to his unsuitability,' Marlborough remarked as he picked up his drink and took a sip. 'I don't think that that's your intention?'

'No,' Mulcahy grinned. 'I think the boy's a genius. I think we need him.' He took another drink. 'If he's allowed to he'll graduate at the top – put him straight in at number one as soon as it comes vacant.'

Marlborough looked at him, now very interested.

'He's a new breed, independent and street-wise. He's spent all of his young life surviving on his wits, no rules. God gave him the ghettos and a pretty face, threw him in at the deep end and made him swim. The boy swam good; he turned to the RAF and not the drug scene for his excitement.'

'That doesn't give me an excuse for his behaviour.'

'I can't give you an excuse for his behaviour, and he won't. He'll take any punishment decided on, no matter how wrong it is, but he won't betray a trust or compromise his integrity.' Mulcahy paused, then continued, 'I think you'll draw your own conclusions, Commander, you're a very astute man. I think that given time you might even come to understand him.' He shrugged. 'I think Elliott will respect your decision.'

There was a brief silence.

'Would he have killed Tyler?'

'Killed him?' Mulcahy shook his head and smiled, 'No, he wouldn't have done that.'

Marlborough looked at him and inquired, 'You sound very definite.'

'If he'd intended to kill Tyler, Tyler would have been dead before we got to him. What he intended to do was put the fear of God into him, and he did.'

'He lacks the killer instinct?'

'The boy can't do right for doing wrong, can he?' Mulcahy smiled. 'He'll kill – when he has to, not for the hell of it.'

Marlborough sipped his drink thoughtfully, then asked, 'Who's in charge here, Mulcahy?'

It was Mulcahy's turn to look quizzical. 'Chief Officer Klein.'

'I didn't ask who held the title, I asked who was in charge.'

There was a pause.

'Does that question compromise your integrity and loyalties, Mulcahy?'

'You're still the same devious bastard you ever were, Commander.'

Marlborough nodded and asked again, 'So, who's in charge here?'

'Tyler.'

Marlborough smiled thinly. 'Tell me about him.'

'You have his file. I'm an instructor: it's my job to train the kids and not back stab my colleagues. I still have to work with them when this intake is history. Let the kids tell you about Tyler.'

'I will. But answer me one question.'

Mulcahy looked at him.

'Does Tyler have a boyfriend?'

'That's a leading question, Commander. You've spoken to Elliott and Purnell; I don't doubt that you'll speak to the rest of the intake through Zader. You don't skim over the surface, you'll find the root. Ultimately you'll speak to Tyler, when you're good and ready. Ask him.'

There was a pause. Marlborough glanced around and drained his glass. He asked, 'Elliott hasn't been in?'

'No.'

'Did he join the trainees for dinner?'

'No.' Mulcahy looked at Marlborough curiously.

'I released him. I think I made a mistake – not a drastic mistake,' he said as he rose to his feet. 'There's no indication that the intake are aware of his release?'

Mulcahy shook his head.

'Good, then it can be rectified.' He hesitated, then added, 'I want the recruits back in training tomorrow, Mulcahy, this isn't a holiday camp. I'm putting you in temporary command, and when you're settling the rotas, consider Mr Tyler to be unavailable.'

He moved towards the doors.

'Sir,' Zader called as he started after Marlborough.

Marlborough turned. 'Zader?'

'You said that we'd be given the opportunity…'

'Chief Officer Klein's office at the end of the recreation period.'

The dormitory was in darkness. Marlborough stepped inside.

'Elliott?'

'Sir.'

Elliott was sprawled across the bed, he sat up.

'I gave you dispensation to join the intake for meals and recreation.'

'I didn't think it was a good idea.'

'You didn't think it was a good idea?' Marlborough questioned, smiling. 'In retrospect, Elliott, neither do I. Why didn't you think it was a good idea?'

'Thought it might give some of the intake ideas it was okay to go around slugging instructors.'

'Or throttling them.'

'Yeah. Why don't you think it's a good idea?'

'Similar reasons.'

Elliott rose to his feet.

'You want me to go back to detention?'

There was a pause.

'No, there's a guest suite. I'm not propositioning you, Elliott, we have more than one.' Marlborough hesitated, then added, 'A low profile I think for the time being. I'll arrange to have meals sent in.'

'Any chance I might eat tonight?' Elliott asked, moving towards him.

'I'm sure something can be arranged.'

*

Zader left his fellow students in the reception area and headed for the administration block. He hesitated outside Klein's door, and rapped on it lightly.

'Enter.'

Zader stepped inside and closed the door.

'Sit down, Zader.'

Marlborough looked up, and indicated towards the seat at the opposite side of the desk.

'Sir.'

He pulled back the chair and lowered himself into it.

'I take it you've been confirmed as the spokesman for the intake?'

'Yes, sir.'

'Someone has to draw the short straw,' Marlborough sympathised. 'Is Elliott popular with his colleagues here?'

'Yes, sir.'

'I suppose that you're all in the same position – homesick; perhaps a little afraid of what is, after all, the unknown; only each other to turn to.'

Zader nodded. He had had things in mind to say but Marlborough overawed him.

'Do you confide in each other?'

'Yes, I suppose so.'

'You talk over your feelings, your anxieties?'

'Yes, sir.'

'And Elliott's, I suppose, are much the same as everyone else's?'

There was a pause.

'I don't know, sir,' Zader answered him finally.

'You don't know?'

'No, sir. He listens to our problems; he seems to know when one of us needs somebody to talk to but he doesn't talk much about himself.'

'He doesn't?'

'He doesn't talk much about himself or about his life. He isn't secretive, but he doesn't talk about his feelings. If he has any problems, he doesn't talk about them.'

'Does he have a volatile temper?'

'No, sir.'

'His record seems to indicate otherwise.'

'I suppose it does,' Zader admitted, 'But it's an unfair reflection.'

Marlborough nodded, and did not pursue this line.

'Instructor Tyler claims in his statement that Elliott has "had it in for him" since his arrival here.'

'That's not true.'

'Then you tell me the truth, Zader, tell me the reality of the situation.'

'Tyler – Instructor Tyler, had it in for Elliott. It started at the medical examinations; he was baiting Elliott. He was saying things like, "we've got a pretty one here" and "the lads in your dormitory had better not sleep on their stomachs". There was no call, sir.'

'And what was Elliott's reaction?'

'He asked Instructor Tyler if he fancied him.'

'That seems reasonable in the circumstances,' Marlborough agreed.

'Instructor Tyler said that he was going to make Elliott's life hell. He said that by the time he was finished with him, Elliott would wish that he'd never been born.

'And what did Elliott have to say about that?'

'He said that it was all right, he was accustomed to bloody-minded morons trying to put him down.' Zader looked at Marlborough and clarified, 'It wasn't said venomously, sir, not like Tyler's tone.'

'Did Tyler bully him?'

'I supposed "picked on" would be more accurate, but Elliott didn't react to it, he just did as he was told with no complaints. I think Instructor Tyler got bored with not being able to elicit any real response. He seemed to turn his attention to Tommy Purnell, running him down with constant sarcasm.' Zader paused, then continued. 'We could all see that Purnell couldn't handle it but we didn't do anything about it. Instructor Tyler's a little intimidating, sir, he's always telling us that he can make or break us and I suppose that we were afraid that if we did anything he might turn on one of us instead. We kept our mouths shut and pretended we didn't notice anything.'

'Elliott also?'

'No, sir.'

The interview was not going how Zader had imagined it. He had rehearsed his speech, gone over the events and assembled them into a comprehensive narration which supported Elliott. Marlborough was not letting him use it, not letting him put it into his own words. It was coming out wrong; it sounded as though Elliott was a belligerent physical bastard.

'What happened on Saturday, Zader, three weeks ago?'

A pause ensued.

'We had physical education. Instructor Tyler took it instead of Mr Mulcahy. We were doing springboard exercises. As Purnell took his turn Instructor Tyler kicked the board. If Elliott hadn't reacted fast – he managed to twist Purnell away so that he landed on his feet – Purnell could have broken his neck. Elliott caught him. Tyler was ridiculing Purnell, and made him jump again. He tripped him as he made the run up. Purnell hit his face on the edge of the box – I'm not sure. He was bleeding, and Tyler was shouting at him to get back up, and was pulling him. He went to hit Purnell and Elliott intervened, stopped him.'

'Elliott hit him?'

'No, sir, just caught hold of his wrist and stopped him from hitting Purnell.'

'Tyler says that Elliott hit him. Did Elliott hit him?'

'Yes, sir,' he admitted reluctantly, 'But Tyler threw the first punch.'

'I see.' Marlborough's tone seemed to indicate that he didn't. 'We'll skip the incidents of insubordination. Was what happened on Tuesday's firearms test an accident?' he asked, looking at Zader. 'How did Purnell come to be trapped in the mechanism?'

'Instructor Tyler overrode the control, sir.'

'That's a serious allegation, Zader.'

'Yes, sir, but it wasn't the first time. He did it whilst Elliott was going through. He brought out seven greens instead of five. Right at the outset he said that he wanted to see every one of us die in there. Elliott was going through it like a hot knife through butter.'

'How was Purnell's performance?'

'He was going pretty good. He was about half-way through when Tyler overrode the computer. He brought out two targets together.'

'Knowing that they were opposite and that Purnell would be trapped between them?'

There followed a pause.

'I don't know, sir. But he certainly knew that Purnell was in there.'

There was a brief silence.

'Is anybody here close to Elliott? Does he have a particular friend?'

'I... I suppose that might be me, sir. We've got adjacent beds in the dorm. We partner each other where exercises are in partnerships and we sit alongside each other in lectures.' He looked at Marlborough. 'You could say that I'm the odd one out in the intake and... I suppose he took me under his wing, made me one of the crowd.'

Marlborough nodded and said, 'It's been an illuminating conversation, Zader. Thank you.'

'Sir,' Zader rose to his feet. 'Sir?'

'Zader?'

'What will happen now? Will Elliott be taken before a court martial?'

'I'll let you know once that decision has been made.'

'Thank you, sir,' he said as he started towards the door, but hesitated and turned back. 'Sir?'

'Yes, Zader?'

'I'd be prepared to file a complaint against Instructor Tyler, sir.'

'That's your decision. I'm not prepared to make any comment on its value.'

*

Zader felt as though he had not slept, his mind had been full. He was thoughtful throughout the breakfast period, and had been oblivious to the inane conversation around him. It was around ten minutes to the first lecture period. He stopped Goodwin.

'I'm going to go and see if I can see the Commander. Will you tell instructor Brackley I'll be late to the lecture?'

Goodwin nodded and asked, 'Do you think it will help – if you put a formal complaint in?'

'I don't know.' Zader hesitated, then added, 'I feel I need to do something. They could shoot Mach.'

'So you're going to sort it all by yourself, Zader?' Feiney asked sarcastically. 'Who do you think you are? Custer?'

'I wasn't...'

'A complaint against Tyler, is it?' Feiney snatched the folded paper which Zader held, and unfolded it.

'Give that back.'

'Like firing a bloody arrow at a fucking chieftain tank,' Feiney responded scathingly. 'Do you think one written complaint's going to get anywhere? Look,' he said, sounding suddenly a little awkward. 'Elliott's an okay bloke, I like him...'

'We wouldn't have guessed,' Zader snapped as he snatched the sheet back, 'You're just a stirrer.'

'No, listen. I know I'm not the most popular bloke around here...'

'You can say that again.'

'The truth is, I don't mix easily, I put on the tough guy act so that people leave me alone. It's not that I like being on my own, I just get, I don't know, scared that if I try to get to know people they won't like me anyway so I put on this act and pretend that I don't care, pretend I don't want to know – but I want to help.'

Zader looked uncertain.

'I'll file a complaint too,' Feiney offered.

'It can't hurt I suppose,' Zader said a little dubiously. 'Against Tyler, not Elliott?'

'What do you take me for?'

'Did you see Tyler override the computer control?'

Feiney nodded and added ominously, 'That won't be my only complaint. I've got other allegations to put to him.'

Zader and Goodwin looked at him quizzically.

'I'll save the details for the Commander.' He did not look them in the eyes but said, 'I think I can give him a pretty good idea of what's really going on around here.' He hesitated. 'Why don't you get the lads together, find out who else saw the override, and if they're willing to say so. I figure that Elliott needs all the support he can get. The Commander knows the staff, he doesn't know us.'

He had a point. Zader nodded and offered thoughtfully, 'It sounds like a good idea.'

'Mulcahy's on the lunch roster,' Goodwin remembered, 'We could call a meeting.'

'Okay, we'll do that. Get up as many complaints as we can and then we'll arrange to see the Commander.'

*

After another chat with Purnell, Marlborough returned to Klein's office. The twenty-eight members of the intake were lined up along the corridor. He stopped and scanned them, then moved on slowly. They watched his progress. Zader waited at the head.

'Are you all waiting to see me?' Marlborough inquired of him.

'Yes, sir.'

There was a pause.

'Come through, Zader,' Marlborough instructed as he pushed open the door of the office.

Zader followed him inside. Marlborough took his seat and looked up quizzically.

'I'd like to lodge a formal complaint against Chief Instructor Tyler, sir,' he said as he offered the folded paper.

'I see.' Marlborough took it, opened it out and read through the statement. 'Thank you, Zader.'

'I'd like to stand witness and give evidence for Elliott in the event of court martial proceedings, sir.'

'Am I to take it that that's the intention of the rest of the intake?'

'I think so.'

'Would this be Instructor Mulcahy's idea?'

'No sir, this is our own idea.' He hesitated, then took a sealed envelope from his pocket. 'Tommy Purnell asked me to give you this, sir; he apologises for his unsteady writing.'

Marlborough nodded, and took it.

'Thank you, Zader, I'll take your statements into consideration. Ask your colleagues to come through one at a time.'

'Yes, sir.'

A further twenty-six delivered their lines and handed over their written statements. Feiney entered last, moved across to the desk and handed his written statement over to Marlborough. He waited whilst Marlborough read through it.

Finally, Marlborough looked up and said, 'Sit down, Feiney.'

'Sir.' He took a seat.

Marlborough studied him, then asked. 'You allege that Mr Tyler has made approaches of a homosexual nature towards you?'

'Yes, sir.'

'And that you responded to those approaches.'

'I became his… boyfriend, sir, in return for his promise that I'd graduate from training centre.'

'Do you have anything to support that allegation?'

'I think you'll probably find that in his assessments I've been given excellent marks. They're unmerited. And I think he's altered my marks in other subjects. If you were to have me assessed by one of the other instructors I wouldn't come up to those standards.'

'What if I were to have you medically examined?'

'I'd agree to that, sir.'

'Are you homosexually inclined, Feiney?'

'No, sir, I've been physically sick every time he… it seems to turn him on. If you don't mind I'd rather not go into too much detail.' He hesitated, then added, 'I just wanted to graduate.'

Marlborough nodded, 'Has Mr Tyler intimated to you that other operatives have graduated training in this manner?'

'Yes, sir.'

'Has he mentioned any names?'

'Yes, sir.'

'Do you remember them?'

'I'd rather not say, sir, on the grounds that it may prejudice their future careers.'

Marlborough nodded. 'Very well, Feiney, I won't press the point.'

'Tyler's a piranha, sir, I know. I know just what he's like. He's a sadistic bastard and I hate him. He knows it but I'm trapped. I'm a student statistic and he can do what the hell he likes.' His eyes rested on the cigarette box on the desk. 'Could I have a cigarette, sir? If you don't mind.'

'By all means.' Marlborough flipped the box open, and watched as Feiney took one and lit it. 'Are you prepared to give evidence?' he asked.

'Yes, sir.'

'Has Tyler had a sexual relationship with Elliott?'

'With Elliott?' Feiney drew on his cigarette. 'No, I don't think so. He's pretty proud of his conquests and he's never mentioned…'

'Has he mentioned Purnell?'

'Yes, sir, he raped him and he was proud of it.'

'He raped him?'

'He raped me.'

There was a silence.

'Would you have any objection to my sending you to DHQ Glasgow for medical investigation and skill assessment?'

'No, sir.'

'My car is outside, Feiney. By the time you reach it the driver will have full instructions. I have to ask that you discuss the matter with no one other than the medical officers and skill assessors assigned to you at Glasgow.' He leaned back in his chair and ordered. 'Dismiss Feiney, and go directly to my car.'

'Sir.'

Feiney headed for the door.

It only took a few moments to make the necessary arrangements. Marlborough moved across to the window and looked out. The communication channel to Zaigham, the Regional Administrator at Glasgow, was open. He watched as the solitary figure of Feiney walked across the quadrangle and slid into the rear seat of the car. The chauffeur pushed the door shut.

Marlborough concluded his instructions to Zaigham, closed the channel, and replaced his communicator in his pocket. He returned to his desk and opened the envelope which contained Purnell's statement. There were two pages; he unfolded them and read through. It was a comprehensive account of his oral allegations. Detailed, sickeningly so, too precise and too believable to be fanciful. Feiney's written account had not been dissimilar. Marlborough's eyes lingered on the hastily scrawled words, then he refolded the papers and pushed them into his breast pocket where he had placed Feiney's graphic statement. The other statements he locked into the drawer of the desk.

*

Elliott stood by the window at the side of the bed in the guest room. It was more comfortable than the detention cell. He had seen Feiney cross the quadrangle and get into Marlborough's chauffeur driven car, and had watched it leave. Lighting a cigarette, he continued to stare out over the grey tarmac. If he was court martialled then fifteen years was likely – execution was not beyond the realms of possibility should he be found guilty of attempted murder. If nothing were to come of it he could still be dismissed from training, and thrown out. He would have no career; there would be no going back to the RAF to pick up from where he had left off. No return; his life would not revert to what it had been before. He was not sure that civilian life held the same attractions. What would be the options? In all probability he would end up where it had been thought that he would – in the gutter – jail bait. Presumably the WIA would discharge him brainwashed and with a new identity, but would that subdue his need for the uncertainty and excitement in his life which most professions did not provide? He doubted it. If he wanted good money, something which was not routine, and if he did not have the forces or the WIA, his best option lay in crime.

He could not give Marlborough any reason for his actions without betraying a trust. A promise was a promise, and whether Purnell had in fact confided in Marlborough made no difference, he had not been released from it. He took a long draw on his cigarette and glanced round as the door opened. Mulcahy stepped into the dormitory and closed the door behind himself.

'All right, son?'

Elliott nodded.

'Marlborough said I'd find you here. As bastards go he's one of the best – but he's a fair bastard.'

'Yeah, doesn't seem a bad bloke,' Elliott said. 'I like him.'

'He's a plain talker, some don't like that. And he's a clever bloke, he doesn't miss much.'

'You don't like him,' Elliott stated.

Mulcahy smiled and said, 'I don't dislike him. You don't miss much either, do you, Elliott?' He hesitated. 'I don't think you'll go to court martial.'

'No?'

'You're not in the slammer, son, you're confined to quarters. Marlborough isn't the sort of bloke to confine potential murderers to their quarters.'

Elliott grinned and said, 'I wouldn't bet on it.' He took a final pull on his cigarette and snuffed it out, then threw it into the bin. 'Sort of bloke you wouldn't want to give any guarantees about.'

'No, he isn't,' Mulcahy agreed, 'Don't let it get you down. I don't think that Marlborough thinks the sun shines out of Tyler. I think he's going to take a long hard look at him and maybe he isn't going to stand up to close scrutiny. There are going to be changes made around here – how much they'll help you I don't know, but things won't be the same after this.'

'I'm sorry.'

'You aren't. Neither am I. Don't worry, son, nine years is long enough to stick in any routine. We need changes, times change, a new challenge. Maybe we need to be kicked out of our complacency.' He turned back to the door.

'You're probably the right bloke to do the kicking. You'd make a good CO.'

Mulcahy hesitated, smiled, and shook his head. 'I don't think so, I'm too old, too set in my ways. And Marlborough and I, we don't see things the same way.' He moved back. 'You'll be all right, son, he said as he rested his hand on Elliott's shoulder, 'Take Mulcahy's word for it.'

Elliott nodded, and watched as Mulcahy left and the door closed. A nice bloke and a good instructor, he thought, tough but fair, the best type. But Elliott doubted that Mulcahy could read Marlborough. Marlborough was too deep, too complex a character and Mulcahy was about as straight as they came.

*

Tyler saluted smartly as he entered Klein's office.

'You wanted to see me, sir?' he inquired of Marlborough.

'Yes, come in Tyler, and sit down,' Marlborough invited. He watched as Tyler obeyed.

'You seem to be none the worse for your experience and it doesn't appear to have affected your vocal chords,' he added with pointed reference to the demonstration. 'Tell me, Mr Tyler,' he leaned back in his chair and asked, 'Why are you having so much trouble with Elliott?'

'Sir?'

'It's a perfectly straightforward question. All of the other instructors report his behaviour and groundwork to be exemplary.'

'I'm sure you've read my report, sir. I stated in it that I believed that he'd singled me out.'

'I have read your report,' Marlborough confirmed, 'And it leads me to wonder why he should do that.'

'He's that type, he's a trouble-maker. He singles out one instructor to play up and make life hell for, while he gives the others the butter wouldn't melt in his mouth routine.'

Marlborough studied Tyler for a few moments, then said, 'It's something he's never done before, Tyler. I've seen his educational and forces training records and they show him to be particularly receptive to instruction. I find myself curious as to why his pattern of behaviour should change now, and why he should single you out in particular as the victim?' He regarded Tyler steadily. 'Why not one of the other instructors?'

'I have no idea, sir.'

'No idea at all, Mr Tyler? Are you sure that there could be no explanation in say, your attitude to him?'

'My attitude to him, sir?'

'You haven't perhaps been particularly critical of him or offhand?'

'No, sir.'

There was a brief silence.

'How do you view the intakes, Mr Tyler?'

'I'm sorry?'

'The young men who come briefly into your care?'

A pause followed.

'I look on them as homeless boys, sir, orphans in need of support, encouragement and guidance, and myself as a father figure.'

He sounds like a bad advertisement for a children's home, Marlborough thought, looking at him expectantly.

Clearly Marlborough wanted more, Tyler knew, and offered. 'I like to think that I'm approachable if they have any problems, if they're lonely or need a reassuring word.'

'Perhaps you're confusing yourself with Mr Mulcahy?' Marlborough suggested.

The comparison washed over Tyler. 'I like to think that all of the instructors have the qualities of patience and compassion. The boys are my life. I take a pride in seeing them mature.'

'You sound like a promotional campaign for an inferior public school,' Marlborough jibed and smiled thinly. 'I shouldn't like to think that any of the officers at this level are unsympathetic.'

'We're dealing with boys, sir, their circumstances in coming here are so drastically changed. It's difficult not to feel sorry for them.'

Marlborough nodded. 'Does much bullying go on amongst them?'

Tyler considered the question, then answered. 'There are invariably stronger characters.'

'Would you say that Elliott falls into that category?'

'It's a possibility; he seems to have a strong personality.'

'He appears to be a good student.'

'I can't fault his work.'

'Only his temperament.' Marlborough smiled briefly. 'You allege attempted murder – are you quite sure about that? Might it not be more accurately described as an assault?'

'I don't doubt that Elliott intended to kill me, sir, or that he would have succeeded had Instructor Mulcahy and some other members of the staff not restrained him. He was like a man possessed, uncontrollable.'

'Is that so, Mr Tyler? I've been given to understand that he had ample time in which to kill you had he so desired, and that he was completely in control of himself.' Marlborough surveyed him for a few moments. 'Tell me about the incident which led to Elliott making his attack on you.'

'There was a computer malfunction, sir. It had manifested itself during Elliott's exercise when seven targets were activated instead of five.'

'And despite that incident you proceeded with the exercise?'

'I could see no harm in it,' Tyler said, regarding Marlborough steadily. 'I didn't anticipate that it would cause any more serious injury than a slap by a blood pellet. I never thought for one moment that there might be such a tragic accident.'

'Purnell, the young man involved in the accident – have you had sufficient time to form an opinion as to his abilities and personality?'

'Yes, sir, he's a very promising recruit, with a good all-round ability, and is popular with his colleagues I believe.'

'You haven't experienced any problems with him?'

'No, sir. Although I feel that he hasn't been working to the standard I would have expected of him.'

'Would you say that he was a close friend of Elliott?'

'I really don't know, sir. They share the same dormitory.'

'It has to be said that Elliott's almost pretty.'

Tyler looked at him, then asked, 'Are you suggesting that there might be some sort of relationship?'

'I'm not suggesting anything, Mr Tyler.'

'I would have thought that Purnell was entirely heterosexual.'

'And is that the way you like them, Mr Tyler?'

A strange question but Tyler did not stop to consider it; he just saw it as an opportunity to strengthen points against Elliott.

'I don't have much time for queers; I feel that you can never quite trust them. Of course, I don't consider myself qualified to pass judgement. I'm sure that Dr Laverne's report contains a more valuable assessment.'

'Dr Laverne's report on whom?'

'Elliott. I mean, he's as bent as a ninepenny piece, isn't he?'

'According to the report, Tyler. However, I don't believe that Elliott has any homosexual tendencies.' Marlborough looked at him and continued, 'Nor do I believe that he's temperamentally unstable.' He hesitated. 'Regrettably I find myself unable to form the same opinion as regards yourself.'

He took Purnell's statement from his pocket and passed it across. Tyler took it and read it through, his expression darkening.

'What the hell is this?'

'It's an extremely serious allegation, Tyler.'

'It's a set of filthy lies.'

'You deny it?'

'Of course I deny it, it's nothing more than a fabrication dreamed up by an overactive imagination.'

'There's no foundation?'

'It's absurd. Does he provide any evidence? Did he seek medical treatment or advice? You don't take this seriously? If there was any foundation he would have reported it at the time and not now. The entire allegation is so ludicrous it would be funny if...' Tyler stopped abruptly as Marlborough placed a whisky bottle on the desk.

'You were saying, Tyler?' Marlborough unscrewed the top, upturned two glasses and continued, 'The entire allegation is ludicrous?'

He filled the glasses and pushed one towards Tyler.

'It's a little early in the day, sir,' Tyler declined, recognising the bottle.

'I don't think so,' Marlborough said, picking up his glass and taking a sip, 'I find that it gets the circulation going, helps to keep the chill out of winter mornings.'

Tyler raised his glass to his lips; the liquid touched. It was strongly flavoured and sweet; he lowered it hurriedly.

'It's a little early in the day for me, sir.'

'Nonsense, Tyler, drink it.'

'I'd rather not, sir.'

'Why not? It's your brand, I took it from your room. I was looking for you at the time.'

'In my wardrobe, sir?'

Marlborough smiled and questioned, 'Now, how would Feiney know where it was?'

Tyler seemed to pale. 'Feiney, sir?'

'And the wardrobe wasn't locked.'

'My room was.'

'I had a key.' Marlborough took another sip of his drink and commented, 'It has a very sweet flavour, very palatable. You must give me the name of your supplier.' He looked across at Tyler. 'You haven't touched yours, Mr Tyler.'

'It's a very powerful brew, sir,' Tyler offered, sounding a little nervous. 'And a little early in the day.'

'It's never too early – but you're right about the strength,' Marlborough conceded with a smile, and drained his glass. He reached again for the bottle.

'I wouldn't have any more if...'

'If you're worried about the cost I'm quite prepared to buy a replacement,' Marlborough said as he refilled the glass.

'No, no it isn't that.'

'I know my capacity, Tyler.' He paused, then swilled the liquid around the glass. 'It has a fair kick – forty per cent Pethaparatrymol I'm told – one glassful is enough to render a man immobile, but not senseless, for up to two hours. Now, I wonder why you should require that?'

He looked at Tyler. There was a silence, no response forthcoming.

'Drink it, you have best malt with a few harmless additives. I left the original contents for analysis,' Marlborough informed him. 'I would have expected a little more caution from a man of your service experience. Mr Feiney has gone to Glasgow DHQ for medical examination and progress testing.' His steel grey and icily cold eyes burned into Tyler. 'As you say, it's unfortunate that Mr Purnell has left it a little late to supply conclusive proof of his story.'

Tyler's colour drained from his skin; his hand trembled as he picked up his glass and drained it.

'Purnell and Feiney must have remarkably similar overactive imaginations,' Marlborough commented dryly as he refilled Tyler's glass. 'As for the matter of the computer malfunction, did you not bear in mind that the master computer would log any override of one of its satellites?' Marlborough pulled open the top drawer of the desk and lifted out the wad of complaints. 'And I have ample witnesses,' he added as he regarded Tyler steadily. 'I seem to be in a strange position, Mr Tyler. Never before have I found myself taking court martial proceedings on behalf of a plaintiff who is himself the intended subject of court martial proceedings.'

Tyler took a nervous sip of his drink. Marlborough hesitated, then topped up his own.

'Since I consider the proceedings against yourself to be the more pressing and certainly the most likely to result in a conviction, I feel that I should seek your views on continuing with the proceedings which you wish me to bring against Elliott. It seems that Elliott was, to some extent, aware of what was going on. It's also clear that, together with the rest of the intake, he saw you override the computer control during Purnell's exercise. Elliott would have considerable mitigation, not least being that had he had any intention of killing you he had ample time and you would almost certainly be dead. You spent, I believe, less than two hours in medical and there was no tracheal damage?'

Tyler nodded.

'Am I to continue with the proceedings against Elliott?'

'I think that would be pointless, sir.'

'I'm sure it would.' He watched as Tyler took a drink. 'I propose to have you charged with two counts of homosexual rape, one count of attempted murder with an alternative of malicious negligence, and one count of deliberate misrepresentation. I'll expect a full list of matters to be taken into consideration, and if that isn't forthcoming I shall order a microscopic investigation into your activities here and add further charges accordingly. Do you understand?'

'Yes, sir.' Tyler took another drink.

'Do you wish to say anything?'

'No, sir.'

'You're in gross breach of the trust placed in you, Tyler. No doubt many young lives have been affected as a result.' Marlborough offered a typed sheet of paper and a pen across the desk. 'The retraction.'

Tyler took the pen and signed the sheet.

'I hope that this is one life which hasn't been damaged beyond repair,' Marlborough commented as he retrieved the paper and activated the communicator.

'Detention?'

'Have an officer come to Chief Officer Klein's office.'

*

Elliott was sprawled across the bed, staring up at the ceiling. There was little else to do and inactivity didn't suit him. He would rather have been with the rest of the intake slogging his guts out under Mulcahy's instruction on a torture session which he laughingly termed as a mild obstacle course – anything to relieve the boredom. Not that he was fretting. He was a realist and worried in no great depth until the event. Time enough to worry about court martial when he appeared before it. The door opened. He looked across and swung his legs to the floor as Marlborough entered the room. Marlborough closed the door and studied Elliott for a moment. He found him a little disconcerting; could not weigh him up.

A decision had been made, Elliott could tell. What it was he did not yet know Marlborough well enough to guess.

'Are you homosexual or bisexual, Elliott?' Marlborough asked him straight.

'No, I'm just pretty,' Elliott responded levelly.

Marlborough nodded, then lowered himself on to the edge of the bed.

'I think, and my opinion is shared by Instructor Mulcahy, that you wouldn't have killed Tyler even if you had not been restrained.'

There was a silence.

'Well?'

'I thought you were telling me – how many times can you have me shot?'

Marlborough smiled thinly and said, 'That can't be construed as attempted murder. Did you intend to kill him?'

'If I'd intended to kill him do you think he'd be around to tell you about it?'

'What did you intend to do?'

There was a brief hesitation.

'You're here, you must have a guess of your own.'

'I think you're a calculating bastard.'

Elliott looked momentarily thoughtful, 'Probably,' he agreed.

'Have you killed – I don't mean in warfare?'

'Not yet.'

Marlborough looked at him.

'It isn't a hobby,' confirmed Elliott.

'There won't be any court martial proceedings brought against you. Is that a relief?'

'It was something to look forward to,' Elliott stated as he reached across to the cabinet and picked up his cigarettes. He took one from the packet and lit it.

'Did you want to be court martialled?'

'I never denied anything.'

Marlborough sighed. 'You still aren't helping me, Elliott, and you aren't helping yourself. You aren't offering me anything. You won't confirm or deny the incident which triggered this entire affair, even though Purnell gave me the whole story. Why won't you talk?'

'Maybe I don't have anything to say.'

'I accept that you were acting to protect a friend…'

'Is that what I was doing?' Elliott interrupted.

'I don't know, Elliott. If you won't tell me I have to guess. It leaves me with the problem of what to do with you. The fact remains that a serious assault took place and whether the same was justified or not, I'm obliged to ensure that there's no repetition.'

A brief silence was in place.

'Your actions weren't unprovoked, Elliott. Why will you not mitigate on your own behalf?' He paused. 'How can I give guarantees to the staff here if you have nothing to say to inspire any faith in you?'

Elliott shrugged.

'There will be court martial proceedings against Tyler.'

Elliott drew on his cigarette and exhaled slowly.

'I assume that you won't be giving evidence?'

'That sounds about right.'

Another pause followed.

'Although none of the instructors have raised any objections to your remaining here I'm not sure that it would be reasonable, in the circumstances, to expect them to tutor you. This is not from the point of view that your presence could be disruptive to the other students, but you realise the considerations which I have to make?'

Elliott nodded. Marlborough believed that he did.

'How serious were you about going operative?'

'I was serious when I said it – nothing's changed.'

Marlborough nodded and conceded, 'All right, I'll play it your way. I'm pulling you out of training. You'll return with me to WHQ London and take up immediate appointment at number one.'

If Marlborough had expected a panic reaction, any reaction, he was disappointed. Elliott's expression gave him no indication of his thoughts or any anxiety which he might have. He was a cool character, Marlborough could not deny that, a difficult young man to weigh up. It was impossible to believe that he was not at the very least nervous.

Elliott's own words, 'Try me, I'll either prove it or get myself killed,' had stayed with Marlborough. He had taken up the challenge, and perhaps Elliott had thrown it down a little rashly. To put a man on agent line fully trained was risky – inexperience accounted for many fatalities. To put him in at number one was rather the equivalent of throwing him into the Thames with concrete water wings and expecting him to swim. Marlborough was well aware of what he was doing, was well aware also that Elliott would have to contend with resentment from established and experienced agents with aspirations to the number one slot despite its mortality rate. He did not however doubt that given a little more time to think it over Elliott would come to his senses. It would be bound to occur to him that he was biting off more than he could chew and that his statement of challenge might become a chillingly accurate reality.

The over confidence of youth! Marlborough was certain that by the time it came round for them to make their departure Elliott would have asked him to reconsider. All he required was that Elliott back down, show some vulnerability. Perhaps then Marlborough would relent and allow him to complete his training. Meanwhile it was a battle of nerves and Marlborough's were unlikely to fail him.

'We'll be leaving at fifteen hundred hours,' Marlborough informed him as he rose to his feet, 'I suggest that you pack such clothing and personal effects as you have. You are no longer under charge or threat of charge and therefore you are not confined to these quarters. I suggest that you take lunch with your colleagues and say your goodbyes.' He moved to the door. 'Report to the Chief Officer's office at fourteen fifty.'

'Sir.' Elliott watched as Marlborough left.

He snuffed his cigarette between his fingers and dropped it into an ashtray at the bedside. Falling back across the bed he closed his eyes. Nervous, anxious, terrified? All of these but the latter was probably the most accurate description. Foolish, sheer bloody mindedness – he knew it but would not renege on the challenge which he had thrown down. Self-confident was how he projected himself, arrogant even. It was a veneer with which he protected himself and behind which he hid his insecurities. He had always demonstrated the survival of the fittest, had always lived his life on a high of adrenaline scared and afraid to admit it. God gave him the ghettos and a pretty face; Mulcahy had hit the nail right on the head. Elliott had not fabricated his life story – it was all tragically true. A lonely kid who had had to learn to become self-sufficient and self-reliant almost before he could walk – to be the fastest and the hardest hitting or be used as a doormat. He had a great urge for self-preservation and a need to prove himself.

Mulcahy met up with Marlborough in the corridor outside the gymnasium.

'There'll be changes, Mulcahy.'

'I'm pleased to hear it, sir.'

'Chief Officer Klein is retiring.'

'Does he know yet?'

Marlborough smiled tightly and continued, 'Doctor Laverne, I think, would be more suited to medical research and will be transferred and replaced. Mr Tyler will be court martialled. You will assume the role of Acting Chief Officer and your permanent appointment will be confirmed in writing on my return to WHQ.'

He made to move on.

'Commander?'

He hesitated, then said, 'Mulcahy?'

'What about Elliott?'

'Mr Tyler doesn't wish to pursue his complaint.' He looked at Mulcahy, and added, 'I don't intend to take that matter any further.'

'The right decision I'm sure, sir.'

'I'm pulling Elliott out of training and I'm taking him back to London WHQ with me. Number one is already vacant, Mr Mulcahy.'

'The boy won't back down.'

'We'll see. I don't intend to.'

'You're as stubborn as each other.' Mulcahy warned, 'You'll see the little bastard get himself killed.'

'That isn't my problem, Mr Mulcahy.'

'With respect, sir, it is. You have the authority…'

'I've given him the opportunity to retract, he still has the opportunity. Don't tell me how to do my job and I won't tell you how to do yours,' Marlborough snapped.

'Sir,' Mulcahy agreed, 'But it would be a shame. He's got the potential.' He hesitated, then added, 'Maybe he'll come through – the boy's got guts.'

'It takes more than guts.'

'You've been there, Commander, number one, you should know.' He looked at Marlborough steadily, and said, 'There's a saying, those who can do, those who can't teach.' He paused. 'I'll stick with teaching.'

'And your own unique brand of sarcasm, no doubt.'

'I get to see the boys alive, and I try to teach them to stay alive. If I helped one of them to commit suicide the law would call it murder.' He smiled wryly, and added, 'If you'll excuse me, Commander, I have twenty-seven other youngsters to keep alive.'

He started towards the door of the gymnasium.

'Tell them that the Commander's a murdering sadistic bastard, Mulcahy,' Marlborough called after him, 'Don't forget to tell them that. You wouldn't want them to leave here unprepared.'

Mulcahy stepped into the gymnasium, the intake falling silent and looking towards him. 'At ease, boys,' he instructed, surveying their expectant faces. 'Commander Marlborough has made a number of decisions. Instructor Tyler is to be court martialled, Doctor Laverne transferred and Chief Office Klein retired.' He hesitated. 'There will be no court martial proceedings brought against Elliott nor will he be discharged.'

The intake cheered.

'But,' Mulcahy silenced them by continuing, 'He is withdrawing Elliott from training – to fill an existing vacancy at number one.'

There was a stunned silence.

'Forewarned is forearmed, boys. The Commander wishes me to make it known that he is, to quote his own words, "A murdering, sadistic bastard".' He smiled grimly and said, 'So let's get down to work; we don't want him to think you're on a cushy number here.'

The young men started towards the apparatus.

'Zader?'

Zader turned back. 'Sir?'

'Maybe Elliott could use a little company.'

*

Elliott folded the last of his clothing into the small suitcase and closed the lid. Lunch time was still a couple of hours off. It would be his last opportunity to be with the lads; from there on he would be pretty much on his own. They were a good bunch, the same camaraderie as the forces to which he had grown accustomed, constantly being one of a crowd, except when he was flying on test. Even airborne he would normally have a team, constant contact with flight control. Agent line, he thought, would be rather more solitary. In so far as he could make out they worked in pairs, had radio contact, but not necessarily the opportunity to maintain it. There would be little glamour involved; the videos had been designed to shatter any illusions which they might have had.

Zader stepped into the dormitory and hesitated.

'Mulcahy says you're leaving,' he stated a little unnecessarily, his eyes on the suitcase.

'Yeah.'

'It won't be the same around here without you.'

'No, you'll be able to get some work done,' Elliott grinned.

'We'll miss you, Mach – I'll miss you. You've helped me through, got me accepted as one of the lads and not treated like some breed apart.'

'Not me,' said Elliott sitting on the edge of the bed. 'You did it yourself.'

There was a slight pause.

'You're going to be number one?'

Elliott nodded.

'You'll be careful?'

'I'll have to be, won't I?'

'Are you scared?'

Elliott looked at him and said, 'Yeah, I'm scared.'

'Can't you talk to Marlborough?' Zader suggested, 'Can't you ask him to let you stay and finish your training?'

'No.'

Zader seemed about to question it, but changed his mind and asked, 'You're all packed then?'

'Yeah.'

'What time are you leaving?'

'Three.'

Zader nodded and asked. 'Do you need any help with anything?'

There was a pause.

Elliott nodded, then added, 'Need help with being number one.' He looked at Zader. 'You get through training, Jan, graduate at the top, uh? I...' he faltered slightly, 'If I manage to keep my brains inside my skull, maybe we could get to work together.' He forced a wry smile.

'The word's going around that Mulcahy's been made up to Chief Officer,' Zader offered to change the subject, 'And Tyler's going to court martial.'

Elliott nodded.

'Tommy's going to be okay.'

'Good.'

'I wish you were staying, Mach.'

'Yeah? So do I. It wouldn't work; I'd be disruptive even without doing anything. I came this close,' he said, putting his finger and thumb together, 'to court martial. I wasn't an innocent party.'

'You stood up for a mate; you did what we all should have done.'

'I slugged an instructor, half-killed him. It isn't the way to do things, is it? It wouldn't be fair, Jan, having me here. You'd get the other instructors worried that if they say something out of place I might go for them.' He shrugged and added, 'And the lads, maybe they'd be looking for me to do something.'

'I suppose so,' Zader hesitated, then sat down on the bed beside Elliott. 'Maybe we could try and keep in touch?'

'Yeah,' Elliott agreed, sounding a little subdued.

'If you don't want to, that's okay. I know I'm not someone you'd chose as a mate. You're just sorry for me, the public schoolboy, the over privileged minority who doesn't fit in.' He smiled a little sadly, and added, 'I never really...'

'I want that we should keep in touch. I like you, you're a good bloke. Do you think I care where you came from, what you've got or haven't got? You really think I care whether you talk Oxford or Hackney?'

'Don't you?'

'It makes no difference to me. We're mates, aren't we?'

Zader nodded. 'Knock them dead, Mach, show them that number one is where you should be.' He rose to his feet. 'You take good care of yourself,' he said, offering his hand. 'Can I wish you luck?'

'Yeah, need all the luck I can get,' Elliott grinned and took the offered hand. 'Thanks,' he continued, 'I mean it, Jan, it'll be good if we get to work together.' He released his grip.

'Will you be in touch?'

'I'll be in touch. Just need to find out how to break into the computer so I can send messages across.'

Chapter Five

At fifteen hundred hours the chauffeur slammed the boot of the car shut over the suitcase and moved forwards to slide behind the wheel. Elliott sat beside Marlborough in the rear seat, staring out of the window as the car rolled towards the gates and out into the world from which he had been isolated. The bleak scenery of the Scottish Highlands flashed by the car windows.

Marlborough was thoughtful. Truly, he had not anticipated that Elliott would be with him when he left. Mulcahy had been right, the boy would not back down. By the same token Marlborough would not relent, and would put him in at number one, untrained and untried. Excellent though Elliott's training record was from the practical and theoretical point of view, it was after all only in the preliminaries. He had not even attempted a simulated assignment, nor had his stress factor been calculated. How well he could co-ordinate his individual skills under the pressure of assignment conditions was unknown.

Marlborough glanced across at Elliott. He looked very young, barely more than a teenager; it was only three years since he had been, Marlborough reflected. His hair had grown rapidly during the weeks at the training centre, curled over his collar and flopped over his forehead. A slim youth, his clothing seemed to hang on him a little loosely. It was harsh to put him at number one, unwarranted – almost legalised murder. It was suicidal of Elliott to progress the challenge but he had thrown down the gauntlet. Marlborough was aware that he had been a little rash in accepting. If Elliott was prepared to ask then he was prepared to relent, but he was not prepared to make the offer.

Apart from the small jet plane which stood at the end of the runway, the secluded private airport seemed to be deserted. Elliott's countenance, Marlborough noted, brightened visibly as he viewed the plane. The chauffeur-driven car raced towards it. Elliott had a love affair with the flying machines: the adrenaline had always started pumping in him at the sight of the metal birds. He slid out of the car, behind Marlborough, and hesitated, his eyes running over the sleek lines of the aircraft before he followed up the steps and inside. They were greeted by the hostess, and took their seats as the door was sealed. Elliott had the window seat. Marlborough glanced at him as he fastened his seat belt.

'It's a nice piece of engineering,' Elliott remarked to Marlborough, 'I co-piloted on test a couple of years ago as part of my training before I was licensed to full test.'

'Your service record was impressive, Elliott. Pilot's wings at nineteen, test class at twenty-one and studying two degree courses part-time. I understand that you got first-class honours in law and maths at nineteen.'

'No, sir, that was physics and maths. I did law last year and I just completed masters a couple of months ago.'

'Which you also passed.'

'Yeah?' Elliott smiled and said, 'That's good.'

'Why law?'

Elliott shrugged. ' Something to do, I guess.

'You didn't have any ambitions in that direction?'

'Almost all my life I wanted to be a pilot – I wanted to fly.'

'Why did you give it up? Why did you agree to come to us?'

There was a pause.

'I'd done it.'

'You would have left anyway?'

'No. Maybe I'd have gone for Wing Commander; I'd signed on for fifteen years. Maybe I'd have taken the option to renew; maybe I'd have tried for the commercial airlines – or maybe I would have been dead – I was active service.'

'How much does dying worry you?'

'It isn't something I spend much time worrying about. It's something that's going to happen sooner or later. I don't think I want to be old.' He unbuckled his seat belt as the light went out. 'I didn't ask to be born, it wasn't my decision. I don't suppose dying will be any different.'

'You're a strange young man, Elliott.'

'You don't approve of me; you don't want me. You wish you could send me back to the RAF and be done with me, then I wouldn't have to be your problem. I don't fit into your stereotypes. I know you don't like me and you sure as hell don't think I'm number one material. It's your way out. With a bit of luck some trigger-happy bastard'll solve the problem for you.'

'Is that how you see me?'

'That's the way it is. It's okay, I can understand it.'

'Then I won't deny it.' Marlborough hesitated, then asked, 'Would you prefer me to lie?'

'No, I like you the way you are.'

'You like me the way I am?'

'Yeah, it's not so strange. It's possible to like somebody who doesn't like you – if they're straight with you, if you know where you stand.'

There was a pause. Marlborough shook his head and said, 'Mulcahy said that you were an enigma – I'm inclined to agree with him – but Mulcahy liked you.'

'And he doesn't like you, but you've got his respect. He doesn't like you because he's too straight and you're too complex. He sees everything in black and white – so do you but you go a different way round to get there. You probably finish up seeing things too much the same to get along. You think you're miles apart when your real problem's that you're too much alike.'

'I don't think we'll have that problem.'

Elliott grinned, and turned to look out of the window.

'Why don't you go up to the flight deck?'

Elliott looked at him, then asked, 'You reckon they might let me near the controls?'

'I should think it's a distinct possibility.'

Marlborough rose to his feet and stepped out into the narrow aisle. He watched as Elliott slid across and out into the aisle, then headed up it.

Thoughtful as Elliott disappeared through the partitioning doorway, Marlborough retook his seat.

'Coffee, sir?' the hostess asked him on approach.

'Please.'

She poured it, handed him the cup on a tray with sugar and cream, and retreated.

Marlborough thought that Elliott was an odd young man, immature and at the same time much older than his tender years. It was a little unnerving to have the feeling that Elliott could get inside his head and also that his assessments were almost frighteningly accurate. He felt that Elliott could read him, yet he would not make such a rash claim in reverse. Did Elliott have any respect for him? He professed to liking him but had made no mention of respect. Was it possible to respect and not to like? By the same token, was it possible to like and not to respect? The former seemed the more likely. Did he respect Elliott? He sipped his coffee. Unexpectedly yes, he rather thought that he did.

There was a break in the cloud, a brief glimpse of a town far below. Marlborough glanced at his watch; another five minutes and the plane should be approaching its destination in Surrey, a small military airbase whose facilities the WIA utilised. He slid across to the window seat and looked out on to a bed of cloud like curly white feathers escaping from a duvet. The warning lights came on, and Marlborough placed his empty cup on the tray and fastened his seat belt. There was a smooth descent as the plane sliced cleanly through the clouds. Distant specks on the ground began to take shape, and the runway became visible as a long narrow ribbon. Flying was not Marlborough's favourite pastime. It amazed him that what were basically chunks of metal could defy the laws of gravity and become airborne. It amazed him also that they could descend at a regulated pace and not be sucked like tissue in a whirlwind to the ground. The landing strip looked minute, too short, too narrow, so he averted his eyes from the window and turned his thoughts in other directions.

His number one, Joachim Latislaw, had been recovered, brutally murdered, from a south coast beach and his partner, Rakim Suleman, was presently in medical suffering from a fractured skull and serious internal injuries. Presumably he had been the victim of the same assailants. Whilst Marlborough had every intention of putting Elliott in at number one he had not yet decided upon who would partner him. Suleman would have been ideal, had he been available. With no aspiration to the number one slot himself and having an easy going personality he would have worked with Elliott without question or objection. Brett Kane, perhaps, based at London WHQ, rated at number eight and presently without a partner, could be a possibility worth considering, although he had ambition to be number one. How enamoured he would be with the position of number two to a number one who had not even graduated training was not easy to guess. Marlborough sighed. There really weren't too many options available; Kane it would have to be.

The plane touched down smoothly and slowed to a halt. The steps were towed into position. Marlborough unbuckled his seat belt, rose to his feet and picked up his briefcase. The stewardess released the door, and smiled as Elliott emerged from the flight deck and met up with Marlborough. He followed him down the steps and across to the Daimler which was waiting on the tarmac. They slid inside, a member of the ground crew loading Elliott's suitcase into the boot.

'I want you available for assignment at ten hundred hours on Friday.' Marlborough glanced at him and said, 'I'm afraid that doesn't give you much time to settle in.'

'Doesn't give me much time to get nervous either.'

Elliott glanced at his watch, and noted that Friday was just a couple of days away.

'We'd better organise a few details,' Marlborough said, pulling his briefcase up on to his knees and opening it. 'You'll be found accommodation, probably an apartment within reasonable proximity of WHQ. A vehicle, currently we have an MG or a Triumph Stag available.'

He looked at Elliott.

'MG.'

Marlborough nodded, and made a note.

'Your ex number one's?' queried Elliott.

'Just spares. Eventually you'll be issued with a revolver custom made to your requirements.' He looked up. 'In the meantime you have your training issue?'

'No, it wasn't given back to me after I was charged. Must have something against murderers wandering around with guns.'

Marlborough nodded and said, 'We'll get something organised. Remuneration will be at Scale One, paid directly into a bank account or building society nominated by you.'

'Any. What happens if I don't live long enough to collect?'

'You can nominate a beneficiary.'

'Yeah, a kids' charity.'

Marlborough looked at him briefly, and noted it, saying, 'Any in particular?'

'No. Barnardo's, NSPCC, Great Ormond Street, whatever.'

'Religion?'

He shook his head, and confirmed, 'Nothing in particular.'

'Any specific requests in case of fatal injury? Cremation, burial…?'

'Local tip.'

'No particular requests,' Marlborough amended. 'You were at the training centre for nine weeks – you won't have had your fingerprints removed yet?'

'No.'

'We'll get it seen to on arrival.'

The WIA building was seven storeys of modern design, close to Westminster and with no identification logo. Broad steps led to the automatic entrance doors of tinted glass. Into a large reception area, sparse apart from eight reception desks, three of them manned, and with offices behind. Directly ahead were two entrances to the inner sanctum and not dissimilar to the detectors through which one had to pass at the airports. They were set into a glass wall, reinforced and bullet-proof, Elliott assumed. Beyond them he could see two personnel, probably security, doors and elevators.

'You have the identification card issued to you at the training centre?'

'Took that off me as well.'

Marlborough sighed, and led Elliott across to one of the reception desks. Each of the three receptionists on duty was female, and wore a uniform of navy blue skirt and jacket, blue and white striped blouse and navy neck scarf.

'Good afternoon, Commander, your identification please?' the receptionist greeted him.

Marlborough handed over his ID card, and the receptionist pushed it into the computer console. He placed his hand on a sensor pad.

'Is your guest also to be admitted, sir?'

'He is.' He removed his hand.

'Sir,' she said and looked to Elliott. 'Place your left hand on the sensor, please.'

Elliott obeyed, and watched as the laser scanned it.

'Thank you,' she said with a smile, 'You have clearance. Welcome to WHQ.'

'Thanks,' he said, and returned her smile a little uncertainly.

Marlborough led Elliott across to the security posts and inserted his ID card into a slot on the right-hand stanchion of the barrier. He passed through. Elliott hesitated.

'Come through,' Marlborough instructed.

Elliott stepped through, and Marlborough retrieved his card as it was ejected.

'What if it hadn't accepted me?'

'Contrary to rumour you wouldn't be vaporised,' Marlborough said as he smiled tightly, 'The computer would activate a barrier to prevent access or egress.'

He stepped into an open elevator. Elliott went after him, and glanced back as the door slid shut.

At the third floor the door of the elevator slid open and they stepped out into a large lobby. Two doors were set on the opposite wall, the one to the left was marked *Personnel* and the one to the right *Medical*. They headed to the left. The door slid open silently and admitted them to a reception room. There was a young woman in a pale green uniform on duty, and she seemed to do a double take as her eyes settled on Marlborough.

'Good afternoon, sir,' she greeted him nervously.

Marlborough acknowledged her with a curt nod as he lifted his briefcase on to the desk and opened it. He took out Elliott's file.

'Take this young man and his file to Doctor Vogel and ask him to have him prepared,' he instructed, and snapped his briefcase shut. 'My office when you're finished here, seventh floor,' he instructed tersely.

'If you'd come this way please.'

The receptionist picked up the file as she slid from her chair and made for a door to the left of her position. The end of the reception counter did not extend to the wall so Elliott moved round it and followed her into a long corridor and down past several offices. They entered one on the left.

It was a laboratory. One man was in the room and sat at a desk at the back. He looked up as the receptionist approached. Elliott hung back a little.

'The Commander requires Mr...' she glanced at the file and continued, 'Elliott, to be prepared.'

She passed over the file.

'Thank you.'

She retreated. Vogel flipped the file open and thumbed through it. He was in no hurry, and did not acknowledge Elliott. Finally he rose to his feet and walked across to a long bench. A machine dominated one end; it resembled a pen on a flexible lead.

'Mr Elliott?'

Elliott walked across.

'Take a seat,' offered Vogel, indicating a high stool. He switched on the machine, unhooked the pen and lowered himself into a seat. 'We'll start with your left hand.'

'Start what?'

'Removing your identity,' Vogel smiled.

A friendly looking bloke, Elliott thought, and returned the smile.

'Rest it on the pad, palm up.'

'Does this hurt?' Elliott asked.

'No – but that's easy for me to say, I haven't been treated.'

The pen buzzed as it touched Elliott's skin. It was not an unpleasant sensation, rather a tingling in his fingertips as Vogel 'coloured' them with the pen. After half an hour's work the prints were erased.

'That's it. That didn't hurt too much, did it?'

'Didn't hurt at all,' Elliott said, scrutinising the surface of his fingertips, 'Is that it?'

'That's it. You'll require an identity card. Do you have your temporary ID?'

Elliott shook his head.

'I should have asked earlier – now we'll have to void your temporary ID without prints – no matter.'

Further along the bench there was a computer console with pigeon holes behind it. Vogel scanned them and took out a blank card which he inserted into a slot at the rear of the console, and then activated the computer.

'Over here please.'

Elliott glanced up from examining his fingers, slid down from the stool and walked across.

'Left hand over the sensor, fingertips only touching,' Vogel instructed, watching the computer screen. 'Okay, and now the right.' He looked at Elliott and smiled, saying, 'It's all quite painless, isn't it?'

'Seems that way,' Elliott confirmed as he changed hands.

'You've been pulled out of training?' Vogel inquired.

'Yeah.'

'I'm getting computer detail. You've been put in at number one?'

'Yeah.'

Vogel nodded and sympathised, 'Tough.' His eyes were on the computer screen as he commented, 'Training's okay, luck's better.'

Elliott nodded.

'We can't analyse luck.' Vogel operated the computer keys deftly. 'I don't go much on your life line but then I'm no astrologer.'

Elliott grinned.

Vogel picked up the card ejected by the computer and scrutinised it. There was raised print and a hologram on the left-hand side, and some sort of bar code – it looked a little like a credit card.

'You want to programme it for half a million?'

'This,' Vogel said as he offered it, 'is a passport to hell.' He smiled. 'There's a test facility over there.' He motioned vaguely to the back of the bench.

Elliott pushed the card into the slot. A computer screen illuminated with his image in the right-hand corner. Data came up alongside:

Elliott, Christopher John. Status: Operative.
Rating: Number One. Vocation: Agent Line.
Clearance Granted. Security Rating: AA.

'Is that me?'

'Does it look like you?'

'Yeah, it looks like me.'

'Poor bastard.'

Elliott hesitated at this comment and asked, 'You through with me?'

'No.' Vogel took another card and inserted it into the console. 'In a moment.' He took the card as the console ejected it. 'Looks okay,' he approved it as he offered it across.

It was not dissimilar to a police warrant card, official looking.

Elliott scanned it.

'I'm a scientist and not an operative.'

Elliott looked at Vogel quizzically.

'If you want my advice,' Vogel offered, and Elliott nodded, 'Run fast and keep your head down.'

*

Super Admin was well guarded. A long desk bisected the room and beyond it three young women worked at computer terminals. Elliott approached the desk; one of the women left her post and moved towards him. She wore the same style uniform as he had previously seen, only in charcoal grey, and he guessed that the departments were colour coded. She seemed maybe a couple of years older than himself, and was attractive enough to give him an interest.

'Yes, can I help you?'

That was a good question, he thought, especially as he had spent a couple of months in exclusively male company.

'Elliott, reporting to Commander Marlborough.'

'Your ID please.'

He handed over his card and she computer checked it. 'Go straight through to Super Admin, please.' She indicated towards the door and informed him, 'It isn't necessary for senior operatives to report here – you deal directly with Miss Martinez or Miss Jenova.' She smiled and returned the card.

'Thanks. Which?'

'Miss Jenova is on duty.'

He moved towards the door, and it slid open.

A large office with an impressive array of machinery, and a spacious L-shaped desk with a fitted computer terminal greeted him. In a recess there was a waiting area with plush seating units. Presiding over the territory was a young woman, probably in her mid twenties, her long blonde hair drawn back into a severe plait. She was rather intimidating in appearance, not unattractive, but humourless – Eastern Bloc he guessed. She looked up as he approached and surveyed him with apparent disdain.

'I've got to report to Marlborough.'

'Commander Marlborough,' she responded stiffly, 'You must be Elliott?'

'Not Mr?'

She ignored him. 'Your residence will be 211 Park Avenue, Bayswater. Sign here.' She swivelled a receipt book round towards him and offered a pen, saying, 'Keys, two sets, sign at paragraph *A*.'

He signed.

'Vehicle, MG, BGT, red, registration W, two, zero, zero. Sign at paragraph *B*, keys, two sets.'

He signed.

'Remuneration by credit transfer to the London and National Bank. Passbook, cheque book, gold card and deposit card. Sign on page three, paragraph *L*.'

He flipped through the pages, located the appropriate place and signed.

'Driving licence, passport, pilot's licence and five hundred pounds in cash. Page five, paragraphs *Q*, *R*, *S* and *T*.'

He signed and gathered up the items.

'You're early; the Commander wasn't expecting you before eight.' She sounded disapproving. 'However, he said that you should be referred to him immediately on arrival. Go straight through,' she instructed tersely.

Marlborough looked up as Elliott entered and hesitated, taking in his surroundings. The office was large, carpeted and brightly lit, with two filing cabinets towards the rear. Marlborough sat at a large desk on which a computer console dominated the back right-hand quarter. A decanter and glasses and an ornately carved cigarette box were positioned to the left. On a tray stood a coffee jug and cups. The room had no windows to give any natural light, and a few paintings of European cities, with spotlights illuminating them, broke the blank walls. There was a door to the right-hand side a little way beyond Marlborough's desk, and an elevator on the rear wall.

'I won't keep you long. You're finding your way around?'

'Yeah – it's a bit tough having to slay the dragon to get to you.'

Marlborough smiled thinly and inquired, 'You've been allocated accommodation?'

'Two, one, one, Park Avenue.'

Latislaw's apartment, Marlborough thought, and nodded. There would be no evidence of the previous tenant – Recovery and Maintenance would have been in to clear it.

'I suggest that you go across there and familiarise yourself with your new home and its facilities, then take the opportunity to wind down. Tomorrow you should report to reception at noon. Kurt Mauer our Senior Security Officer will introduce you to our various departments. At fourteen thirty you will report to computer, and Mr Sherratt will introduce you to its operation. Your apartment also has computer facilities. I shall expect to see you on Friday at ten. That's all Elliott; dismiss.'

Had he remained in the RAF and saved seriously he might, in around fifteen years, Elliott supposed, have sufficient funds to run a new MG and rent a place in Park Avenue. He parked up in one of the reserved parking bays and surveyed the elegant row of large Georgian houses. Number 211 had its own entrance hallway and stairs, two flights, to the top floor apartment. He took his keys from his pocket and unlocked the external door, stepping inside on to rich carpeting. His eyes roved over the polished wood half-panelled walls. He sprinted up the stairs to the door of his apartment and hesitated. The key slid easily into the lock and turned. He pushed the door open and stepped inside.

It was like nothing he had seen before – spacious with expensive lounge furnishings. It was a little out of his range. He spent some time exploring – two double bedrooms with beds made up, and his suitcase on top of one of the wardrobes in one room, the clothing unpacked and put away, a bathroom, shower room, and fully equipped kitchen with all mod cons. There was food in the well stocked fridge, drinks in the lounge cabinet, and a small study with computer facilities. He supposed that the property in its entirety was WIA owned and that WIA personnel occupied the two lower floors.

His apartment had probably previously been Latislaw's, but the poor sod would no longer be needing it. Perhaps he himself would not be needing it for long – that was a sobering thought.

Elliott had five hundred pounds in his pocket, practically five weeks' wages in the RAF before deductions and he had reckoned that he had been on good money. He took his bank passbook and gold card from his pocket. The passbook showed a ten thousand pound credit balance and the gold card had no limit. It was now several months since his last leave so he decided to take a look in town. He was not in the mood for self-catering, and he could afford to take in a restaurant more expensive than the corner grease café which he normally frequented, maybe go on to a club. After a shower and shave and a change of clothes he was ready to hit the town. Clubland was not too far away so he decided to walk: the car would limit him to a couple of drinks and he was in the mood to celebrate his freedom. Sprinting down the stairs he let himself out on to the street, and locked the door.

He came upon a busy wine bar. When he stepped inside and glanced around he noted a scarcity of apparently 'unattached' clientele. He made his way across to the service bar and ordered a whisky and soda, his eyes running again over the clientele and lingering on a slender brunette in the company of three young businessmen. She looked bored. A couple of years older than himself, he guessed, attractive, and he could see no rings on her wedding finger. He sipped his drink and watched her.

Her eyes wandered frequently from her companions and he waited for them to rove in his direction. Finally they did. She noticed that he was watching her and smiled. Should he wait and see whether she moved away from her companions or should he go across? He decided on the latter.

'You look bored rigid, maybe you need rescuing?'

'Excuse me but the young lady is with us,' one of the young men intervened, objecting to Elliott's approach.

'It was the young lady I was talking to, you're not my type,' Elliott responded. 'Does she want to be with you? Maybe she'd like to answer for herself.'

She looked a little uncertain.

'Yes or no should do it,' he suggested as he grinned. 'Do you want rescuing or not?'

There was a pause.

'Yes,' she answered with a smile.

'Can I buy you another drink?' he asked as he eyed her almost empty glass.

'Thank you, a sweet Martini with ice and lemon.' She followed him to the bar.

He ordered her drink, 'Chris Elliott,' he offered, introducing himself.

'Jayne Marshall.'

'Is one of them your boyfriend?'

'No, they're just colleagues.'

'I'm not likely to find the heavy mob waiting for me outside then?' He paid for her drink and passed it to her, then said, 'I was thinking of going on to a nightclub, do you want to come?'

She studied him for a few moments, then said, 'I don't know. I don't know you.'

'I don't know you either.' He took a drink and asked, 'Does that make us quits?'

'Why not? What do you do?'

'I used to be a pilot.'

'Used to be? What are you now?'

'I'm not sure. How about you?'

'I'm a solicitor.'

He resisted inviting her to solicit him any time but asked instead, 'Interesting job?'

'It can be, if we get a prosecution which isn't run of the mill.'

'You're a prosecutor?'

'You sound a little scathing. Do we usually find you in the dock?'

'No, I didn't mean to sound scathing. Shall we move on?'

They went to a nightclub, had a few more drinks and a meal. She looked good by candlelight; with a little luck he might score.

'I think you should sleep with me tonight.'

He looked at her. He had not expected it to be her suggestion.

'I want to know if you're as good as you look,' she teased.

'I look good?'

'You look as though you should be.'

'What happens if I'm not as good as I look?'

'I put you out with the milk bottles.'

He nodded and asked, 'And if I'm good?'

'I might keep you for another night.'

A pause.

'Sod off!'

'What?'

'I said, sod off; I could put it stronger.'

'You don't want to sleep with me?'

'I had it in mind but I'll get by without. Do you want me to get you a taxi?'

She looked a little uncertain, then asked, 'You don't even want to try?'

'For marks out of ten?' He took a drink. 'You're a clinical professional and it sounds like it extends into your private life.'

'And what's wrong with that?'

'If you want to put it into that context, I know your sort better as prostitutes.'

Her hand whipped across his face. He barely flinched as he had expected it. It was a hard slap which left a livid red print on his cheek and drew the attention of the patrons in the proximity. He took his cigarettes from his pocket and lit one.

'You've got time to find yourself another bloke for tonight – I don't lend myself out on approval.'

'So you're supremely confident?'

'No, I just don't get a lot of pleasure out of measuring performances.'

She smiled and suggested, 'My place, no points?'

'No criticism?'

'No criticism.'

He was good. She had not expected him to be. Those who showed promise were usually a let-down. It wasn't often that good looks and good sex went together; the good-lookers were usually too egotistical to care. Their agreement prevented her from giving points – but it could be nine – nine out of ten was brilliant, with a little room for improvement.

'You need to loosen up a little, sweetheart,' he said as he sank back against the pillows and slid his arm beneath her shoulders. 'You're too busy trying to be good to let yourself go.'

'No criticism, you said.'

'I'm not criticising,' he clarified, looking at her, 'I'm just suggesting that you might enjoy yourself a bit more.' He paused, then added, 'Do you want me to go home now?'

'Please yourself.'

He slid from between the sheets and began to dress.

'Will I see you again?' she asked.

'Do you want to?'

'Call me some time.'

'Okay.' He pulled on his shirt and fastened it.

'I won't wait in.'

'I wouldn't expect you to.' He tucked his shirt into his trousers, leaned across the bed and kissed her. He picked up his jacket as he straightened up and made for the door.

'Maybe I'll see you on the wrong side of the dock,' she commented.

'Don't hold your breath.'

*

Midday brought a tour of the WIA building, with Kurt Mauer as the guide. The female members of the staff made the scenery more interesting and Elliott's eyes roved frequently although his concentration did not. His session with Sherratt, the senior computer technician, did not run its anticipated length. Computers were not new to Elliott, and his basic grasp of their operation was sound. He knew sufficient to operate the terminals to the extent required of operative level who needed only to know how to extract information. The RAF had not been without technology. Sherratt needed to tell him little, other than his access code.

Brett Kane was twenty-nine years of age, tall, lean and dark haired, with chiselled features. Operative level on agent line for four years he had been brought in to take up the number two slot temporarily, with a possibility of the posting being made permanent. His reaction to a non-tried, non-graduate at number one had been sceptical but it was not his place to question Marlborough's decisions. Any questions were for Elliott.

Elliott looked up as a shadow fell over him. It was not a break period, so there were plenty of vacant tables in the refectory.

'Brett Kane,' he offered, introducing himself as he took a seat. He studied Elliott for a few moments. 'Looks like we're going to be working together.'

Elliott nodded.

'So what gets you to number one straight off when I've been climbing the ladder for nearly five years?'

'Sheer bloody-mindedness maybe.'

Kane nodded, then jibed, 'So we're taking agents straight out of nursery school now? Well, I'm not in the habit of babysitting.'

'It's a long time since I had a babysitter.'

'Just so long as you know you're going to have to look after yourself.'

'I think I get the idea.'

Kane leaned back in his chair and asked, 'You've never done assignment before?'

'Not without an aeroplane under me.'

'Simulated assignment at training centre?'

'No.'

'I intend only to look out for me.'

'Sounds like a good idea,' Elliott agreed, offering his cigarettes.

Kane took one and leaned forward for a light.

'You won't mind if I do the same?' He lit his own cigarette and looked at Kane. 'In the RAF I worked as part of a team and I worked solo. I preferred solo; my life's easier if I'm not responsible for somebody else. I never had any problems looking after number one.'

'Confident little bastard, aren't you?'

'Think you'll find we're about the same size,' Elliott said, drawing on his cigarette. 'I need to be confident, don't I?' He smiled vaguely. 'If you aren't into babysitting I'm not going to get the benefit of your experience.'

'Too right, I've worked for where I am.'

'I'm not arguing.'

'So we'll get along – just so long as you understand the position.'

'I'm reading you loud and clear. If you don't like what I'm saying you're going to go your own way. If you're right you'll come through and if I'm right I'll come through. That sounds fair enough.'

There was a pause.

'Have you got anything planned for tonight?' Kane asked.

'No.'

'I think we ought to go out on the town. Off duty we'll get along okay. Tomorrow, when it comes down to it, you're where I want to be and I'll fight you for it – nothing personal.' Kane grinned and stated, 'I'll pick you up about eight.' He rose to his feet. 'You're at Latislaw's place?'

'Latislaw's in a drawer in forensic, I'm at my place. I'll be waiting.' He watched as Kane left.

There was obviously not going to be much of a partnership. He held number one and Kane wanted and probably had more entitlement to it. At least he had the benefit of knowing what the hell it was about, had been in it for four years and was still alive.

*

Kane arrived on time, and pressed the car horn as he pulled up outside the mews. Elliott stepped out on to the pavement and pulled the door shut, walked across and slid into the passenger seat.

'Have you read the rules?' Kane steered the car away from the kerb, 'You can do what the hell you like so long as you don't get married. *Carte blanche* to love 'em and leave 'em.' He grinned. 'The art's in moving on without leaving a forwarding address before the complications set in.'

'That's an example of some of the experience you're willing to pass on?'

'You're number one without graduating – if you're that good there's nothing for me to teach you. I haven't worked to give it all away. I'll accept that maybe you're experienced in life,' Kane conceded, half smiling. 'So we aren't going to talk work tonight, and we don't know what we're going to be in tomorrow, so let's get out and enjoy ourselves.'

'Sounds good enough to me.'

At an expensive nightclub on the outskirts of the city Kane parked up on the car park. They both slid out, Kane locking the doors. Elliott followed him into the foyer. It was membership only, and Kane signed him in. The plush club room was crowded, so they pushed their way through to the bar and Kane ordered the drinks. His eyes roved over the clientele as he waited.

'It's the big day tomorrow, we need to get to bed early,' he grinned and said, 'Seen anything you fancy?'

'One or two possibilities.' Elliott looked back to the bar as the barman set the drinks down. 'Thanks,' he acknowledged, as he picked up his glass and took a drink.

'You can go down to the local spit and sawdust and drink bitter,' Kane remarked, 'We're a bit more upmarket. This is a class joint.'

'So I like bitter, I've never been into cocktails and I don't intend starting now. And I figure if you're going to be drinking straight whiskies, I'm driving.'

Kane nodded and agreed, 'You've got yourself a deal. We'll go back to your place. I'm going to try the brunette in the red dress.' He moved away. Elliott watched after him. A good looking bloke, he thought, shouldn't have much difficulty in scoring.

'Good evening, Mr Elliott.'

He turned to see Maryana Jenova. She looked completely different with her hair loose – less severe and more attractive. Definitely more attractive, he decided, something of a stunner.

'This is not the sort of place I would have expected to find you. Mr Kane's idea, no doubt.'

'I get ideas of my own.'

She nodded and said, 'I suggest that you have a clear head when you see the Commander in the morning.' She made to move away.

'You could make sure of it.'

She turned and looked at him quizzically.

'Can I buy you a drink?'

'I'm with friends.'

He looked across to where her party stood chatting. 'They seem to be getting along okay without you. You could take the chance to act over and above the call of duty and make sure I keep in line.'

'That would be too far over and above the call of duty, Mr Elliott. By no stretch of the imagination do my duties extend to chaperoning operatives.'

'Is there ever a time you come off duty and turn into a human being?'

'Excuse me, Mr Elliott,' Maryana dispensed with his company.

He grinned, took another drink and glanced around. Kane appeared to be making good progress. Personally, he was not really in the mood, the following day being too much on his mind. He had the same feeling as he used to have before taking a new plane on test; the adrenaline was already beginning to flow and the nervous energy was building up. He turned back to the bar. Chatting with the lads at RAF Flyingdale, the training centre and Mulcahy – they all seemed to be a long time ago. The WIA was going to be a lot different to service life. Still, being on his own was nothing new.

'We meet again. Isn't this place a little above your usual haunts?'

'Depends on where my usual haunts are. It beats hanging around in courts and police cells.' Elliott hesitated, then asked. 'Can I buy you a drink or are you with somebody?'

'Just girlfriends. In these surroundings I expect nothing less than champagne. Do you want to withdraw your offer?'

'Do you want it by the glass or the bottle?'

'By the glass will do.'

Elliott placed the order. 'Put any poor bastards behind bars today?'

'You weren't there,' she teased.

'But you're following me.'

'Maybe I'm looking out for you incriminating yourself.'

'If I find myself in the dock I'm likely to register an objection to the prosecutor – unless I'm guaranteed sentence of a personal supervision order.'

She smiled and added, 'That's outside the court's jurisdiction.' She took the glass which he offered. 'However, a private arrangement might be acceptable, on a short-term basis,' she suggested, taking a sip of her drink and looking at him. 'Until tomorrow morning maybe?'

'I already told you that I don't give guarantees.'

'That would appear to preclude the possibility of bail.'

He nodded and took a sip of his drink. 'I was thinking of taking an early night.' He studied her for a moment, then asked, 'My place? With a bottle of champagne?'

'No caviar?'

'I don't like caviar. How about crisps?'

'Champagne and crisps don't have the same air of sophistication,' she said sarcastically.

'So we'll just stick with the champagne.'

'And your place?'

'You're not into slumming it?'

'Just this once.'

At twenty-two thirty hours Kane and the brunette in the red dress made up the foursome. They were both well oiled. Elliott had watched Kane make frequent excursions to the bar and he had with him a large bottle of whisky. Maryana Jenova watched as the foursome made for the doors, disapproval registered on her face.

'Where did you steal the car?' Jayne asked as she slid into the front passenger seat.

'From him,' Elliott said, nodding towards Kane who was climbing into the back seat after the brunette. 'He's in no fit state to drive.'

He passed her the bottle of champagne which he had bought, and glanced over into the back seat. Kane didn't seem to be particular about waiting until he was in bed. He was engaged in a mutual groping session with the brunette.

'Is your friend on heat?' Jayne asked, looking across at Elliott as he started up the car.

'No, just oversexed and impatient.'

'And you aren't?'

'I figure that if something's worth having then it's worth waiting for.'

There were gasps and sighs from the back seat. Jayne looked round and turned back quickly, 'Oh, my God, that's disgusting.'

Elliott glanced round. 'Yeah, like a couple of dogs in the park. You want me to stop off at a police station and you can have them arrested for indecency?' he offered as he grinned, 'Give you something to prosecute tomorrow.'

She turned back. 'I hope you enjoy cleaning upholstery.'

'His car, it's not my problem. I just wish they'd stop steaming the windows up.' He glanced into the rear view mirror and commented, 'It's like looking through frosted glass.' He looked across at her and grinned. 'I wouldn't bother watching, they're not doing anything we can't do better.'

Half an hour's drive got them back through town. They were now only a couple of minutes from the apartment, and the back seat passengers were making themselves presentably decent.

'Is it his apartment too?' Jayne asked emerging from the car. Her eyes moved over the façade of the mews.

'It's borrowed.'

'And I thought that ex-pilots must make good money.'

'They get by.'

Elliott tossed the car keys to Kane and moved to unlock the door to the apartment. He switched on the light and guided Jayne along the hallway and up the stairs.

Chapter Six

Kane stumbled through to the kitchen and dropped into one of the chairs.

'Coffee?' Elliott asked as he glanced round.

'Sweet and black. What time is it?'

'Almost nine.'

There was a silence.

'Where are the girls?'

'I ran mine to work and yours home.' He placed a mug of coffee in front of Kane, and added, 'Yours was called Linda, incidentally; she couldn't remember if she mentioned it. I told her you were called Arnold.'

'Thanks.'

'How much did you have to drink last night?'

'I lost count. Do I look as bad as I feel?'

'Worse.'

Kane picked up his drink and took a sip. 'Have you got a couple of aspirins?' he asked.

Elliott pulled open a cupboard and took out a bottle, which he passed across. 'Do you want anything to eat? A couple of slices of dry toast maybe?'

'Fuck off,' Kane snapped as he tipped three aspirins into his hand and fired them into his mouth. He took a drink and commented, 'It was some night, she was some girl.'

'I'm surprised you remember.'

Kane looked at him. 'Is Marlborough going to think I look like the morning after the night before?'

'It depends if you've improved on grey green by the time we get there,' Elliott said, carrying a fried breakfast across to the table and setting it down.

'You're going to eat that?'

'I thought I might.' Elliott pulled back a chair and lowered himself into it, then offered, 'Unless you want it?'

'I think I'm going to throw up.'

Kane rose hurriedly to his feet and bolted for the door. It slammed behind him. Elliott grinned.

At nine thirty Kane returned and gulped down his almost cold coffee. He looked across at Elliott. It was not up to him to inform Elliott that Marlborough had old-fashioned ideas on standards of dress, and that he expected his operatives to wear a suit, shirt and tie unless otherwise directed. That was part of the etiquette taught at the training centre.

'Are you about ready?'

'I've been waiting for you,' Elliott said, lifting a leather jacket from the back of his chair and pulling it on. 'Are we taking both cars or are you going to fly there on the back of a pink elephant with wings?' He grinned.

'Not unless you're going to go out and catch it. We might be going in different directions.'

'Both cars then,' Elliott acknowledged, 'You're looking better.' He made for the door.

Kane followed, asking, 'Nervous?'

'I'd be a fool if I wasn't.'

'Got everything?'

Gun, ID, communicator, keys, Elliott checked and nodded.

'Did I see Jenova at that club last night?'

'Yeah.'

'Oh, God.' He stumbled down the stairs and out on to the street, waiting whilst Elliott locked the door. 'I suppose she was drinking tomato juice and making notes?'

'It was tomato juice? I thought it was blood,' Elliott grinned and suggested. 'She probably knows how many whiskies you had, if you want to ask her.' He walked across to his car.

Kane hesitated, then walked to his own with little enthusiasm, and let himself in. Starting up the engine he manoeuvred out of the parking space and followed Elliott towards the city centre and WHQ. His mind was wandering as he drove – number two to an untried and basically untrained number one – there were enough risks without that sort of a liability.

Maryana Jenova greeted their arrival with a scowl, then checked her watch – nine fifty-three.

'Is he in?' Elliott asked.

'Presumably *he* is the Commander?' she responded coldly. 'Yes, the Commander is in. You are early, you will have to wait.'

'Okay,' Elliott agreed, and perched on the edge of the desk as Kane moved across to the waiting area.

She was probably around twenty-five or -six he guessed, about five feet six and with a curvaceous figure. He wondered whether she had ever had sex or whether her legs were welded together. She didn't seem to like him too much, or maybe she just didn't like men.

'Do you mind?' she snapped.

'No, the view from here's pretty good.'

'Chairs are for sitting on, my desk is not. Kindly remove yourself.'

'You want me to go and stand in the corner or should I write a hundred lines?' He remained on the desk. She ignored him. He leaned across the desk and viewed the computer screen.

'This is of no concern to you. Will you please go away?'

'I'm just interested.'

'It is not your place to be interested.'

'What is my place?'

'Whatever it is, Mr Elliott, it is not on my desk.'

'No, miss,' he conceded as he slid down and moved away.

She hesitated, and watched him out of the corner of her eye. He stood in the corner by the door and faced the wall.

She looked across and asked, 'What are you doing? Will you please behave yourself.' She paused, then continued, 'At least try to behave like an adult.'

'Maybe, if you try and treat me like one.' He turned and looked at her. 'Do you talk to everyone like they're about ten?'

She did not respond, but turned her attention back to her work. Elliott shrugged and moved towards Kane.

'Rubbing the boss's PA up the wrong way isn't a good idea.'

'The chances of rubbing her up any way would be something! Do you think maybe she's an automaton?'

'You tell me, you're the one intent on winding her up.'

The communicator on Jenova's desk buzzed.

'Yes, sir?' she responded.

'Have Elliott and Kane arrived?'

'Yes, sir.'

'Send them through please.'

She looked across, 'The Commander will see you now.'

'Yeah? Be in trouble if we didn't have you to interpret for us, wouldn't we?'

Her scowl deepened.

Elliott led towards the door. It slid open as he approached. Marlborough looked up, his eyes travelling slowly over Elliott – jeans, tee shirt, leather jacket and no tie.

'I expect certain standards of dress from my operatives. You appear to fall short of them.'

'Will I shoot faster if I'm wearing a suit?' Elliott responded, 'Or would I just make a better-looking corpse?'

Marlborough hesitated, decided not to pursue this line and instructed, 'Sit down.'

Kane and Elliott took the seats at the opposite side of the desk. Marlborough studied them briefly. Two good-looking young men, undoubtedly academically clever, one to an extent proven on assignment and the other...?

'As you're no doubt aware, you're coming into this assignment part-way through, and with the target on the alert.' He paused, then continued, 'Latislaw is dead and Suleman is in the intensive care unit. He hasn't as yet regained consciousness, and so our information finishes at the time of the last report some five days ago.' He surveyed them a little doubtfully. 'The investigation, gentlemen, is into the supply of arms, ammunition and explosives to terrorist organisations. They shouldn't be getting into the country but they are, and how and where has not yet been established. We're talking about quantity; this is big business and the importers will go to any lengths to protect it. Obviously Latislaw and Suleman were on to something...'

'And now they'll be waiting to welcome us with open arms, uh?' Elliott asked. 'We could just shoot ourselves now and save Recovery a lot of trouble.'

Marlborough ignored him. 'We know that Latislaw and Suleman's inquiries have produced a couple of suspects,' he informed them, and tossed a slim file across the desk. 'A Spaniard, Miguel Espachio, and an American, Denver Mackintosh – both are strongly suspected of arms dealing and neither has ever been convicted. Neither of them was in the United Kingdom five days ago.'

'Is anybody watching them?'

'Observation. Mackintosh is presently in Warsaw and Espachio is at his Costa Brava villa.'

'So Latislaw and Suleman were on to something but we don't know what. Our two main suspects are thousands of miles away and putting on a show for Observation and we don't know how or where the arms are getting in?'

'I believe that's what I said,' Marlborough agreed.

'I was just checking that I heard you right.'

'If you wanted more, I'm sorry,' Marlborough offered almost sarcastically, 'Unfortunately, we rarely have information handed to us on a plate.'

'So what do we have?' Elliott asked.

Marlborough looked at him. He was not accustomed to being interrupted and questioned.

'We've got a whole bunch of negatives. You must have something for us. Where were Latislaw and Suleman working?' Elliott again interrupted.

'Does it matter?'

'It's all we've bleedin' got.'

Marlborough's eyes held Elliott's but Elliott's did not deviate. That question at least was one which Marlborough could answer.

'Brixton.'

A Spaniard, an American and Brixton – that was some combination, Elliott thought.

'Didn't wander too far from base, did they?' Elliott hesitated. 'There's no way the arms are coming in Port of London.'

'And you would know?'

'I was brought up on the streets of London. I reckon Suleman and Latislaw upset the drug barons, not arms dealers, with their sniffing around. We should be looking some other place.'

Marlborough frowned and inquired, 'That's your opinion, is it, Elliott?'

'You've got one agent dead and one agent in intensive care. If I can do worse than that maybe I'll just go home and change into a suit. It'll save a lot of time in laying me out; I could climb straight up on to the forensic bench if you want.'

'Don't tempt me, Elliott,' Marlborough snapped. 'Acknowledging the fact that you were brought up on the streets of London, do you have any contacts?'

'You reckon the kids I went to school with are running around with Kalashnikovs?'

'I'm sorry, Elliott.' Marlborough clearly wasn't. 'Do you resent that inference?'

'No, I was just thinking that if that's the way things are I might have seen more action if I hadn't joined up.' He looked at Marlborough and asked, 'What sort of brief are we working on here? Find the nearest thing to suicide alley and jump?'

Marlborough's eyebrows raised.

'Okay, so there's plenty more where I came from. I'm expendable and life comes pretty cheap, uh?' Elliott took his cigarettes from his pocket, lit one, 'I'm only twenty-two, I've only just started living and I'm not going to die just because you say so. I want a better reason than that. I don't even think you expect me to do that. I've cost you money, you want some sort of return on your investment.'

There was a silence.

'I think you should dismiss,' Marlborough decided finally. 'Return for further briefing tomorrow at noon. Dismiss gentlemen, thank you.'

Maryana Jenova watched their silent exit, Kane following Elliott. They left Super Admin and stepped out into the corridor. Elliott summoned the elevator, Kane glanced along the empty corridor.

'What the hell did you think you were playing at?' he demanded.

Elliott looked at him quizzically.

'I asked what the hell you thought you were playing at? You get instructions for assign, you jump. Marlborough says, you do.'

'Is that right? I've got my own ideas on God and he doesn't fit.'

'Around here that's exactly what he is.'

'Tough.'

'You don't get it, do you, Elliott?'

'Get what?'

'You're nothing, you're just another piece of software. There's another programme waiting to replace you.'

'Are you telling me I'm shit, Kane?' Elliott stepped into the elevator as the door slid open. He turned and asked, 'Disposable software? I didn't see Marlborough press exit.'

'So you got lucky. There's no way I'm going to go down with you.'

'Then split. You're not my worry, you don't have to work with me, Kane. Tell Marlborough you don't want to.'

The elevator commenced its descent.

'He'll have you for this.' Kane gloated.

'For what? What the hell did I do?' Elliott asked him. 'If I wanted to get myself killed I didn't need to leave the RAF – all I needed to do was walk into a Belfast bar in uniform. I might be daft, I'm not stupid. I don't want to be where Latislaw is.'

'There were suspects.'

There was no reply.

'So what do you propose to do tonight?' Kane asked.

Elliott grinned.

'Did you get her address?'

'Yeah, but I fancy a change.'

Elliott didn't elaborate and Kane didn't pursue it. No plans were made that they should meet up that evening. It was too early for any sort of friendship to have formed and they had nothing to discuss.

It was a little chilly in the basement car park of the WIA building as they headed for their cars. Elliott stopped, his eyes resting on a rather battered Vauxhall Cavalier.

'You know who that belongs to?'

Kane stopped and turned, his eyes following Elliott's. 'One of the mechanics, I think.'

That figures, Elliott thought and nodded. 'Thanks.'

He veered away from his car and towards the bottom end of the car park where the mechanics' workshop was located. Kane watched him for a few moments and shrugged. The Vauxhall was no great age, just knackered, and he could see no reason for Elliott's interest.

There was a radio blaring loudly in the workshop as Elliott approached. In each of the service bays there was a vehicle, and seven or eight mechanics either wandered around or had their heads stuck in various parts of vehicular anatomy.

'Yeah, can I do something for you?' a young lad asked. He was younger than Elliott and wearing greasy overalls. He looked up from a tyre which he was wrenching off a wheel.

'I'm told somebody down here owns the green Cavalier out there,' Elliott said, indicating vaguely towards the car park.

'The chunk of scrap metal that's only held together with rust?' The lad grinned. 'It's mine, every last flake of it,' he yelled over the din.

Elliott moved towards him. 'Don't suppose you'd consider lending it to me?' he asked.

'Lending it?' the lad repeated.

'Just until tomorrow lunch time. You can have my car until I bring yours back – the MG.'

There was only one MG out on the car park and that was an agent line vehicle. Elliott took the spare key from his pocket and offered it.

'Do we have a deal?' he asked.

'You bet,' the young mechanic agreed and fumbled in his pockets, finally drawing out a grubby key with sellotape wrapped around the fob. He offered it and grabbed the key to the MG. 'I don't score tonight I'll never score, uh?'

Elliott grinned, 'I reckon you could be in for a hell of a night.' He tossed the key into the air and caught it deftly. 'Thanks for the loan.'

The car was no better inside than it was out, a mobile ashtray with grime and oil ingrained and frayed upholstery. It juddered as Elliott turned the key in the ignition and came to life grudgingly. Every joint, rivet and screw creaked. He smiled – it was perfect for Brixton. The gears grated crashingly, he could feel the clutch slipping and the brakes screamed of metal on metal. He hoped that that was what was responsible for the smell of burning.

His clothing was a little on the new side and of designer label. A brief stopover at a side street flea market produced a more appropriate outfit: very well-faded denim jeans, denim shirt, broad-buckled belt and cowboy boots. He checked himself over in the mirror. Not too bad, he reckoned, but he looked as though he was stuck in a time warp. Was the black cowboy style hat going too far? He tried it – way over the top, he looked a complete bozo – best keep it that way.

He took an early dinner over in Chinatown. The restaurant was quiet as it was too late for the lunch time trade and the evening trade had not yet commenced. The waitresses in their colourful silk outfits had nothing better to do than flutter around his table and that in turn gave him something to look at and relieved him, to some extent, of his own company. He enjoyed the best of service and the best of cooking since the chef was not distracted by other orders. His strange style of dress appeared to perturb no one; he was just another prat. The cashier didn't turn a hair as he settled his seven pound account with a fifty pound note.

Elliott had known the Brixton area pretty well and it hadn't changed much. It was still a dump, still a ghetto. Not that its residents were dregs, it was just that nobody in a warm and cosy office could be bothered to try and make things any better. In return for such apathy the response was anarchy, and the powers that be could apparently not understand why.

*

Marlborough's shift had finished and Omaru had taken over command. Nevertheless Marlborough remained in his office. He had been unsettled all day. Elliott – Elliott was a mistake, and all the more unfortunate a mistake because he talked sense. Marlborough was not accustomed to being challenged. Somewhere amongst the aggravation of having his authority undermined a small voice asked why the hell it shouldn't be. It was a new experience and, he had to admit, not one which he liked. If the little bastard wasn't right maybe it wouldn't be so bad. That was what had unsettled him – Elliott was right. What right did he have to send agents in cold and with a reception committee waiting? Absolutely none, but no one had ever questioned his authority – until Elliott had come along. There was nothing to work on, nothing to justify the assignment. He hauled himself up from his seat and made for his quarters. A shower would refresh him but it would not wash away the dissent. The uncertainty of his own fallibility had lodged in his mind.

Latislaw was dead and Suleman was now only holding on. And for what? Absolutely nothing. There had been nothing gained. What was the point of sending two more in? Marlborough lay across his bed. It was strange how even after all these years he missed his wife. How he longed to turn to her for comfort, advice and sympathy.

Elliott looked like a boy, a child, young enough to be his son, Marlborough admitted to himself. He would have liked children, but his daughter had been lost at the same time as his wife... Self-pity would get him nowhere, so he turned his mind back to the current events. It was an abortive assignment; it had to be left to Observation, shelved until there was something new on which to work.

*

The Dyers was around the roughest dive in Brixton and not a place which Elliott usually frequented. He parked the car up amongst others of similar ilk, and checked that his gun was fully loaded before sliding it into his belt. There was a tattered leather jacket in the back seat. He dragged it out as he slid out of the car and pulled it on. It was a little on the tight side for his build – the mechanic was a short skinny youth – but it covered the butt of his gun. He retrieved his hat from the passenger seat and planted it on his head, slammed the car door shut and checked it. Pausing to light a cigarette he crossed the street, dodging between the still busy traffic and stepped into the Dyers.

All eyes moved towards the door, and a silence descended as the patrons looked him over. He made for the bar and the conversation resumed. The barman took his time in reaching him. He had the looks of a man whose face had stopped a few bottles.

'Yeah?' he asked disinterestedly.

'Pint of your strongest bitter.'

'You over eighteen?'

There were younger looking kids in the pub.

'Yeah, what are you over? The fuckin' hill?'

'Haven't seen you in here before.'

'Exclusive membership is it?' Elliott responded belligerently. 'You want to get a bit more beer and a bit less head in that glass?'

The barman scowled at him, and finally slammed the filled glass down on the counter, the liquid spilling over the sides.

'Asked for a pint, not paying full price for a half pint in a pint glass.'

'You asking for trouble?'

'Just asking for what I'm paying for. I'm looking for some action but I wasn't figuring on finding it so fast.'

The barman hesitated, retrieved the glass and topped it up.

'So who's in on the action around here?'

'You a cop?'

Drinkers in close proximity fell silent and rested hostile eyes on Elliott.

'Sure, and you're a robber, I don't see no price list around.' Elliott pulled a handful of change from his pocket.

'Fifty-six.'

'Yeah, you're a robber, I must be a bleedin' cop.'

Elliott paid out and took a drink. His eyes roved.

There was a young black guy holding court, and Elliott watched him. He looked like the type to have his finger on the pulse. The patrons were back about their business, so he headed towards his prey. There were interested spectators but nothing was said that Elliott wanted to hear. Drugs were going down but again he wasn't interested, although he watched the transactions.

'You want?' the black guy turned to him.

Elliott shook his head, 'I don't get my kicks out of dreams.'

The young man shrugged.

'I'm looking for power, fire power.'

'Sell matches at the bar,' retorted the young black guy.

'Comedian, uh? I want Kalashnikovs or something similar – in bulk. What's your language?'

'When's the revolution?'

'That sounds like my language,' Elliott grinned and introduced himself. 'Chris Elliott.' He offered his hand.

'Pushto,' the youth offered as he accepted.

'Nice name.'

'Park your butt.'

Elliott hesitated. The youth had sprawled across the fitted padded bench seat. He pulled a stool up to the small table and lowered himself on to it, looking at Pushto quizzically.

'Tell me about the revolution?'

'You want to enlist?'

'Hell, man, I got a business to run,' Pushto took a slim cigarette from his pocket, lit it and inhaled deeply on it. 'I don't have time for no revolution, there ain't no money in it for me.'

He offered the cigarette across to Elliott. Elliott accepted it, took a drag on it and passed it back: pot, nothing he couldn't handle.

'Haven't seen you around here before?'

'Just got back.'

'From where?'

'Korea.'

'You isn't so brown.'

'I didn't go sunbathing – not exactly the climate.'

Pushto grinned and asked, 'So you're looking for fire power?' He looked Elliott over thoughtfully, then added, 'I don't know nothing about you.'

'You want I should advertise?' Elliott took a drink and continued, 'I got friends, we go where the money is, services rendered to the highest bidder. Take with us what we need, makes us popular. You know what I'm saying?'

Pushto nodded. 'So what are you looking for?'

'Serious hardware.'

'And plenty of it?' Again Pushto offered the cigarette and Elliott accepted it. 'What's the crack?'

'We've got funds.'

'As serious as the hardware?' he asked, retrieving the cigarette and taking another pull on it.

Elliott nodded.

'You don't want to talk about it?'

'I don't know who I'm talking to, this isn't my territory. I'm not talking serious money with somebody who's maybe got serious intention of relieving me of that money and giving me nothing but a cracked skull in return.'

Pushto considered Elliott as he drew in a leisurely fashion on the cigarette. 'Don't think I've ever met a mercenary before. How'd you get into it?'

'Joined up when I were sixteen, got into the commandos. Found out there was better money to be had if I hired myself out, so I deserted.'

It sounded plausible to Pushto and Elliott looked and sounded sufficiently off-beat. He no more wanted to talk arms and cost with Pushto than Pushto would want to talk drugs and wholesale supply with him. Pushto had met dupes before; usually they were too keen or too laid back and Elliott was neither. Also, he looked young, nineteen or maybe twenty; dupes were usually older. He was the right age for drugs maybe; Pushto wouldn't have figured him for firearms, but figured that he was genuine. Now in his mid twenties, Pushto had been doing drugs and a few other profitable sidelines since junior school, and had the experience to trust his instincts – but not one hundred per cent.

'Maybe I know somebody,' he offered lazily.

'I don't have much time, I'm not looking for maybes,' Elliott drained his glass and rose to his feet.

'You can spare a couple more minutes.'

Elliott hesitated and retook his seat. Pushto took a long draw on the cigarette and exhaled slowly.

'If you check out I'll fix an introduction.'

'Check out?'

'Only got your word you're what you say you are.'

'I don't have much on you.'

'I'm not asking you for anything,' Pushto grinned.

Elliott nodded. 'How long is this going to take?'

'Tomorrow, same time same place.'

*

Marlborough was not asleep. Nevertheless, he did not acknowledge for a few moments that the buzzing sound which was invading his room was coming from his communicator. Realisation dawned. He hauled himself up the bed, fumbled on the bedside table, located the communicator and activated it.

'Marlborough?' he mumbled as he sought out the bed-light.

'I need a cover.'

The voice seemed familiar and unfamiliar. 'Who is this?'

'Elliott. I need a record that I deserted the commandos a couple or three years ago, and I need it pretty fast. I'm being checked out.'

'What the hell are you talking about?'

'Buying arms. They want to check me out before they deal...'

'You're doing what? Where are you?'

'About to head out of Brixton and...'

'My office, fifteen minutes,' Marlborough snapped, and deactivated the communicator.

*

'You're an idiot, Elliott!' Marlborough thumped the desk and continued his tirade, 'Nobody gave you instructions to...'

'I figured it was safer than going in cold with a neon sign over my head.'

'And the assignment was cancelled.'

'Adjourned.'

'You went in alone and without giving any notification!'

'I went in with a plan.'

'On a wing and a prayer.'

'That was my plan.' Elliott took the hat from his head. 'And now I need help. If I don't get it I'll live – if I don't go back.' He set the hat down on the desk and asked, 'Let me do it.'

'Do it?'

'You want to wait years? I'm working for you, I want what you want. I can't do it on my own, I need your help – and I need it now.'

'You've spun some sort of line about being a deserter?'

'From the commandos, maybe a couple or three years ago. Mercenaries need guns.'

'And you've approached an arms dealer?'

Elliott nodded and conceded, 'Sort of.'

'Has the thought occurred to you that he's seen the pound signs and might be stringing you a line?'

'Yeah, that's the chance I take.'

Marlborough hesitated, then activated the communicator.

'Yes, sir?' the night secretary Veronica Martinez responded.

'Get me the armed forces records department.'

Elliott lit a cigarette and leaned back in his chair. It seemed that he was right in thinking that Marlborough would have contacts and the authority. He was probably also right in thinking that Marlborough was presently not in the best of moods. It was a long telephone conversation, Marlborough was precise in his requirements and a perfectionist. Clearly if he arranged cover it was good cover. He closed communications finally.

'This is something you don't ever do to me, Elliott,' he snapped, looking at him coldly, 'If you ever do anything like this to me again, without discussion, without authority, I'll have you court martialled for insubordination so fast your feet won't touch the floor. Do you understand me?'

'Sir.'

Marlborough didn't doubt that he did – or that it would make any difference.

'You're young, Elliott, maybe you think you know it all. You'll find as you grow older – if you grow older – that you don't know as much as you thought you did. Give yourself the chance,' he suggested, smiling thinly. 'Don't make the mistake of thinking I'm stupid. Where you are, I've already been.'

Elliott didn't disbelieve him, but he wasn't Marlborough. 'You just did as you were told and never asked questions?' he looked at Marlborough and shook his head. 'I don't think so. If you were a yes man the WIA wouldn't exist.'

'And if that's flattery, Elliott, it will get you nowhere. You have an appointment for briefing at twelve noon. That gives you considerably more time to sleep than I'm likely to get. Dismiss and let me get back to bed.'

'Sir.' He retrieved his hat as he rose to his feet, then added, 'Thank you, sir.'

'Don't patronise me, Elliott, just get out of here.'

It was a little late for finding company unless he wanted to buy it and that had never been Elliott's style. He had seen enough money grease his mother's palm and it had sickened him. The pleasure he could handle, but the payment – no way.

'Hi there.'

He stopped in the process of locking the car and looked round.

'Where have you been all night?'

'Jayne,' he smiled and asked whilst locking the car door, 'You care?'

'No.'

'You just want my body, uh?'

'It's a nice body.'

He grinned, walked across the pavement and made to unlock the door.

'Am I invited in?'

'Sure,' he agreed, and turned the key in the lock, 'I'll fix us a drink.'

He held the door open for her and followed her inside.

'I'd just have slipped away quietly if you hadn't been on your own,' she led up the stairs, 'I'm not the possessive type.' She watched as he opened the door to his apartment. 'And I wanted to say goodbye.'

He cast her a quizzical glance as he switched on the light.

'I leave for Carlisle tomorrow.'

'Permanently?'

She nodded, and lowered herself on to the sofa as he headed for the drinks cabinet.

'I'm getting married on Saturday.'

'Congratulations. Does your boyfriend know...?'

'I'm entitled to a last fling, aren't I?'

He nodded, relieved that she did not have him in mind as a long-term prospect.

'What can I interest you in?'

She looked him over.

'Besides my body.'

She smiled and said, 'Dry martini.'

He scanned the bottles and reached for one. 'Yeah, I can manage that.' He poured a large glass, picked up a can of lager and moved towards her. He offered the glass, 'I don't think I've ever been a last fling before.' He sat down beside her. 'What do I have to do?'

He pulled back the ring on the can and took a drink, then slid his right arm around her shoulders.

'This is my last free night as a bachelor girl; I want it to be memorable.'

She wasn't drunk. He reckoned that she hadn't had a drink all day. He took another drink, rose to his feet and offered his hand. She looked at him, then drained her glass in one long gulp, set it down and slid her hand into his. He pulled her to her feet and lowered his lips to hers. Her arms folded around him, her body pressing closely to his. His tongue entered her mouth and explored a little, then he pulled away from her and took another drink from the can. His left hand slid over her body identifying the obstacles. Nothing complex, he thought, and steered her through to the bedroom.

A back kick and the door closed. She was already on the buttons of his shirt. He drained the can and tossed it towards the bin. His left arm slid around her, his right hand ran up her back and his fingers located the pull of her zip. He slid it downwards, easily, to below her waist, then his hand ran back up over smooth skin and rested on the fastening of her bra. A deft movement and the fasteners released. She offered no resistance as he slid her dress from her shoulders and over her body, her bra travelling with it. His shirt was open, her hands massaging his chest. She sucked at his neck.

As her dress slid down to her ankles he pushed her back on to the nearby bed, and followed her down. Her fingers worked almost desperately on the button and zip of his jeans. He slid her briefs over her hips and down her legs. Her legs folded upwards, and her thighs caressed his hips.

'Bear with me, sweetheart,' he said, hauling himself to his feet.

His shirt and trousers were loose. He kicked off his boots and tore off his socks, then discarded his shirt and trousers.

'Chris...'

'Wait for me.' It was both a threat and a promise, his eyes lingering on the view. They roved over her body and held her eyes. 'What do you want me to do?'

'What do you want to do?'

'It's your bachelor party.'

'I want you to try for ten.'

'Yeah?' He hesitated, then asked, 'And how am I doing so far?'

No marks, no criticism, she thought. She looked at him. He had said that it was her party.

'Nine... and a half.'

He grinned, finished undressing and joined her on the bed. His left hand slid over her body as he lowered his lips to hers. Between her legs she was already wet with anticipation, and his fingers slid inside her easily. She felt him massaging the wall of her vagina, and her arms tightened around him.

'Relax, sweetheart,' he whispered. 'It's more fun if you let yourself go.'

He slid down a little. His tongue lapped at her right nipple as he continued to stimulate her with his fingers. Her hands folded over his shoulders, her fingers digging into his skin. An eruption was building up inside her; her fingers relaxed as her body reacted to the arousal and she moaned softly. He slid across her, and she grasped at him clumsily. She was ready. He withdrew his fingers and penetrated her, and she arched towards him. He was taking leisurely exercise; winding down, there was no emotion involved, only the physical pleasure. There was no pleasure to be had if she did not share it; he had never just taken from any girl.

Jayne's body went into spasm; her muscles contracted around him, drawing on him erratically. Her body no longer resisted the impulses and she was carried by the ecstasy. He pumped into her. Her drawing on him made him lose his control and eventually his head exploded as he came to climax. Breathlessly he fell across her. Her arms folded around him, her heart beating rapidly. Neither could speak; waves still ran through their bodies. He rested his head between her breasts and inhaled her heady perfume.

'Ten,' she whispered audibly.

'I'm not even started yet, sweetheart, that was just warming up.' He nuzzled briefly at her breast.

'How are you fixed for the rest of the night?'

'Yes.'

*

Elliott blinked his eyes open at ten fifteen. There was a watery sun filtering through the curtains. Jayne was laid on top of him and his arm was folded around her over the top of the sheet. Her head rested against his shoulder, and he stroked her hair.

'You awake?'

'I don't know. Did I dream you?'

'I don't think so, I feel pretty real to me.'

He looked pretty real. She hauled herself up a little way and brushed his lips with hers. He raised no objections. She locked her lips to his and he responded, his left hand sliding down to her buttocks.

'So what's he like, this bloke you're going to marry?'

'Matthew?' She looked at him, rolled from him on to her back and stared up at the ceiling. 'He's sweet.'

'Good in bed?'

She turned to face him and related, 'Good enough. That isn't everything.'

He supposed not. There must be something more to keep couples together.

'In love with him?' he asked.

'Yes.'

She looked back towards the ceiling. He rolled on to his side and looked at her. Attractive and brains. Matthew had himself a pretty good catch.

'How are you going to explain the love bites on your neck to him?'

'What!' she screamed as she shot up the bed.

He grinned, 'Just kidding.'

Her eyes moved to the clock at the bedside. 'I have to go. Can I use your shower?'

'Sure. Can I keep you company?'

It was a tempting offer but she shook her head. 'Last night was brilliant, I don't want to lose it.'

She slid out of the bed. He watched as she gathered up her clothes and headed for the door. As he slipped out of the bed he reached for his shorts and pulled them on. His body was hirsute and retained the almost excessive slimness of youth; it had not yet filled out.

He was getting a little pushed for time, he noted as he checked his watch and switched on the kettle. It was already ten fifty-six and he had an appointment with Marlborough at noon. It would be ungentlemanly not to drop Jayne off at home, and he still needed a shower and a shave. He heard the water of the shower slow and stop. He moved out into the passageway and rapped on the door of the bathroom.

'I don't want to hurry you, sweetheart, but I'm on a bit of a tight schedule.'

The bolt on the door slid back and Jayne appeared, clutching a towel to herself.

'The kettle's just boiled. I think there's a hairdryer in the bedroom.'

*

It was almost noon as he stopped the car outside her apartment block. He looked at her.

'Good luck, I hope he turns out to be all you expect him to be.'

'He will. He is.'

'Don't send me a forwarding address, I was never much of a letter writer.'

'I wouldn't want you to be. You were fun.'

'Just a fling,' he smiled.

'I couldn't have picked anyone better,' she said, looking at him uncertainly.

'Make sure he takes good care of you.'

He leaned towards her, curled his arm around her neck and drew her towards him. Their lips met. It was not a short embrace. They parted finally, she turning away from him, fumbling with the handle and pushing the door open. No goodbyes. He watched as she slid out, pushed the door shut and briskly crossed the pavement, disappearing into the apartment complex without a backward glance.

*

Maryana Jenova looked at the clock pointedly as Elliott stepped into her office. It was almost half past noon. There was no sign of Brett Kane.

'I'm late,' he admitted to the unspoken accusation. 'I'm sorry.'

She said nothing, just activated the communicator. 'Mr Elliott has arrived, sir.'

'Send him through.'

'Yes, sir,' she said, closing communications, and looked up. 'The Commander will see you now.' Her attention returned to her work.

Marlborough glanced across as the door opened, 'I'm very pleased you could make it, Elliott. I trust I'm not inconveniencing you too much?' The sarcasm was acute.

'I'm sorry I'm late. I don't have any acceptable excuse.'

Kane watched as he took a seat.

'Kane and I have occupied ourselves with small talk,' Marlborough leaned back in his seat and looked Elliott over, 'Perhaps now we can get down to business?'

It wasn't a rhetorical question.

'The position, in so far as Observation are concerned, hasn't changed. Suleman is stabilising but has not yet regained consciousness.' He looked thoughtful. 'It seems, if we are to stand a chance of making any immediate progress, that the only avenue open to us is to pursue the rather tentative channel which Elliott encountered.'

There was no praise in it, he was not commending the action. Kane glanced at Elliott with a hint of amusement. Clearly Marlborough had put him in the picture.

'Tomorrow at noon, Kane, I'm sure that you can find something to occupy your time.

'Sir.' Kane rose to his feet and asked, 'I'm not required tonight, sir?'

'I don't believe that my assistance was sought anything other than reluctantly,' Marlborough responded, his eyes resting on Elliott momentarily, 'We appear to be flying solo.'

Kane smiled, and thought to himself that Elliott wasn't going the right way to become a permanent fixture. 'Sir.'

Marlborough watched him leave, then looked at Elliott and asked, 'Did you ask the RAF to postpone the war?'

'No, sir.'

'No, Elliott. It may be that we don't have bombs and aerial combat, but the threat is the same. When I give you a time I expect you to be here. I require, as a minimum, the discipline employed by the forces – do I make myself clear?'

'Sir.'

'I don't propose to ask why you were late; had there been good reason I would probably be aware of it.' He poured himself a coffee from the thermos jug, then said, 'You have an appointment this evening. I trust you intend to be on time?'

Elliott nodded.

Marlborough pulled open his desk drawer, 'This may be useful.'

Elliott took the dog tag which he offered, and looked at him.

'You deserted, you weren't discharged; there's no reason why you shouldn't have kept it.'

No, Elliott thought as he looked at it. He still had his RAF tag – would never part with that.

'For the time being you continue to fly solo. I advise that you proceed with extreme caution.'

'Yeah,' Elliott agreed, pushing the dog tag into his pocket, 'I'm not in any hurry to view the afterlife.'

'You surprise me.'

The youth in the mechanics department raised no objections to Elliott's request that he keep the Cavalier on loan a little longer. Whether the MG had enabled him to score or not he didn't say, but he was in no hurry to part with it. It occurred to Elliott as he emerged from mechanical that he was hungry. There seemed little point in joining in the hassle of finding a parking space in town when the refectory menu suggested that there were perfectly good meals to be had.

His arrival in the refectory had coincided with the end of the six to fourteen hundred hours shift and most of the tables were occupied. He walked across to the service bar and scanned the chalked up list of additions to the menu.

'What would you like?' a matronly assistant asked.

He hadn't realised that he had reached the front of the queue. 'Lasagne, please.'

'Green beans, asparagus or broccoli?'

'Any chance of some of each?'

She smiled and added, 'You're a growing boy, about the same age as my son, and he takes some filling.' She headed out to the kitchen.

The refectory prices were subsidised and the portions were generous. Elliott surveyed his well-filled plate as he picked up his coffee. He turned away from the service bar and scanned the tables of unfamiliar faces. His eyes rested on Maryana Jenova sitting alone at one of the tables, and he made for it.

'Okay if I join you?'

She looked up and looked around: the refectory was quite full. 'I don't have any monopoly on this table, Mr Elliott.' Her tone did not suggest that she welcomed his company.

He set his plate and cup down on the table, pulled back a chair, and lowered himself into it. Her lunch appeared to consist of cottage cheese, a green salad and two crispbreads. She surveyed his plate disapprovingly as she took a delicate nibble of a crispbread.

'Maybe if you ate decent meals you wouldn't be so thin,' he commented as he dug his fork into the lasagne.

'I eat what I like to eat, thank you.'

'Maybe you're conditioned. You see the models and think that that's what you're supposed to look like – that that's what the blokes want.'

'I don't care what the blokes want, Mr Elliott, I care about my health. I look after my body.'

'Yeah? I wouldn't mind helping you out.'

She threw him a withering look and stabbed at the shredded lettuce.

'What've you got against blokes? Or is it just me?'

'I have nothing against blokes, and you, Mr Elliott, are an agent and I have no feelings one way or another towards you.'

'So the fact you treat me like dirt's nothing personal?'

'If you don't mind I came to the refectory for lunch.'

He chewed on an asparagus spear, then said, 'You know, you're a real stunner. I fancy you like hell.'

A forkful of cottage cheese froze en route to her mouth, and she stared at him.

'How about a date?' he asked.

'A date?'

'Yeah, you know – I pick you up from your place, we take in a show, go for a meal after and indulge in a little small talk, and then I take you home and kiss you goodnight on your doorstep.'

She looked away from him, the fork finalising its route to her mouth. There was no doubt that she was nervous; she was perspiring.

'Sweetheart, I never forced my way into a girl's knickers.' He looked at her and continued, 'Maybe you had a bad experience some time. I don't know what your problem is, why you should want to starve yourself,' he smiled, 'but I like you.'

'You like me?'

'Yeah. You're still beautiful, you turn me on. I figure

there must be some way of melting the ice.'

'Why don't you just eat your lunch and let me eat mine?'

He shrugged.

Chapter Seven

The Dyers was no less busy than it had been the previous night. Pushto was plying his trade openly, his customers gathered around him. Elliott elbowed his way through to the bar, where the same barman who had been on the previous night was on duty.

'Yeah?' the barman grunted, acknowledging him eventually.

'Pint of bitter.' Elliott reached into his pocket for change.

He was wearing the same outfit as he had worn the night before. His gun nestled in his belt, pushed well back towards his side. He paid over his money, picked up the glass and took a drink. A few minutes elapsed, then he pushed his way through to Pushto's table, where Pushto was still dealing. Elliott pulled back a stool and took a drink as he lowered himself on to the seat. There was a brief acknowledgement in the form of a curt nod – Pushto was in no hurry. Elliott took his cigarettes from his pocket. As he lit up, he let his eyes rove as though he was wary – he was a little.

Around twenty minutes later, Elliott drained his glass and rose to his feet. Pushto snapped his fingers, and a youngster, about fifteen years old, Elliott guessed, appeared at his side.

'The glass wants a refill,' Pushto snapped, and shot a finger towards Elliott, 'Get it.'

The youngster nodded and walked across to Elliott.

'Get you a full glass, mister,' he said, and snatched the glass from Elliott's grasp, 'Draught bitter?' he asked, waving the glass briefly under his nose and smelling, 'Be right back.'

Elliott dropped back on to the stool. He looked across to Pushto, who winked. Was that a good sign or was he just supposed to think that it was?

After another fifteen minutes Pushto's clients had dispersed. 'Beat it, kid,' he instructed the youngster, 'I want you I'll call you.' He looked at Elliott as the youngster sidled away. 'So, do you check out or what?' he asked.

'Or what?'

'You ain't that confident?'

'I know about me, what I am. I'm not in a pub full of my mates.'

Pushto grinned, took two reefers from his top pocket and offered one to Elliott. Elliott took it.

'Smoke plenty of that stuff and stronger in Korea, uh?'

'Yeah, plenty.' Elliott took his lighter from his pocket and lit the reefer. 'So?'

'You check out.' Pushto drew on his reefer and exhaled slowly, 'So you can have a meeting.'

'When?'

'You got time to finish your drink.'

'I don't have the money on me.'

'I don't have it in mind to do for you down some dark alleyway,' Pushto said, looking at him evenly. 'A flick knife ain't gonna match up to a guy with a gun in his belt.' His grin broadened and he added, 'Course, it's depending how fast you are on the draw on and I ain't about to find out.'

'I get an introduction?'

'Thought that was what you were angling for?'

'Yeah. Who…?'

'They want you to know names they'll tell you.'

Elliott nodded and took a long pull on the reefer. He was on his own, didn't have his communicator with him. Marijuana wasn't particularly powerful but it had a soporific effect on him. His brain was already fighting off the effects – clouds of apathy were beginning to infiltrate his thoughts and he needed his wits about him. He drained his glass, and Pushto rose to his feet.

'Let's move.'

Elliott nodded.

He followed Pushto out of the pub and on to the street.

'Got wheels?'

Elliott indicated towards the Vauxhall. Pushto looked it over and shrugged.

'So where are we headed?' Elliott asked as he started up the car.

'Barbican.' Pushto sucked on the reefer.

Concentrating on the driving gave Elliott an excuse to allow the reefer to burn at a distance. Even so, the smoke as it smouldered and the smoke from Pushto's was a little heady.

The apartment block overlooked a pool, Elliott noted as he glanced through a distant window on stepping out of the elevator. Pushto strode along the corridor, the plaque stating the existence of apartments 307–349. He followed, stopping once to stub out his reefer in one of the raised ashtrays. Pushto was maybe five yards ahead as he stopped outside a door. Elliott quickened his pace to join him on Pushto's beckoning command. The door was shut firmly. Pushto again pressed the bell push briefly and looked at him.

'They said half ten; it's thirty-two minutes.'

'I guess they're calling the shots.'

'I've got other places to be, I'm doing you a favour,' Pushto drawled as he took a long drag.

'So I'm grateful.'

'You oughta be.' Pushto pulled another reefer from his pocket and lit it. 'An introduction and I'm out of here.'

'So you want a commendation?'

Pushto grinned and pressed again on the bell push. 'I just want my commission.'

'And I just want the means to earn my living.'

Pushto nodded and conceded, 'Sure, I see that.'

'I don't think you see. You don't know what my life's like.'

'Fighting for some bastard you don't know, some bastard you don't even care about.'

'Aren't you doing the same thing?'

'I guess so.'

There was a click, then the door opened.

'I got a buyer.'

'Fine, bugger off.'

Elliott saw an envelope change hands.

'See you.'

Pushto swung round and winked at Elliott as he moved away.

Elliott stepped into an unlit, uncarpeted hallway.

'Pushto says you carry a gun.'

'Yeah,' Elliott agreed.

'So do we.'

He followed the footsteps and shadowy figure towards a door, at the base of which was a thin crack of light. The light flooded into the hallway as the door opened, and Elliott saw a dark brown suit and neatly trimmed blond hair.

There were three men, including the blond, all looking like city bankers. The eldest was in his fifties, a plump, comfortable-looking man, balding and wearing glasses. The other two were in their thirties, Elliott guessed, the blond being a good-looking bloke in a bland sort of way. His eyes travelled over the third. He was around five feet six, mousy haired and maybe a little academic looking. The room had a square of carpet and a three piece suite, and French windows opened on to a balcony which, he supposed, overlooked the pool.

'Take a seat, Mr Elliott,' the blond instructed rather than invited.

The sofa was vacant. He lowered himself on to it.

'You've been in Korea?'

Elliott nodded.

'And going to?'

'Cambodia.'

'How many?'

'Around a dozen of us.'

'And you're looking for?'

'Decent arms.'

'You know decent arms?'

'I want to stay alive.'

The older man smiled thinly.

'What are you looking for?' the blond continued with the questioning.

'What do you have for sale?'

'I was told Russian.'

'Off the top of my head. Can you get American?'

All three men looked at him.

'Does that give you guys a problem?' Elliott asked.

'It doesn't give us a problem.'

'Good.' Elliott knew that more was expected of him but was not in a position to know what.

'We'll meet.'

'I thought we already had.'

'We want more. Not all deserters turn into mercenaries.'

'What do you want?'

'Your blood.'

Elliott looked at him.

'We want to know if you match up.'

The academic peeled the sterile wrapper from a syringe.

'I've got a guarantee you're taking out and not putting in?'

'We don't give guarantees.'

Elliott hesitated. Rising to his feet he slipped his jacket off, unbuttoned the left cuff button of his shirt and began to fold the material back.

The man with the syringe moved towards him. Elliott folded the sleeve up past his elbow and offered his arm. He felt the point of the needle pushing against his skin over a vein. The barrel of the syringe was opaque, and he could not tell if there was already something in it.

'If I'm carrying hepatitis I'd rather not know about it.'

The mousy-haired academic looked at him quizzically.

'There weren't too many five-star hotels out in Korea.'

The older man laughed and said, 'Hepatitis could be the least of your worries.'

'I'll worry about swamp fever when I'm showing the symptoms.'

The needle broke the skin, and Elliott watched as the milky opaqueness of the barrel darkened. He was offered a cotton wool pad as the needle was withdrawn.

Elliott left the apartment not entirely sure that things had progressed. Money, hardware and ammunition had been discussed briefly. Whether he had been accepted he would know only if they contacted him. No names had been exchanged, and the apartment was nothing more than a meeting place. Back in the car, he folded his arms against the steering wheel and rested his head against them. He had hoped for something to take back to Marlborough, something which would not only justify his existence but his place on agent line.

The slamming of a car door made Elliott raise his head a little and he caught sight of the blond behind the wheel of a dark coloured Granada. A few seconds and the car pulled away. Elliott made sure that his car lights were dead, swung the Vauxhall round and followed. He couldn't travel blind all night, so on a convenient right-angled corner he activated the lights and picked up a view of the Granada.

A few hours' driving later, he had been welcomed into Wales and was driving on coastal roads. He was intentionally losing and finding the Granada, not staying on its tail, and there was no indication that he was making the driver aware of his presence. It was quiet at the wheel. The cassette player was past its use-by date and no longer played, and the radio picked up spasmodic sections of airplay and static interference. They were headed towards the far westerly coast, having passed Carmarthen. The road they were travelling was a normal main road and it was getting more risky. If he stayed too close he was bound to be spotted; if he held back too far he could lose his quarry at a junction.

They were now in Pembrokeshire. The leading car led down into a small fishing village near Newport and parked outside a neat terraced cottage. Elliott drove on past and turned up a side street where he parked up. He waited a while, to give the blond an opportunity to go indoors – or maybe to do an about turn if he had realised that he was being tailed.

After ten minutes he slid out of the car and walked back down to the sea front. The car was still there and unoccupied. The night air was chilly. Elliott pulled up his collar and plunged his hands into his pockets as he strolled along the promenade. It was an end terraced cottage outside which the car was parked, an unremarkable building. He turned up the side street on which the gable stood, a six feet high brick wall enclosed a modest back yard. A cobbled back street ran behind the terrace, and on the other side there was a single storey workshop-type building with double doors. Elliott's eyes rested on the fascia above the doors – O'Brien's Boat Repairs, Boats Bought and Sold.

*

It was around seven hundred hours when Elliott fell, heavy eyed, into his bed, the alarm clock set for eleven hundred hours. He slept deeply, undisturbed by the building traffic outside. An insistent electronic bleeping sound woke him and he fumbled blindly for the reset button on the alarm. The noise persisted. He forced his eyes open.

'Aw, shit,' he muttered as his eyes rested on the figures.

It was twelve thirty-seven. The alarm had been set to go off at eleven hundred hours, but he had omitted to press the reset button after setting the time and it had not activated. He snatched up the communicator from which the noise was emanating.

'Elliott?'

'I'm in my office, Elliott,' Marlborough informed him evenly, 'So where the hell are you!'

Elliott cringed a little, then said, 'I overslept.'

'Get yourself over here now!'

The line went dead. Elliott closed the channel and replaced the communicator on the cabinet. He slid out reluctantly from between the warm sheets and pulled on his shorts, before heading for the bathroom. His head felt a little muggy and his eyes were still heavy. He blanched as he stepped into a barely tepid shower, as he was afraid that if the water was warm he would probably fall asleep. After five minutes he stepped out shivering and a little more awake. He towelled himself down and pulled his shorts back on. In the mirror he saw that the stubble shadowed his jaw darkly. He reached for the razor.

It was almost thirteen thirty as he stepped into Super Admin to be greeted with a withering look from Maryana Jenova. She made to speak.

'I don't need any aggro from you, sweetheart, so shut it before you even start,' he snapped, 'I take it I've got to go straight through?' He made for Marlborough's door.

Marlborough was alone in his office, and did not look up from his paperwork. Elliott stopped in front of the desk and waited; he felt as though he had been sent for an audience with the headmaster.

'You overslept?' Marlborough questioned as he looked up finally.

'I didn't get to bed until seven. I set the alarm for eleven but I forgot to switch it on.'

Marlborough looked suitably unimpressed. 'I expect my operatives to take their work seriously, Elliott, and clearly you have other priorities.'

'Yesterday, being here on time should have been priority and I made the wrong choice, but this isn't a job where the hours can be rigid, and I'm not intending to be disrespectful. I didn't get to bed until seven but it wasn't what you think.'

'You're an expert on what I think?'

'You think I've been out on the town, spent the night with some girl,' Elliott guessed aloud as he took his cigarettes from his pocket.

'And do you intend to proclaim your innocence?'

'No, and I wish I'd found time in between having blood taken out of me and trailing one of the intermediaries down to some village near Newport,' Elliott mused as he lit up.

'This Pushto character arranged a meeting?' Marlborough inquired, showing an interest.

'An apartment at the Barbican, three blokes.'

'Are they going to deal?'

'They're serious about checking me out – wanted a blood sample.'

'Did you oblige?'

'Yeah.'

'You were taking a risk.'

'I thought that was the name of the game. I didn't see I could do anything else without losing any chance I might have of getting closer. And I don't have a custom-made gun yet, so I didn't rate my chances against three.'

'Would you be able to identify them?'

Elliott nodded and explained, 'When I got out of the place I was a bit psyched up. I hadn't been able to tell whether there was already anything in the syringe, and my nerves were a bit raw.'

Marlborough nodded as that was understandable.

'While I was sat in the car one of the blokes left and I followed him. I don't think the arms are coming in on merchant shipping. The bloke went to a terraced house, there was a boat repair workshop behind it – O'Brien's – boats bought and sold. It could be they're buying small seagoing boats and using them to bring arms in – anywhere along the British coastline.'

It was not beyond the realms of possibility, Marlborough acknowledged.

'Why don't you get Kane to sell a boat?' Elliott suggested.

Marlborough looked at him.

'Maybe you don't think the job's worth the price of a boat?' Elliott questioned.

'I think it would be well worth the price of a boat,' Marlborough confirmed and smiled. 'Would it have hurt to have kept me informed?'

'I didn't take my communicator.'

'You went in without communications?'

'I figured that if it was spotted it wouldn't be good for my health. Didn't help Latislaw and Suleman much. You think I'd have got a chance to use it if anything had gone wrong?'

'Probably not,' Marlborough conceded to himself. 'I'll arrange to take possession of a boat. Perhaps you could go down to computer and look through some photographs.'

'Okay. Noon tomorrow?'

'I'll call you.'

Viewing photographs on a TV screen for five hours made Elliott's eyes even heavier. He found the older bloke and the blond; both had form but not for gun running. George Bentley, aged fifty-four, had previous convictions for fraud, and Stephen O'Brien had previous convictions for possession of small quantities of heroin and assault.

Down in the basement he exchanged keys with a slightly reluctant young mechanic, and retrieved the MG. It was a relief to get into a car whose floor didn't threaten to cave in at every bump in the road. He waited for a gap in the traffic and steered the car in a right turn out of the WIA car park. His eyes ached and his head was beginning to thump. No night out on the town tonight, he thought. His recent late nights combined with the erratic hours kept at the training centre had caught up with him.

Kane was at a loose end. It was up to Marlborough to get hold of a boat for him to sell. So far his part in the assignment hadn't been particularly strenuous. He figured that pretty soon the number one slot would be his – Elliott's ideas were good but his approach wasn't creating a good impression with Marlborough.

The communicator buzzed as Kane unlocked the door of his car. He slid inside and activated the button on the dashboard.

'Kane?'

'The Commander requires you to report in at nine hundred hours,' Veronica Martinez's voice came over the air, 'Confirm please.'

'Yeah, confirmed.' He sighed as he deactivated the control. It looked like he was in for another early night.

Elliott received a similar communication, and he pushed his communicator back into his pocket. His guess was that Marlborough had found a suitable boat to offer for sale and that he didn't intend to waste time over it. He pulled open the fridge and took out a can of lager, flipped back the ring pull and took a drink. The doorbell rang as he headed back through to the lounge. He sighed. Setting the can down on the table he moved out on to the landing and sprinted down the steps to the door.

'Hi,' Kane greeted him as he shepherded two young women inside, 'Don't have company already, do you?'

Elliott shook his head, and watched mutely as the threesome headed up the stairs. He hesitated, then went after them a little bemused. The girls were settling themselves down, one on the sofa and the other in an armchair.

'Okay, girls, what do you want to drink?' Kane scrutinised the contents of the drinks cabinet. 'Martini and lemonade?' He glanced at Elliott and asked, 'You've got some lemonade?'

Elliott nodded and made for the kitchen. He was tired, and had had it in mind to take a shower and go to bed. He certainly had not been planning on having company. Snatching up the bottle of lemonade from the draining board he walked back through to the lounge. Kane took the bottle from him and topped up the long glasses, then pushed them into Elliott's hands. Elliott looked at him with a questioning expression.

'Oh, sorry. Haven't made any introductions, have I?' Kane steered him towards the centre of the room. 'Chris, this is Amanda, Amanda – Chris.'

'Hi,' she smiled as she took her drink from him.

A pretty skinny girl with waist-length dark brown hair, Elliott noted.

'Chris, this is Rachel, Rachel – Chris.'

Elliott passed her her drink and picked up his can from the table. He noted that Rachel was a cherubic-looking blonde, only around five feet, and of a more voluptuous build than Amanda.

'Have you got any crisps or peanuts or anything?' Rachel asked, looking up at him.

Kane carried a large whisky across and lowered himself on to the arm of Amanda's chair.

'I'll put some music on while you go and find some crisps,' Rachel offered, rising to her feet.

Elliott looked at Kane, then headed for the kitchen.

Kane leaned against the door frame and watched as Elliott rummaged around in the cupboards. 'What do you think of Rachel?'

'If you'd told me I was having a party I'd have bought some peanuts. You think she'll settle for Ritz crackers?'

'I'm sorry, I thought you'd like some company.'

'I don't have any particular dislike for my own company.'

'Maybe you prefer Amanda. I'm easy.'

'You're on permanent bleedin' heat,' Elliott said sharply as he emptied the crackers on to a plate.

'Hey, make the best of it. You're on assignment, you don't count on tomorrow.'

Elliott picked up the plate, walked towards him and muttered, 'I like to sleep occasionally.'

Kane grinned, 'So I brought you a teddy bear.' He followed him back through to the lounge.

There was no denying that Rachel was a bonny kid and a chatterbox. Right now Elliott was getting her life story as she nibbled her way through the crackers. She was nineteen, twenty in a couple of weeks, worked in the typing pool of a large insurance office and thought that Elliott was 'really the cutest boy' she'd ever met. He wasn't too sure about that but she was pretty cute herself. The round-necked tee shirt which she wore exposed interesting mounds and a deep cleavage, her jeans fastening around a trim waistline.

'You look tired.'

He nodded in agreement. Kane and Amanda were engaged in a heavy petting session.

'Why don't we go to bed?' Rachel looked up at him and asked, 'Or would you rather sleep alone?'

'I'd sleep with Snow White and the seven dwarfs so long as they just let me sleep.'

'I was hoping for a little sex.'

'I'm tired, sweetheart, or I'd be happy to oblige. You think you could get by on half an hour?'

'Get by? The blokes I've met on half an hour – I'd be delirious.'

'You want to give it a try?'

Elliott emerged from the bathroom; Rachel was already between the sheets. Slipping off his shorts he joined her. His right hand ran across her firm, generously proportioned breasts. She rolled on to her side and his lips located her right nipple. He sucked gently on it, his right hand roving over her body. He stopped and looked at her.

'You've stopped talking.'

'I want you to kiss me.'

He smiled, curled his left hand beneath her neck and pulled her towards him. His kiss was long, sweetened by his massaging of her body. She barely noticed as he pushed her down on to her back, his lips not parting from hers, and slid across her. The fluids were running. He penetrated easily and felt her gyrating beneath him. He was swelling inside her; her body arched towards him and she gasped as he came further. She could feel him thrusting into her, controlled, holding back. Her hands massaged his chest, and tremors were beginning to run through her body. He was tired, knew that he did not have the concentration to maintain control for much longer, and hoped that she was ready. The climax overtook him. He thrust violently into her and she screamed, clutching at him as her body reacted with rapid powerful contractions and brought on his ejaculation with such force that a blinding pain shot through his head. Exhausted, he sprawled across her. For a time there was no sound other than their breathing.

'That was so good,' she whispered.

Not that good, he thought. He had come too quickly. He liked to take the time to make the girl feel good. Still, if she was satisfied he supposed that that was all right.

'You're tired,' she sympathised, folding her arms around him, 'You were wonderful.'

He nuzzled up to her, his head resting against her soft breasts. His eyes were closing; he tried to keep them open but it was impossible.

'I'm sorry, sweetheart.' He yawned, gave up on the battle and fell asleep.

Elliott awoke at seven thirty to a dishevelled but empty bed. He lay for a few moments staring up at the ceiling. Hauling himself from between the sheets he pulled on his shorts, and looked round as the door opened.

'Thought I'd better check you were up,' Kane said, poking his head round, 'Three times late would be pushing your luck a bit.'

'You sure that wasn't what you had in mind?'

'Bringing the girls round last night?' Kane stepped into the room. 'I wasn't out to nobble you, just thought it would help you wind down. Rachel liked you.'

Elliott rose to his feet.

'There was nothing intended but a good time.'

'So, did you apologise to her for my falling asleep on her?'

'Didn't need to, she thought you were brilliant. Amanda's interested in you; I think I should keep my girls well away from you.'

'Do that,' Elliott agreed as he headed for the bathroom.

Kane shrugged. 'I'll make coffee,' he called after him.

Elliott stepped into the shower. Kane was okay but there was resentment and he couldn't blame him for it – some pipsqueak still wet behind the ears just walking in and taking the top job. Nobody seemed to care about or consider the mortality rate, it was like Everest – there. Elliott knew that despite his denials, Kane had intended him to be late, and had been checking that he was asleep and not awake. In Kane's place he would probably have done the same thing.

He stepped out of the shower and folded a towel around his waist, grabbed another towel and rubbed at his hair as he walked across to the washbasin. The overnight stubble was dark and coarse. It would grow back again by evening, he reflected as he reached for the razor, whoever his dad was he must have had hair like an ape. He grinned at the idea.

*

Kane picked up the telephone and dialled nine for an outside line. The number of O'Brien's was written on a note pad. Kane checked the outside line and dialled. It rang five times before it was answered. Kane nodded to

Marlborough. Elliott took a draw on his cigarette as Marlborough switched on the amplifier.

'O'Brien's, can I help you?'

'Yes, I'd like to speak to somebody about a boat I've got for sale,' Kane responded to the female voice.

'Would you hold please?' The line went dead.

'O'Brien's,' said a male voice.

'Yes, hi,' Kane acknowledged, 'My name's Brett Kane, I've got a boat moored in Fishguard I'd like to sell. Understand you buy?'

'That's right.'

'My company's moving me out to Canada, so I need to sell. She's called *Blue Velvet*, forty feet, seagoing and in good condition. Would you be interested?'

'There's no reason why we shouldn't be. Can we meet?'

'Well, I'm in London now,' Kane said, checking his watch, 'I could make it across to Fishguard for four.'

'There's a wine bar, the Lobster Pot.'

'I know it,' Kane confirmed as he looked down at the town plan which was swivelled towards him by Marlborough.

'We could meet up there, say four fifteen?'

'That's fine. I'll meet you there then.'

'Just ask for me, Stephen O'Brien.'

'Stephen O'Brien, no problem. I'll see you there.' He replaced the handset and looked at Marlborough. 'He sounded interested.'

'Then you'd better go and meet him.' Marlborough switched off the amplifier. 'Set your communicator on open line and keep it well out of sight.'

Kane nodded.

'All right, go.'

'On my way,' Kane said as he headed for the door.

Marlborough looked at Elliott and instructed, 'If things start to move you'll need to be awake. No number one travels as a passenger. Go home and get some sleep – it could be a long time before you get another chance. You need to get the training centre out of your system.'

A human side! Elliott had not been sure that Marlborough had one.

'Go to bed, Elliott, anorexic is one thing, an anorexic panda I can do without.'

Elliott rose to his feet.

'Alone, Elliott.'

Elliott looked at him.

'No bedmates, no girl, just go to bed and sleep. If no call comes through from your intermediaries I'll have you called in when I think you've slept long enough.'

*

The Lobster Pot was a wine bar and restaurant on the coast road in Fishguard. It was three minutes past sixteen hundred hours as Kane turned on to the car park and parked up. He slid out of the car, locked it, and walked across to the entrance. It was quiet. He walked over to the bar and, from the photographs which Elliott had selected, he mentally picked O'Brien out of the few patrons.

'Whisky and soda please.' He placed his order and watched as the shapely barmaid prepared it. 'Thanks,' he acknowledged, offering a five pound note in payment.

'Don't you have anything less?'

'Sorry. Get yourself one.'

She smiled and headed for the till. His eyes followed her, and he thought that maybe he should call back nearer to closing time. In a few moments she returned with his change and handed it to him.

'I'm looking for Stephen O'Brien. Do you know him?'
'Over there,' she indicated, pointing out the man he had picked out.

'Thanks.' He picked up his drink and walked towards O'Brien's table. 'Stephen O'Brien?' he asked.

O'Brien rose to his feet, 'Mr Kane?'

Kane nodded and offered his hand.

'Pleased to meet you.'

O'Brien shook hands, 'Take a seat.' He retook his own.

'*Blue Velvet*, I glanced over her on the way in, she looks good.'

'You're interested?'

'I'll need to take a proper look at her, but if she comes up to expectations then it's down to negotiation.'

'Good,' Kane approved, taking a drink, 'I leave the country in a couple of weeks. I've been trying to put off selling *Blue Velvet*. I hate to part with her but it's too expensive to take her with me.'

O'Brien nodded and drained his glass. 'Ready when you are.'

The two men walked along the quayside parallel with the moored boats. *Blue Velvet* was the largest. Kane led on board. He had never previously set eyes on it.

'Why don't you just take a look around and I'll wait on deck? I think I'd just like a little bit of time.'

'It's okay, I understand,' O'Brien empathised, and moved away.

Kane leaned against the rail of the deck and lit a cigarette. He stared out over the other boats as he drew on it.

It was around twenty minutes before O'Brien returned. 'You don't have anything left on board?'

'No, I had her cleared out last weekend – no point in postponing the inevitable any longer. I had her cleared while she was down in Hastings. The moorage is cheaper here.' Kane hesitated, then inquired, 'What do you think?'

'What are you looking for?'

'I've had her valued at a hundred and seventy-five thousand.'

'That's a bit steep. How far are you prepared to come down?'

Kane considered the question, then answered, 'One hundred and thirty-five thousand.'

'It's still a bit steep.' O'Brien looked thoughtful and offered, 'She's a nice boat.' He looked at Kane and asked carefully, 'Come down to a hundred and twenty-five thousand?'

There was a silence.

'I think I could hold out for the hundred and thirty-five thousand if I took her round to Plymouth,' Kane mused.

'She'd need fuel, crew,' O'Brien pointed out, 'And maybe you wouldn't sell so fast – the climate isn't right.'

'Split the difference?'

'One hundred and twenty-seven and a half and that's the highest I can go. I'll be making nothing out of it at that.'

A short silence followed.

'Okay, it's a deal,' agreed Kane, offering his hand.

O'Brien took it. 'Why don't we finalise the details over another drink?' he asked.

It was a reasonable deal. Whilst it was true that the boat was valued at one hundred and seventy-five thousand Marlborough had purchased it from a liquidators at ninety-eight thousand, and Kane's instructions had been to let it go for as low as a hundred thousand. He had not wanted to seem too anxious to make a sale, did not want to rouse any suspicions. Computer and Recovery Personnel had been on board overnight fitting a sophisticated tracking system into its navigational instruments which even a highly specialised technician would be hard pressed to detect.

Kane checked himself into a class hotel for the night. It was, after all, expense account and no one would expect a top flight executive to take bed and breakfast guest-house lodgings, particularly one who had just sold an expensive toy for a barrowload of cash. He had made arrangements to meet up with O'Brien the following lunch time in the hotel restaurant when he would hand over the papers to *Blue Velvet* in exchange for a banker's draft. The idea of owning a seagoing yacht quite appealed to him. Perhaps if he lived long enough to retire from agent line this idea might materialise.

It was still only early evening, and Kane had booked dinner for twenty one hundred hours. He strolled along the quayside and up on to *Blue Velvet*, leaned against the rails and watched the smaller boats bobbing on the water. *Blue Velvet* was beautiful, rising pale out of the water, and the blue deepening almost imperceptibly into a rich navy. The rails around the deck gleamed and the tinted glass of the cabin windows reflected the rising moon on to the water. Right now her papers were in his pocket, and stated in black and white that she was his. It was a good feeling, he grinned and thought to himself. Tomorrow a banker's draft for a hundred and twenty-seven and a half thousand, made out in his name, would probably not be quite as good. Unfortunately, neither option was to be long-lived.

He straightened up and slid his hands into his pockets. It was getting a little cold and there was a chill breeze blowing in from the sea. Slowly he walked down to the quayside and back towards the hotel. Although it was nearing the end of the low season the area was still quiet, and he wondered if there was somewhere in town with some action.

⋆

Elliott got to bed at around noon and slept through nineteen hours, undisturbed. It had been the mental and not the physical stress of the training centre which had drained him. The prospect of court martial and the possible consequences had affected him deeply, and maintaining the façade had not been easy. He lay in the bed staring up at the ceiling. His head was clear and he felt fresher than he had felt for weeks. There was a relief in the lack of responsibility; at the training centre he had not been able to take a detached view but on agent line he had only himself to worry about – and Kane, to a limited extent. It felt good; there was no hassle in making his own decisions.

Maryana Jenova looked across as the outer door to her office slid open. Surprise registered briefly as Elliott stepped through – it was only a little after eight o'clock.

'Okay if I go through?'

She nodded mutely, and watched as he made for Marlborough's office.

Marlborough barely glanced up, motioned vaguely towards the chairs at the opposite side of the desk and continued with his paperwork. Elliott took a seat and leaned back, let his eyes rove around the room. There wasn't too much to look at, and his eyes lingered on the coffee pot on the desk. He took his cigarettes from his pocket and lit one. He noted there were three cups and saucers on the tray. Reaching out he upturned two cups and filled them from the jug.

'You take sugar and milk?'

Marlborough shook his head. Elliott pushed a filled cup towards him, stirred a spoonful of sugar into his own and left it black.

After ten minutes Marlborough pushed his paperwork aside. Elliott drained his cup and reached again for the jug.

'How do you feel?'

'Better,' Elliott said, refilling his cup, 'I needed to wind down from training centre.'

Marlborough nodded and reached for his coffee. 'That was quite an experience for you.'

Elliott nodded.

'You're a strange creature.'

There was a silence.

'It isn't something you want to discuss?'

'Training centre? No.'

Marlborough smiled thinly.

'Does anything in connection with the training centre matter now?' Elliott asked.

'Does it matter to you?'

'I don't think so. I'm not there, I'm here, it's history.' Elliott hesitated, then continued, 'Or were you thinking of sending me back?'

'I think it's too late now.'

'I don't want to go back.'

Marlborough studied him for a few moments. 'I wouldn't send you back now, Elliott, you know that. You're number one, that can't change. Number one stays number one until he's dead, disabled or deprocessed. At this level there's no demotion.'

'A mile high with an enemy fighter on my tail there's no going back. You think he cares I got my wings yesterday?'

'So this isn't the first time you've been there,' Marlborough acknowledged. 'Kane appears to have made a sale.'

Kane looked good in a suit, and would pass as a high-flying executive. And he had looks. Who was going to believe that he was willing to risk his face?

'The money and papers are due to change hands at lunch time.'

'No phone call?'

'No – but I give you credit for progress.'

'Thanks.'

'Grey matter, Elliott, initiative. This is not an approval.'

But it was the nearest thing, Elliott thought, although it could not be construed as such.

'I wanted to get somewhere,' Elliott shrugged. 'Nothing I do's going to impress you.'

'I'm not here to be impressed.'

'So what are you here for?' Elliott asked. 'What do you want from me?'

'One hundred and fifty per cent.'

'I want to be here and I'll give you everything I've got. I just want you to be on my side,' Elliott suggested.

Marlborough nodded. It was a reasonable deal. 'Have you come in for any particular reason?'

'I've slept, and I figured there might be more going on here than on morning television,' he offered, taking a drink.

'I don't think so.'

'Suppose I'll get myself some breakfast then.'

*

Kane rolled over on to his side, lifted his communicator from the bedside cabinet, and flipped the channel open.

'Kane?' he responded as the buzzing ceased.

'How's it going?' Elliott asked.

Kane rolled on to his back, looked at the girl beside him, and smiled. 'Oh, it's going pretty good,' he confirmed.

'Thought I'd just give you your early morning call.'

'Thanks but I was already awake.'

Kane switched off the communicator and replaced it on the cabinet. He rolled on to his side and his lips met the girl's.

'What did you say your name was?'

'Jennifer.'

'I love you, Jennifer. Did I tell you that last night?' He slid across her. 'Did I tell you I'm a liar?'

Any response was silenced by his lips on hers.

'Do you want me?'

Her arms folded tightly around him.

*

Elliott stabbed at a mushroom and ate it. Kane had been ready for him and wasn't going to let him put a damper on his activities, he thought, and smiled. So Kane had the upper hand, was dictating the game of one-upmanship. And why not? He was four years on agent line and knew the ropes.

'Is this seat taken?'

He looked up to see Maryana Jenova. He shook his head, and she took a seat. Her breakfast was a half grapefruit and lemon tea.

'I don't have to sit here,' she snapped after a few moments' silence.

'I didn't ask you to,' he pointed out as he glanced around, and then looked at her, 'The refectory's almost empty.' His attention returned to his breakfast.

'I'm sorry.'

With his fork almost at his mouth he stopped, and his eyes rose quizzically.

'You're very young.'

'Sometimes I don't feel to be.' The fork continued to his mouth.

'You need an explanation.'

'Of what?'

'My attitude.'

A brief silence ensued.

'I guess you don't like me,' he broke the silence.

'I don't know you,' she responded. 'Agent line come and go, no one lasts long. If I know you, it hurts when you don't come back. I've felt that hurt enough times; it's easier not to get close, involved.' She looked away from him and dug into the grapefruit. 'Keep your distance please, don't make me start to like you,' she added.

'I'd like somebody to miss me when I'm gone,' Elliott said and smiled thinly. 'I don't see Marlborough missing me. Kane would miss me like a headache.' He scooped up a piece of egg. 'I'm nothing, sweetheart, I already know that.'

'The Commander cares. No one who works for the WIA is nothing,' she hesitated, then asked. 'Are you very sad?'

'Sorry?'

'You've left behind your friends, your family, and you're under a lot of pressure.'

'I don't think sad's the word, sweetheart, lonely maybe. You don't think you could maybe like me a little – keep me company?'

'Please don't call me sweetheart.'

'Miss Jenova's a bit of a mouthful.'

There was a pause.

'I suppose you could call me Maryana.'

A hell of a concession, he thought, then said, 'And you can call me anything you like.'

She smiled.

*

Kane knotted his tie, pushed it up to his collar button, and straightened it in the mirror. He turned, picked up his jacket and walked towards the bed.

'I'll have some lunch sent up,' he suggested as he stooped and kissed Jennifer's forehead. 'Just got some business to settle. I'll be back,' he smiled and added, 'to celebrate.'

O'Brien was already waiting in the restaurant. Early, Kane noted as he glanced at his watch and made for the table.

'Been waiting long?'

O'Brien looked up and shook his head. Kane took a seat.

'I've got the papers; do you have the draft?' Kane reached into his inside pocket. 'We agreed on one hundred and twenty-seven thousand five hundred.' O'Brien offered the draft. Kane took it and checked the details, then pushed the papers across the table.

'That's business out of the way,' confirmed Kane, reaching for the menu, 'Let's eat.'

*

Marlborough looked at Elliott as the line went dead. There had been an open line over lunch but the conversation had been general. O'Brien had steered clear of talking business beyond the purchase of the boat, and although Kane had tried to draw him a couple of times he had had the sense not to push.

'What if the deal turns out to be innocent?'

'We'll have made almost a thirty thousand pound profit.' Marlborough reached for the coffee pot and refilled his cup, upturned another cup and filled it. He pushed it towards Elliott. 'Observation remain with Mackintosh and Espachio; sooner or later...'

The buzz of Elliott's communicator interrupted him, and for a moment Elliott made no move.

'I don't appear to be calling you,' Marlborough pointed out.

Elliott took his communicator from his pocket and activated it. 'Yeah?'

'Mr Elliott?'

'Yeah?'

'Perhaps you'd like to come and look at some samples?'

'Some samples?'

'And discuss quantities. You said you were talking serious money. We term serious money as being in excess of fifty thousand. If you don't have that sort of minimum we don't need your business.'

'I'm not playing games. Serious hardware, serious money.'

'We need a deposit, as a token of good faith.'

'What sort of a deposit?'

'Five thousand, cash.'

'So that would make me pretty faithful. What would it make you apart from an easy buck?'

'No guarantees, Mr Elliott. If you want the hardware you have to trust us. In Cambodia you run the risks; here the risk is all ours. Do you want to deal?'

'Yeah, I want to deal. I guess I have to accept your terms.'

'We'll meet this evening. At ten o'clock be waiting outside Tiffany's, you'll be picked up. Have the money with you.'

The line went dead. Elliott switched off the communicator and pushed it back into his pocket.

'Petty cash?' he asked, and looked at Marlborough.

'Are you going?'

'You think I shouldn't?'

'Alone, without a communicator?'

'I'd feel safer with a custom-made gun.'

Marlborough nodded and instructed, 'Ballistics will meet you in Computer. They don't have much time, but do you have specific ideas?'

'I want nine chambers, double speed, and it needs to feel good.'

'Then make it,' Marlborough suggested, and looked at him. 'You need to go in with something besides the five thousand.'

*

At almost twenty hundred hours Elliott watched as the grips were fitted to the butt of the gun.

'Try it for size,' offered the ballistics technician handing it over.

Elliott took it. It rested comfortably in his hand and was neither heavy nor light. It had nine chambers but it was no wider than a normal six chamber – the divisions were narrow.

'Feel?'

'Okay.'

'Weight?'

'Okay.'

'Try it,' the technician instructed, and nodded towards a door.

It worked fine. Its trigger was on a hairspring, and the next shot was out almost before the trigger had dropped back. Nine bullets pumped out one after the other, every one hitting the centre of the moving target.

'Nice shooting,' approved the technician, standing in the doorway.

'Nice gun,' Elliott confirmed, walking towards him.

'Marlborough authorised five boxes of ammunition, that's ten rounds. Future authority for supply on demand.'

Elliott followed him back through to the workshop, and examined the gun as he walked.

'It's a prototype; in a couple of days it'll be perfect.'

'What?'

'That's the prototype. You can take it. In a couple of days we'll take it back and replace it with the actual.'

'I'm happy with this.'

The technician shook his head, 'The replacement will have had the rough edges taken off.'

'I like rough edges – this is fine.'

'It'll be made up anyway.' The technician lifted five boxes from the shelf and set them down on the bench. 'That's your ammunition.'

'Thanks.' Elliott opened one of the boxes and reloaded the gun. 'If I'm still happy with the prototype in a couple of days?'

'We keep the top model until you want it. The other agents keep the prototypes in stock as a spare.'

Elliott tipped the remaining ammunition in the box into his hand and pushed it into his jacket pocket. 'I'll see you when I run short,' he said, as he picked up the remaining four boxes and headed towards the door.

Marlborough looked up as Elliott returned to his office. He said, 'I would have preferred you to go in wired.'

'Think that's a risk I don't have to take, feel safer wired to dynamite than for sound.'

Pulling open his desk drawer Marlborough drew out a wad of notes and offered it across. 'Money comes cheaper. If it turns out that they're looking for easy money let them take it and get out.'

'You want to give me that in writing?'

'Just go out there and do it – but remember that money isn't everything. Five thousand is nothing – you take no risks over that.'

'Fifty thousand and you'll try and bite your tongue?'

'A couple of weeks in training costs more than that. Right now I suppose you're running in credit.' Marlborough smiled slightly and said, 'I derive no pleasure from dead agents.'

'How about pretenders?'

'Pretenders? You told me you were agent potential.'

'And if I lied?'

'How much do you like being dead?'

'It doesn't rank.'

'No, I don't suppose it does.' Marlborough considered him for a few moments. 'What do you believe in, Elliott?'

There was a silence.

'I didn't know I was being interviewed for Mr Universe.'

Marlborough smiled and glanced at his watch. 'It's almost time. Be careful.'

★

At twenty-one fifty the night had drawn in and the air was chilly. Elliott leaned against the wall at the side of the entrance door into Tiffany's and slid his hands into the pockets of his jacket. His gun nestled reassuringly in his belt, five thousand pounds in twenty pound notes secure in his inside pocket. The traffic was still heavy and casting a thin spray up on their wheels from an earlier rainfall.

'You're early,' O'Brien commented as he walked towards Elliott from the side street.

Elliott straightened up.

'You've brought the money?'

'Yeah.'

'This way.'

Elliott followed him down the street to a transit van with blacked-out windows and a partition between its rear and the driver's cab. O'Brien pulled open one of the doors and watched as Elliott climbed inside. A glance around and he followed, and secured the door behind himself. There was a bench seat.

'Check you over before we move off,' O'Brien stated.

Elliott hesitated, then leaned with outstretched arms against the wall of the transit. O'Brien checked him over, took the wad of notes from his inside pocket, fanned through it, and returned it. The gun didn't seem to worry him; he left it in Elliott's belt, but checked Elliott's pockets.

'Okay.'

Elliott turned and lowered himself on to the bench. O'Brien rapped on the partition and the van pulled away. The bench seat wasn't too comfortable. It was made of unupholstered wooden slats and the driver didn't go easy on the corners. Elliott made no attempt to make conversation and O'Brien showed no inclination to talk.

It wasn't too long a journey, around half an hour, but long enough on the hard uncomfortable bench, in a limited space with virtually no light. The van came to a sudden halt throwing O'Brien against the partition. He hammered on it and swore colourfully. A few seconds later and the rear door opened. A boiler-suited youth grinned up at them. Elliott emerged into brightly lit surroundings. They were in a warehouse with the doors sealed. He blinked a little at the light, and his eyes rested on Bentley as they refocused. There was high metal shelving all round, fully loaded. A bulk distributing warehouse of hangar-like proportions, with rails of clothing, soft toys and electrical goods. Bentley looked towards O'Brien who nodded.

'So you want to see some samples?' he asked, looking at Elliott.

'That's what I came for.'

Bentley moved away up the warehouse. Elliott followed with O'Brien trailing along behind him. There were workers, and fork-lift trucks carrying boxes and cartons down to loading bays. They gave barely a second glance towards the small party. Bentley unlocked a door at the top end of the warehouse and stepped inside. He switched on the light as he held the door open. Elliott followed, and O'Brien dropped the catch.

It was an office. There was a window through to the warehouse but a venetian blind covered it. There was a large desk with nine weapons – automatic rifles and sub-machine guns laid out on it.

'That's your choice in high-powered arms.'

Elliott walked towards the desk. His eyes roved over the hardware. 'Okay to touch?' he asked.

'You're the buyer.'

He picked up a high velocity rifle, checked that the barrel was empty, raised it up to his shoulder and adjusted the telescopic sight. His finger was on the trigger, it tightened, caught, sprang back and was ready. Bentley watched as Elliott went through the weapons. The boy knew what he was looking for; they rested easily in his hands; he knew how to handle them; he matched up to their inquiries.

'This one's nice,' said Bentley, reaching towards a rifle, 'Chinese.'

'I'm not looking for nice. I don't want to look at it and I sure as hell wasn't thinking of holding a conversation with it.' Elliott glanced at it. 'Kalashnikov?'

He swung round, a repeater in his hands. Bentley nodded and eased it aside with the back of his hand.

'How much?'

'Three thousand, they aren't easy to come by.'

'Maybe I should fly out to Russia and get my own.'

'You wouldn't find much availability.'

Elliott replaced it on the desk and picked up a machine-gun.

'Hewson Dwight.'

'I'm not illiterate, I can read the label.' It rested easily in Elliott's arms. He tried it: easy trigger action and it rattled through imaginary ammunition rounds. 'What's the ammo give away?'

'Two boxes on each.'

'How many a box?'

'Two rounds.' He hesitated, then asked, 'To buy?'

Elliott nodded.

'As many boxes as you need. Kalashnikov, three hundred, Hewson Dwight, five hundred.'

'Eighteen Kalashnikovs, twenty-four Hewson Dwights; ammo – twenty boxes of each.'

'No problem.'

'When?'

'Next week.' Bentley stabbed at a calculator. 'One hundred and forty-two thousand.'

'Lose the two thousand.'

'Cash payment?'

'Five thousand deposit, all cash.'

'I lost the two thousand.' Bentley smiled and said, 'I want the deposit.'

Elliott reached into his inside pocket and withdrew the wad.

Bentley snatched it and stated, 'We'll be in touch.'

'I don't get to take a sample?'

Apparently not, Elliott observed. O'Brien headed back to the door and pulled it open. Bentley tucked the wad of notes into his briefcase.

'We'll call you. Don't change your telephone number.'

*

Marlborough had not retired to his quarters but remained in his office. Kane had not yet returned, had been distracted, Marlborough didn't doubt. He suspected that Elliott would return, if only to retrieve his communicator. In the meantime, there was a good deal of paperwork to keep him occupied.

Chapter Eight

Espachio's villa in Marbella was painted a pristine pale pink, stood in its own high-walled grounds. Observation shifts kept a discreet watch but Espachio had not ventured out for several days. His curvaceous dark-haired live-in girlfriend made brief excursions to the food store but for Observation those excursions were rare highlights, rare occasions when something moved.

The Mackintosh Observation camp was faring no better. Mackintosh had had no meetings, and only rarely left his hotel room. The hotel staff had instructions that he had recently been seriously ill and had come to Warsaw to relax and recuperate. Nothing had been discovered to substantiate the story, and Warsaw seemed a strange place to choose.

Marlborough checked the computer loggings, progress zero. Unless something came out of Elliott's attempts to create his own action the wait was likely to be long. It was incredible that quantities of arms – any quantity never mind large quantities – were finding their way into the country undetected. Customs and Excise and the Security Services had been striving for long enough to seal the channels but without success. The assistance of the WIA had been sought reluctantly, and Marlborough had no desire to be accused of failure. Something needed to come up soon, and if it didn't he couldn't afford to keep the number one team tied up with it.

'Mister Elliott for you, sir,' Veronica Martinez informed him over the communicator.

Marlborough glanced up at the clock – one seventeen. 'Send him through.' He leaned back in his chair and looked towards the door expectantly. Elliott stepped through to the office.

'You been to bed and got up again or have you been here since I left?'

'I've been here since you left.'

'Always wondered what it was like to be waited up for.'

'Coffee?'

'Yeah, thanks.'

Elliott pulled back a chair and dropped into it. Marlborough reached for the coffee pot, filled two cups, and reached for the milk.

'Leave it black and hot,' said Elliott as he reached for the cup, and folded his hands around it. 'Kane not back yet?'

'Not that I'm aware of.'

Elliott took a sip of his drink. 'I got separated from the five grand. Placed an order for eighteen Kalashnikov automatic rifles and twenty-four Hewson Dwight sub-machine guns. Hundred and forty thousand, a hundred and thirty-five still to pay, cash.'

'Where were you taken?'

'Hard to say, there were no windows. Some warehouse, maybe a mail order distribution not too far out of town. Seemed like we did a lot of cornering, so I figured maybe we were doing some circles.'

'When do you take delivery?'

Elliott shrugged, 'They'll call me.'

'Or not as the case may be.' Marlborough smiled thinly and ordered, 'Go and get some sleep. Take time off until I send for you – or the telephone rings.'

Elliott found himself driving towards Brixton rather than Bayswater. It was getting late but he was not feeling tired; rather, the adrenaline was pumping. He was growing impatient, and taking risks had always been a part of his life. The streets of Brixton were reasonably quiet even though youths gathered in groups on street corners. Elliott parked up on a side street and secured the car. There were lights on in the Dyers – he had not expected it to abide by the licensing laws. The door was unlocked, so he stepped inside and glanced around. Pushto was holding court at his usual table, laughing and joking with friends, but no dealing. The bar was open. Elliott bought himself a pint of bitter and took a drink, moved towards Pushto's table but not up to it.

It was a few minutes before Pushto noticed him. 'I got business,' he informed his audience as he rose to his feet and moved away from the table towards Elliott. 'You not finished around here?'

'Yeah, so far as my doing business is concerned.'

Pushto looked at him quizzically.

'Who looks out for you?'

'I look out for me,' Pushto stated.

'Not sure that's enough.'

Pushto grinned, 'Hey, man, get a life.'

'I've got a life, that isn't a problem. Holding on to it, that's what I've got in mind.'

'You want to deal?'

'That isn't life; you don't take what you push, you've got more sense than that,' Elliott observed as he took a drink, 'I want to talk death, reality.'

'You've been to 'Nam, not me; sounds heavy.'

'Korea – one white, one Asian. I figure they died round here.'

Pushto smiled.

'You know what's going down. Am I on a deal or am I marked down?'

Pushto shrugged, 'Not my interest.'

'You've got a guarantee you aren't on the list?'

Pushto lit a reefer and sucked on it.

'I reckon you saw what happened,' Elliott stated, 'I reckon maybe you led them to it.'

'I deal – shooters aren't my scene.'

'How long do you think they'll let you live – knowing what you know?'

Pushto's grin faded. 'What you sayin'?'

'Come on, Pushto, we're both playing a dangerous game here. I don't want to be found down some dark alleyway with my skull caved in and rats using me for breakfast. It's my guess that if I show up with a hundred and thirty-five thousand to complete the deal that's what's going to be waiting for me.'

There was a silence. Pushto didn't deny it.

'So what about you? What do you reckon you're worth to them?'

There was no response.

'I'll tell you what you're worth – fuck all,' Elliott snapped, 'and you know it.'

'I don't need to listen to this.'

'So tell me I'm wrong – tell me these guys are really going to come up with the goods and I'm going to walk away.'

A lengthy silence followed.

'You want to ride?' Elliott broke the silence.

Pushto nodded.

'I made a mistake, they weren't legit,' he said, finally.

Elliott looked at him.

'You checked out, they didn't. They're nothing to worry about. I just get the detail, arrange a meeting. It's not my involvement.' Pushto pulled hard on the reefer, and then exhaled. 'I just supply names. These two blokes were at the bar, and they were making like, noises about buying guns. I passed them on and they didn't check out – that's not my problem.' He glanced across. 'You've gone upmarket.' His eyes ran over the MG and he observed, 'Nice car.'

'Yeah.' Elliott unlocked it and slid behind the wheel.

'Look – you're okay.'

Elliott glanced across.

'They've checked you out, you're legit. Those guys you're talking about, they didn't even make it to first base.'

There was a silence. Pushto reached for a packet of cigarettes on the dashboard and pushed in the cigarette lighter. His hands trembled a little as he shook a cigarette out, placed it between his lips and lit it.

'How did you get yourself mixed up with them? How do you know O'Brien?'

Pushto looked at Elliott sharply.

'He's got previous for possession. Maybe you were his supplier?' Elliott quizzed.

Pushto nodded, 'This isn't my scene, man.' He hesitated. 'He's got some heavy friends, real nutheads. I wasn't asked if I wanted to get mixed up in this.' He pulled hard on the cigarette.

'Are these guys really producing the goods?'

'On pre-order, not to casual buyers.'

'What am I?'

'I dunno. What did they tell you?'

'Next week.'

'So you're pre-order. They've got to get hold of the goods.'

'And do they?'

'How the hell should l know? Maybe they just take the money and run.'

'Yeah, that's what worries me.' Elliott remained silent for a few moments. 'What happens to you when they find out almost too late I'm not legit?'

'You what?'

'If they go fishing and they find my cover isn't that deep.'

'Aw, Jeesus.'

'They're going to think you set them up. Or maybe I'm winding you up,' he grinned and continued, 'I don't know whether I've got me a deal or a one-way ticket into the afterlife. I just know I'm fond of my skin, I need it to keep the rest of me in place and I don't give a bugger about you any more than you give a bugger about me. I just want to be around tomorrow.'

'You and me both,' Pushto looked at him.

'So what about the other two blokes?'

A pause followed.

'Same routine. I just fixed an introduction, and took them across to the Barbican. That's me out of it.'

Elliott glanced across. Maybe he believed him, maybe not. He believed that he probably didn't know much, and from that point of view was not worth wasting his time over.

'So where do you want dropping off?'

'You okay for Peckham? Hordle Promenade?'

Elliott nodded.

'You sure know how to spook a bloke,' Pushto stubbed the cigarette out as the car sped through Peckham. 'You can drop me any place along here,' he said.

*

Kane's car was parked up outside the Bayswater Mews. Elliott parked up in his reserved parking bay and slid from behind the wheel. He stooped to lock the door, his eyes on the dark silhouette inside Kane's car. He straightened up and walked across. The driver's seat was reclined and Kane appeared to be asleep. Elliott rapped on the window. For a few seconds Kane seemed to be disoriented. Finally he straightened up, pushed open the door and slid out.

'Where the hell have you been?'

'Where have I been?' Elliott echoed, 'You've been screwing around Newport for the past three days and you want to know where I've been?'

'According to Marlborough you left WHQ hours ago.'

'And it's compulsory I come straight home, uh?'

'You making coffee?'

Elliott hesitated, nodded then offered, 'Yeah, come on up.'

Kane followed him across the pavement, waited whilst he unlocked the door and then followed him up to the apartment.

'Sugar and milk?' Elliott asked as he headed through to the kitchen.

'Both, thanks. And a bed for the night.'

Elliott reappeared at the kitchen door and looked at Kane quizzically.

'It's best I don't go home tonight.'

'How come?'

'I'd made arrangements for the past couple of days. Looks like they didn't like being stood up.'

Elliott grinned, 'What happened to love 'em and leave 'em and don't give a forwarding address?'

'There's a couple of exceptions to the rule.'

'A couple?' Elliott's grin broadened.

'Seven or eight.'

'And the rest.' Elliott turned back into the kitchen. 'What was she like?' he shouted.

'Who?'

'Miss Newport?'

'Yeah.'

'That good, uh?' There was amusement in Elliott's tone, 'I usually take the front bedroom.'

'I don't mind a view of the Post Office Tower.'

'Reminds you of great things, does it?'

Kane grinned broadly, 'Like it was a part of me.'

'I bet she screamed.'

'You'd be on a pretty safe bet.'

Elliott carried coffee through and passed a mug to Kane, 'And modest with it.' He lowered himself on to the sofa, took a drink, and said, 'I'll overlook the park, you can overlook VD.'

'I don't mess around with sluts,' Kane retorted as he took a drink, 'I don't catch anything.'

'You believe that, Kane, you want cutting off.'

Kane looked at him.

'I'm taking my coffee to bed, it's late,' Elliott yawned as he rose to his feet, 'Isn't any way you can tell until you've got it.' He pulled open the door and stepped out of the room, and hesitated. 'You should be knackered enough to sleep good. Me, I'm just tired,' he said, glancing back. 'You weren't thinking of bringing your harem round tonight?'

'If you want...'

'No, I don't want. Just making sure.'

*

Elliott slept well and did not waken until late, almost noon. Pushto came immediately into his mind, and he supposed that Pushto had not slept too well. He slid out of bed, pulled on his shorts and padded through to the bathroom. His hand slid over his jaw, the overnight stubble felt coarse and dark. He shaved, switched on the shower and stepped into the flow of tepid water. He preferred it that way as it made him feel good, comfortably warm and it put his brain to sleep again. There was a rap on the bathroom door. He slowed the flow of the water.

'Yeah?'

'You in there?' Kane shouted.

'Yeah.'

The door opened and Kane stepped inside carrying a steaming mug of coffee. He leaned against the wall beside the shower unit and took a drink.

'Marlborough called. *Blue Velvet*'s on the move, headed south.'

'How long has she been on the move?' Elliott asked.

'A couple of hours, she's running out from the Cornish coast in deep waters. Could be she's just changing moorings, heading for the Cinque ports maybe.'

The water slowed to a stop. Kane pulled a towel from the radiator and offered it as the shower door slid back.

'Thanks.' Elliott took it and wrapped it around his waist. 'Does he want us in?' he asked.

'No hurry, about three. Time to take lunch at the steak house over in Leicester Square.'

'I'd prefer Chinese.'

'Malaysian, down off the Edgeware Road?' Kane suggested.

'Okay.' Elliott picked up another towel and rubbed at his hair.

'Skinny bastard, aren't you?' Kane commented.

'I'm still only a kid,' Elliott said as he grinned, 'If I stick around a while maybe I'll fill out a bit.'

'I'll buy you lunch towards it,' Kane offered as he took another drink, 'Fatten you up for the kill.'

'I'm in no hurry but I'll let you pay.' Elliott discarded the towel and pulled on his shorts.

'Move yourself a bit,' urged Kane, setting the cup down on the wash basin, 'I don't need indigestion as a dessert.'

'Book a table, I'll be ready in five minutes.'

'I'll book us a bit of company,' Kane added as he headed for the door.

*

Elliott followed Kane into the restaurant. It was a small, rather cluttered room with only around ten tables, most of which were occupied. Kane headed towards a table at which two girls of oriental origin were already seated. He glanced at Kane, and didn't doubt that he would expect something from them in return for lunch. Both were pretty girls. It was clear that one of them recognised Kane, as she smiled on the approach to the table.

'Hi, poppet.' Kane took the seat beside her and inquired, 'Who's your friend?'

'San Ling.'

The other girl smiled and looked down demurely.

'Mai Li, San Ling – Chris.'

'Hi,' acknowledged Elliott as he took the vacant seat.

'We don't have much time, we'd better order,' Kane reached for a menu.

San Ling cast a sidelong glance at Elliott, looked at Mai Li and both girls giggled coyly.

'Will we meet later?' Mai Li asked Kane.

'Sure, we'll meet later,' Kane assured her and looked at Elliott. 'They're built the same,' he clarified.

Elliott looked at him quizzically.

'Oriental girls, they're built the same,' Kane reiterated.

'Never suggested they weren't.'

'Some blokes get funny ideas about oriental girls; they think that because they're small there's something different where it matters.'

'Not something I've turned my mind to,' Elliott admitted.

A waiter walked towards the table and he asked, 'Ready to order?'

The girls wore dresses which were split to the thigh. Kane's left hand was unsighted and Mai Li's expression suggested that its absence wasn't innocent. San Ling did not look at Elliott. Her eyes remained cast firmly downwards, and he felt that she realised that something was expected of her and that she expected something of him. All he had had in mind was lunch and that was still all he had in mind. The waiter brought satay as an entrée, together with a cucumber and onion side salad and set down a peanut sauce. Mai Li slid beneath the table. Elliott reached for a satay and placed it on San Ling's plate.

'Stay right where you are, sweetheart, I only came to eat,' Elliott advised San Ling.

San Ling looked at him and smiled unsurely.

Kane was clearly enjoying himself, but wasn't showing much interest in the food. He took his cigarettes from his pocket, lit one, and slid a little further down in his chair.

*

Later, at WHQ Elliott followed Kane into the elevator. 'Beats me how you ever find time to work.'

Kane grinned. 'Practice. Nothing like sex for recharging the batteries. You'll learn that you take what you can today; tomorrow you might be sat on a cloud playing a bloody harp.'

That much was true, Elliott conceded, and sex was better than any other exercise he knew. He was pretty sure that Kane had paid for the sexual company of the Chinese girls, and Elliott wasn't into that, as he had seen what that sort of life had done to his mother.

The elevator slowed to a halt and the doors opened. They stepped out into the corridor outside Super Admin.

'Hope Marlborough doesn't have anything for us – I'm on more than a promise for tonight,' Kane said as he led through to Maryana Jenova's office, 'You wouldn't believe the energy that girl has got. She is incredible – legs up to her armpits – and when she's got them wrapped round my neck...'

'Mr Kane!' Jenova snapped in horror, 'You are in mixed company.'

Kane hesitated, 'Sorry, I find it hard to put gender to a computer.'

She scowled.

'Okay if we go through?' Elliott asked.

'It would be preferable to your remaining here.'

'I think you upset her,' Elliott whispered as they headed towards Marlborough's office.

'Sit down, gentlemen,' Marlborough instructed, glancing up briefly, 'The purpose of this briefing is to update you on the situation. The tracking system on *Blue Velvet* is working efficiently, and she's presently travelling along the south coast with no indication of moving out into off-limit waters. Espachio and Mackintosh remain static in Spain and Poland respectively. And Suleman died of his injuries early this morning.'

'That's tough, he was a nice bloke,' Kane acknowledged.

There was nothing for Elliott to say; he had never met Suleman.

'You remain on standby. Don't leave your communicators unattended.' Marlborough looked up then, 'Thank you, gentlemen. Dismiss.'

Kane started to his feet.

'Can you spare me a few minutes?' Elliott asked.

Marlborough hesitated then inquired, 'Do you require Kane to stay?'

Elliott shook his head.

'Then don't let me delay you, Kane, clearly you have plans.'

'Sir.' Kane headed for the door.

Marlborough looked at Elliott quizzically.

'Pushto,' Elliott suggested.

'Is that the drugs dealer?'

Elliott nodded. 'I'm not sure his staying on the street's a good idea. He made a mistake introducing Suleman and Latislaw to the arms dealers. If they really start digging I'm not sure how well I'm going to hold up and another mistake wouldn't look good for him.'

'He takes the money, he runs the risk.' Marlborough stated.

'He told me that O'Brien had some heavy friends, Espachio or Mackintosh maybe.'

'Have you made promises?' Marlborough asked.

'Not sure I'm in a position to.'

'You aren't. What promises haven't you made?'

Elliott shook his head, 'Thought we might be able to arrange him a couple of weeks' vacation in Brixton just to keep him out of circulation when things start to hot up.'

'Things are going to start to hot up?'

'I'm an optimist.'

'And this Pushto character would be willing to spend a couple of weeks in custody?'

'It's a marginal improvement on being dead,' Elliott offered.

Marlborough smiled a little grimly. 'I suppose that that's a matter of opinion,' he sniped, then nodded. 'All right, I don't need unnecessary casualties. Perhaps a little concern for your own situation wouldn't go amiss,' he suggested as Elliott rose to his feet.

'Sir.'

Maryana Jenova looked across as Elliott emerged from Marlborough's office, and then returned her eyes to her work quickly. Obviously she did not want to pass the time of day, nor did she intend that the hard veneer should drop again. It was not too early to go looking for Pushto, Elliott decided, he had a living to make and was hardly likely to limit his trading to an hour or two in the evening.

It was a nice day – he hadn't noticed earlier. The sun was out even if the shadows were beginning to lengthen and it was cool rather than cold. Elliott slid behind the wheel of the car and started up the engine. Brixton in the daylight would be a novel experience, he thought as he pulled out into the traffic.

The Dyers was clearly one of those places which was never quiet. Elliott pushed and negotiated his way through to the bar.

'Oh, it's you again,' the barman cast a glance in Elliott's direction whilst serving other patrons.

'Pushto at his usual table?' Elliott inquired.

'If he is his customers are having trouble finding him,' the barman muttered sarcastically, turned to the open till and threw a handful of change into it.

'What time's he usually come in?'

'First through the doors. You drinking?'

'No, just looking,' Elliott retorted as he turned away and headed back towards the door.

He sat for a few minutes behind the wheel, thoughtful. Pushto liked to be surrounded by people, he thought: he was safer surrounded by people so why the hell wasn't he? What was the stupid bugger playing at. He would do himself no favours by running; or maybe he hadn't run, maybe he couldn't; maybe he was already out of it. Elliott started up the engine and the car roared away from the pavement.

Elliott remembered Hordle Promenade. It wasn't too much to go on, but Pushto had asked to be dropped off there and it was no guarantee that that was where he had digs. Maybe it was not even the area of his digs; it would be easy enough to jump on a bus or into a taxi and go elsewhere. Elliott parked up, and his eyes roved along a row of shops. He recognised the premises of a Caribbean takeaway; the last time he had been in that neck of the woods it had been an English chippy.

Reggae music filled the air, and a largely Rasta clientele looked him over curiously. It was not the sort of place where he could blend into the background; he felt like a flake of snow in a coal cellar.

'Hi,' he acknowledged the teenager in front of him in the queue, 'What do you recommend?'

There was a silence as the teenager surveyed him. He then looked up at the board and suggested, 'Seventeen, twenty-three, thirty-two.'

'Sounds a bit light up top but I like the twenty-three, thirty-two.

The youth grinned and said, 'You could take forty-one with it.'

'That sounds good, forty-one, twenty-three, thirty-two, but I think maybe she'd fall over.'

He waited a long time, half an hour, for his order – forty-one, twenty-three, thirty-two – knowing only that he was getting hungry, not knowing what he had ordered.

'Anything else?'

'Pushto…?'

Silence descended like a blanket.

'I guess he isn't popular around here?'

The man behind the counter shook his head. Elliott decided not to push it, but paid and gathered up the package, and headed outside. He lowered himself on to the narrow ledge of the neighbouring shop window, looking something of a dejected figure.

'Here.'

He looked up. The teenager stood over him and offered him a slim reefer.

'Thanks.'

'You'd better find yourself a new pusher,' the teenager recommended as he lowered himself on to the ledge.

'How come?'

'Pushto bunked off last night – took off like he'd got a rocket up his arse.'

'You don't know where he might have gone?'

'No,' he said and shook his head, 'Hackney maybe, or Lewisham; got family in both them places, although he isn't much of a family man.' He hesitated, then continued, 'You don't want to hang around here too long. Pushto comes late, goes early, right now he isn't around at all; better for you if you aren't.'

Elliott looked at him. 'Yeah, right,' he said, and rose to his feet. 'How much do I owe you for the reefer?'

'I don't deal, just a favour.' He moved away.

*

Elliott pulled up in a quiet side street and switched off the engine. He reached for the take-away, thinking that there seemed to be little point in looking for Pushto. If he had decided to go to ground he was not Elliott's problem. He leaned back in his seat and ate, and supposed that he might as well go home. The communicator buzzed. He reached out and flicked the dashboard switch.

'Yeah?'

'The latest report is that *Blue Velvet* has moored at Lyme Regis,' came Marlborough's voice over the airways.

'Nice area,' Elliott commented, continuing to eat, 'You want me to go down and take a look?'

'No, this is merely a further update. All of the indications are that the tracking system is efficient. I have a static trace on your vehicle Elliott and it appears to be on the outskirts of Peckham, some distance from home.'

'I was looking for Pushto but he's done a runner. Maybe I'll go across to the Barbican, take a look around the flat.'

'I'll tell Kane to meet you there.'

'I'll be okay on my own; Kane's probably made plans.'

'Then he will have to un-make them. What time?'

Elliott glanced at his watch and offered, 'Around an hour?'

'Nineteen forty,' Marlborough confirmed, 'I don't want you going in before he gets there.'

'Okay,' Elliott acknowledged, and closed communications.

*

'Damn!'

Kane tossed the communicator down on to the bed. He had a date fixed for twenty-thirty hours; a few drinks with an elegant blonde by the name of Louise at a quiet out-of-town pub followed by dinner in its restaurant and sex in a room with a four-poster bed. Elliott was a bloody pain. Why couldn't he just do what he was told to do; there was no bonus for coming up with ideas of his own. A fraud or not, he was already in at number one; there were no Brownie points needed to take him up the ladder. Kane snatched up the telephone and stabbed at the numbers bad-temperedly. It rang maybe a dozen times before it was answered.

'What took you?' he snapped.

'I was in the shower.'

'Yeah?' Kane licked his lips and asked, 'What are you wearing now?'

'Nothing but water,' she murmured seductively.

He hesitated, then said, 'I need to call a rain check, something came up.'

'And what's her name? Don't bother phoning me again, Brett, I've got better things to do with my life.' She hung up.

He looked at the receiver for a few moments. 'Well, thanks a lot, Elliott,' he muttered, and slammed down the phone.

He wouldn't be needing the dinner suit and bow tie now, he thought, so he grabbed a pair of jeans and pulled them on, then dragged a tee shirt over his head.

*

Elliott parked up outside the Barbican Centre. He was on single yellow lines but the parking limitations had expired until morning. His eyes roved briefly along the street but there was no sign of Kane's car, so he surveyed the first few floors of the building. He didn't need Kane there, he was only checking out an empty flat – any indication that it was not empty and he would leave – he wasn't looking for trouble.

Kane came in from the opposite direction and parked up. Elliott slid out of the car and locked it, walked the couple of hundred yards and sank to his haunches, his right hand on the wing mirror. Kane wound down the window.

'This had better be good.'

'I didn't ask for you to be here,' Elliott snapped, looking at him, 'I guess you reckon I'm just around to make your life hell, it isn't intentional. What was she like?'

'I was hoping to find out,' Kane muttered.

'Surprise me, Kane, I thought you were working your way round for at least the second time.'

'You're too young, Elliott, you've got no excuse for being a sarcastic, perverse little bastard.'

'I've got every bleedin' excuse. I was never brought up on a cushy number, nobody ever did me any favours. I've spent my entire bleedin' life just surviving and I'm not about to break my heart on account of you missing a screw.' His eyes held Kane's. 'You'd got plans, that's tough. Left to

Marlborough you'd be running your ass off and maybe getting a bullet up your rectum. I didn't see you objecting to assign being stood down.'

Kane looked towards the Barbican Centre, 'She was no virgin. She was playing hard to get.'

'So you're playing harder; that's something of a novelty, uh?'

'Shut up.'

'Fifth floor,' Elliott straightened up, 'Right out of the elevator, seventh right.' He walked away.

Kane hesitated, wound the window back up and slid out of the car. He checked the lock. Taking his cigarettes from his pocket he lit one before slouching after Elliott. He caught up with him at the elevators.

'You aren't normal, Elliott.'

'No?'

'At your age your hormones should be running riot – we should be having to prise you off the girls.'

The elevator doors opened and they stepped inside. Kane leaned back against the wall.

'Is this going to take long?' he asked.

'Don't suppose so.'

'The whole night isn't going to be wasted then?' Kane brightened a little, then suggested, 'We could go on for a drink when we're through here. We could go down to the Chocolate Box.'

That was a new one on Elliott. He looked at Kane quizzically.

'Trixabelle's, always a good selection and plenty of sweet centres,' Kane's voice held an insinuation. 'I'm not talking prostitutes, just girls who like a good time. You're out of touch, Elliott; these days we're the game and the girls are queuing up to jump us.'

'How about we just get the job done?'

Kane shrugged, 'Suits me.'

Elliott led to the door of the apartment and rapped on it. They waited. There was no response so he rapped again on the wood.

'So what are we going to do now, break the door down?'

Elliott reached into his pocket and drew out a penknife, opened out a narrow blade and pushed it into the keyhole. A few seconds and the barrel turned.

'The school you went to must have been interesting,' Kane commented.

Elliott turned the handle and pushed the door open silently. They stepped through into the dark hallway. Kane followed, closing the door behind him and shutting out the last vestige of light. Locating the door to the lounge Elliott opened it; the dull grey of twilight was filling the room.

'What are we looking for?' Kane whispered.

Elliott shrugged. It was a sparsely and shabbily furnished room, a door from it leading, he guessed, to the dining-room and kitchen.

'You take this side and I'll check out across the hallway,' Elliott decided.

There were three doors on the opposite side; the first led into a bathroom. It was empty, no towels or toiletries, the bathroom suite was a long time uncleaned. The second door led into a bedroom, uncarpeted and unfurnished. A part of the door seemed to have been scrubbed recently. Elliott walked across and sank to his haunches, and scrutinised the boards. Taking his penknife again from his pocket he opened out a wider blade and dug it into the narrow crack between two floorboards. The blade emerged stained. He studied it – blood perhaps, he thought. Straightening up he returned to the hallway and headed for the second bedroom. He could hear Kane in the lounge, and heard the doors to the balcony being slid open. The door to the second bedroom creaked as it swung open. Elliott stepped inside and recoiled from the stench.

A body lay crumpled on the floor. He moved towards it but then stopped – it was alive with maggots. The build, he guessed, was right for George Bentley but that would be for forensic to establish. The head had been completely smashed in.

'Okay, there's nothing here, let's stop wasting our time and… Aw, Jesus, what the hell was that?' Kane retreated into the hallway. 'Come out of there. Just leave everything as it is for Forensic and Recovery to sort out,' he snapped as he drew his communicator from his pocket and activated it.

'Marlborough?'

'I'm with Elliott at the Barbican apartment. We've got a murder victim, identity unknown.'

'Probably George Bentley,' Elliott suggested as he emerged into the hallway.

'Remain on site?' Kane asked.

'Forensic will be with you within half an hour,' Marlborough confirmed, and closed communications.

'Doesn't look like we'll be left with much drinking time,' Kane muttered, heading back through to the lounge.

Elliott hesitated, then followed him. 'I reckon there's been blood spilt in the other bedroom – the floorboards have been scrubbed,' Elliott commented.

'You're an expert on housekeeping, uh?' Kane dropped on to the sofa and muttered, 'Should have brought a six pack.'

Marlborough arrived with the forensic team. He hesitated as he crossed the threshold and sniffed the air briefly and disdainfully. He walked through to the first bedroom and his eyes lingered on the dark silhouette of the body.

'Light,' he snapped.

A forensic officer flicked the light switch with the tip of his ball pen. Marlborough walked towards the body and looked down at it impassively. It was, what, four days since the meeting at the warehouse and that could be around the length of time the body had been decomposing.

'Elliott!' Marlborough barked.

'Sir?' Elliott was standing right behind him.

Marlborough glanced round. 'If this is Bentley, I want your assurance that you left him alive.'

'I was gone for around three and a half hours. I walked from HQ to Tiffany's and I spent around an hour touring London in the back of a van. I was back in your office wearing the same gear I went out in. Don't recollect finding anybody's brains in my pocket or carrying any bodies across London.'

Marlborough nodded.

'The floor in the other room's been scrubbed; you want to get forensic to check it out,' Elliott asked.

Marlborough turned. 'All right, make a start,' he instructed the waiting forensic team. 'Your leads appear to be diminishing, Elliott,' he said as he strode out into the hallway.

Elliott followed. 'Maybe I should check O'Brien out,' he suggested.

'For what?'

'Signs of life.'

A pause followed.

'The local police…'

'I'd sooner take a look before everything disappears under size nines,' Elliott interrupted.

'Are you implying that there may be something to disappear?' Marlborough asked.

Elliott shrugged and said thoughtfully, 'We've got Bentley feeding the sprogs of bluebottles, and Pushto's done a vanishing act. Somebody must know the set-up.'

'That may make your position precarious.' Marlborough observed.

'I figure maybe it's rival gangs. Unless my cover fails, I think they're more likely to be after my custom than my blood.'

Chapter Nine

The passenger seat was in full recline but Kane was not asleep, he was simmering.

'You sure you were in the forces?' he asked.

Elliott glanced at him.

'Never volunteer for anything, that's the first rule of service. You've got a hell of a lot to learn.'

'You made it pretty clear you don't intend to teach me,' Elliott retorted.

'Even a complete bloody moron should grasp the basics,' Kane snapped.

'So I'll throw my lot in with the amoebas,' Elliott responded.

'We're robots, Elliott, we aren't paid to think. We've got computers and a whole back-up team to do the brain work. Why the hell do you insist on thinking for yourself?'

'I don't like the idea of somebody else thinking me dead; I'd hate to be terminated by a computer error.'

The silence was lengthy.

'I could have been screwing a real stunner tonight,' Kane lamented.

Elliott grinned. 'You make it sound like that sort of action's only for the night hours. What happens if you try making it in the daylight – you turn into a pumpkin?' He hesitated, then added, 'Found yourself a girl over in Newport, didn't you? Maybe you could look her up again?'

'We had a good time for a couple of days, that's long enough or the girls start to get ideas.'

It was a pretty lengthy journey, something over a couple of hundred miles. Driving relaxed Elliott, and out of London he could put his foot down. Night had drawn in, the sky was black and there was no moon. Kane was silent, sulking again, Elliott supposed. He was a moody bastard and lazy, not the type to put himself out. Presumably he worked well enough when the heat was on.

Newport had been coming up on the signposts for some time now: only another fifteen miles to go. Elliott glanced at the dashboard clock. It was a little past twenty three hundred hours and it had taken around two and a half hours to make the journey. In Newport, Kane straightened his seat as the car slowed to a halt opposite a row of terraced houses. They were all in darkness on the front aspect. Elliott slid out of the car, and Kane followed suit a little reluctantly. The night air was chilly and a little damp; there was also a touch of frost.

Elliott crossed the road and moved along the side of the house which O'Brien occupied. There were no lights on at the rear either. Elliott's eyes swept briefly over the rear façade and then moved on to the boatyard. He walked across to the double doors. They were secure and solid with security locks, and he moved away.

'Not going to try the magic penknife?' Kane asked.

'Only as a last resort and with a couple of hours to spare,' Elliott retorted.

There was a high surrounding wall at the rear, around ten feet high. Elliott looked up at it.

'Are you going over or am I?' he asked.

'You are,' Kane responded as he cupped his hands.

Elliott caught the top of the wall, hauled himself up and sat astride it, 'Want to wait in the car and I'll call you?'

'It's an improvement on freezing to death.'

Elliott tossed him the keys. Kane waited and watched as Elliott disappeared from the top of the wall. He heard the impact as Elliott dropped down into the yard. Turning, he walked away.

Elliott steadied himself, turned and surveyed the dark silhouettes which nestled against the skyline. Carefully he picked his way across the yard towards the buildings. The rear door to the building was on a standard lock, so Elliott picked it expertly and pushed the door open. An alarm sounded on a time-switch before it connected with the monitoring office. One, two, three, four, reset, four, three, two, one; he tapped in the engineers' code in the hope that it had never been voided. He was in luck: the alarm deactivated. He located the light switch panel and threw the switches; the shipyard and buildings illuminated.

There was a boat, stripped and being worked on in the workshop. He moved past it and towards the offices. The reception was deserted, the switchboard switched through to an answering machine. There was a door through to another office. He opened it and switched on the light as he stepped through.

So O'Brien was filed from A to Z, or at least that was as far as the blood extended. Like Bentley the identity was a matter for forensic – there was little identifiable from the shoulders up. Elliott stepped back through to the reception. There was a wall with a window through to a small waiting area. He walked across to the door which led out and pulled it open. He almost fell over the body of a young woman. There was blood on her temple and bruising on her throat. Sinking to his haunches he pressed his fingers against her neck. There was no pulse – he had not expected there to be. Straightening up he made his way back through to O'Brien's office. He supposed that he had better alert Kane. His eyes roved as he reached for his communicator and lingered on a photograph on the desk. It was of O'Brien, a young woman – the young woman who lay dead a few yards away – and a baby. He guessed that it was a recent photograph.

'Yeah?' Kane sounded bored when he answered.

'Two bodies – O'Brien's wife and probably O'Brien. Same SP as Bentley. There's a kid somewhere, think you'd better find your way into the house.'

Elliott closed the channel. He thought then that he should notify Marlborough. About to reopen communications he hesitated. Just visible beneath the desk there was a mobile phone. He retrieved it and pressed the last number redial – 010 34 52 364620 came up on the small screen. He ended the call procedure, and activated his communicator.

Kane's method of entry had not been subtle, as the glass panel in the front door of the house was smashed and the door lay ajar. Elliott stepped inside. The pitiful cries of an infant were audible.

'Kane!'

'Yeah, upstairs.'

Elliott sprinted up the stairs and towards a lit room where Kane stood by the side of a cot.

'What the hell are you doing?' Elliott demanded.

'What the hell am I supposed to be doing?'

The child was around four months, wet through and apparently hungry. Elliott lifted it carefully. A little girl, he thought. 'You see any nappies?'

'Nappies?' Kane asked horrified.

'Forget it, I'll take a look downstairs in the lounge. How about you find your way to the kitchen and see if there's some Cow and Gate or something around.'

'Some what?'

'Powdered baby milk, to make a bottle,' Elliott explained.

'You want me to make a bottle?'

'Would you prefer to change the nappy?'

It was not as easy as it looked, Elliott decided, as he tried to fasten a clean disposable around flailing little limbs and a sob-wracked little body.

'I found this,' offered Kane as he appeared in the doorway, a feeding bottle in his hand, 'In the fridge.'

'Full marks for initiative. If there isn't a bottle warmer stand it in some hot water for a while.'

'Right,' Kane acknowledged, heading back to the kitchen, 'You're quite an expert – got a few sprogs of your own running about?'

'Not that I know of.' He wrapped a thick towel around the small body and lifted it up. 'How's that, sweetheart? Better, uh?' he said tenderly as he stroked her face with his fingers. 'Come on, Kane, must be hours since the poor little mite was fed, bring it cold, for Christ's sake.'

Kane watched as Elliott held the baby gently and winded her.

'You sure you haven't done this before?'

'Shut up, Kane,' Elliott snapped, then grinned, 'Cute little thing, isn't she?'

'She's a bit young, Elliott, even for you.'

She looked drowsy, and he cradled her in his arms. Poor little basket. Her parents were lying with their skulls embedded in a concrete floor and the callous bastards who had done it hadn't even given her a thought. If they didn't know it was no bloody excuse.

Recovery and Forensic were swarming all over the boatyard, and Social Services had arrived at the house. Elliott handed the child over a little reluctantly, and squeezed the tiny hand which found its way out of the towel.

'You through with babysitting now or were you thinking of adoption?' Kane asked, 'Let's head back.'

Elliott nodded.

*

Marlborough looked at the mobile phone, then looked at Elliott quizzically.

'Picked it up from under O'Brien's desk. I pressed redial and got an 010 34 number. I figure that's Spain and maybe Espachio.'

'I'll have it checked out,' Marlborough decided and took custody, 'You deserve praise for observing the child; an infant of that age can't tolerate too much neglect. Another twenty-four hours and it may have been too late.' He looked momentarily thoughtful. 'It's late, you need to rest. This may be our turning point – I'll have investigations put under way.'

*

Elliott undressed and fell into his bed. Although he was tired he knew that he would have to fight to sleep and that the nightmares would come as soon as he closed his eyes. Even with his eyes open he saw only the carnage, the battered bodies in the gloom. He fell asleep eventually into a restless perspiration-soaked sleep.

He grimaced and forced his eyes open. His eyelids felt heavy and his body still needed to recharge. There was a constant hammering and for a moment he thought that it was in his head. He realised that it was from the front door, distant and muffled. Sliding wearily out of his bed he pulled on his shorts and jeans, and fastened them as he headed through his apartment.

'We got fed up with three in a bed, so Rachel suggested breakfast at your place.'

'Why don't you go to hell, Kane?' Elliott snapped, not feeling in the slightest bit sociable.

'I knew you'd be pleased to see us. We brought the bacon, eggs and mushrooms – can we help ourselves to the cornflakes?'

'Help yourself to anything you want, I'm going back to bed.'

'Can I help myself to you?' Rachel asked.

'Yeah, will you mind if I sleep through?' Elliott asked making his way back to the bedroom. His head touched the pillow and he was asleep.

When he reawakened he was not alone, Rachel was moulded around him.

'On prior performance you were worth waiting for,' she whispered alluringly.

'I wouldn't hold my breath,' he responded as he rolled on to his back.

She raised herself up on her elbow. 'You look stressed,' she said, then kissed his forehead, smiled, and lowered her lips to his.

It felt good. His hands massaged her soft skin and palpitated her breasts. His tongue pushed between her lips and explored her mouth.

She pulled away from him and asked softly, 'How do you like your girls?'

'Hot and in bed.' He pushed her over on to her back, 'I don't have stereotypes, if I like the girl.'

'Do you like me?'

'Yeah, you're okay.' He slid across her.

'Do you like the way I feel?'

His hands cupped her breasts. 'Yeah.' His right hand slid between her legs. 'I like what I feel,' he said evocatively, massaging her clitoris.

Her hands slid downwards.

'Just one, sweetheart,' he whispered.

Her left hand slid back upwards and ran across his chest.

'How does that feel?' she inquired.

'Pretty good.'

Her stomach muscles were beginning to spasm and he penetrated her. She arched towards him and he thrust into her, her fingers digging into his back, and his tongue exploring her mouth as he kissed her.

She lay cradled in his arms, her head resting against his chest. Her body still tingled with residual excitement, her heart beating a little rapidly. Elliott had enjoyed the exercise but the aftermath was always an anticlimax. He supposed that couples who were close talked to each other or didn't need to. Rachel was just a girl; he knew nothing about her and had no real desire to change that situation. It was just a limbo; nothing to talk about and not knowing her well enough for silence to be appropriate.

He managed a sly look at his watch by raising his left arm momentarily a little way from her – it was approaching thirteen thirty.

'Reckon it's time I was getting up,' he said more to himself.

She looked at him. 'Should I make you some breakfast?'

'No,' he looked up at her and offered, 'I'll buy you some lunch some place before I go in to work.' He slid his arm from around her and suggested, 'You could maybe make coffee while I take a shower.'

*

The telephone number was Espachio's. Perhaps it was time to pay him closer attention, Marlborough thought. *Blue Velvet* was confirmed to be still static at Lyme Regis. That too might warrant further investigation unless it moved on soon. Elliott appeared to have taken them from having no leads to several and a surfeit of bodies. Forensic had confirmed the identities of Bentley and O'Brien from dental records, and Pushto had been placed on the Police Missing Persons Record.

It had been a long day, Marlborough thought as he glanced at his watch, almost sixteen thirty, a thirty-six hour long day. He reached for the communicator and activated it.

'Yes, sir?' Maryana Jenova responded.

'Call in Elliott and Kane,' he instructed, 'I'll see them at seventeen thirty.'

The deaths were a strange development, Marlborough thought, one which he could not work out. It seemed to be apparent that Bentley and O'Brien were associated with Espachio, and that being the case Mackintosh became suspect as being behind the murders – except that he was in Warsaw and there was nothing to suggest that any of his agents were in the United Kingdom. Both Espachio and Mackintosh were being uncharacteristically quiet.

Both Elliott and Kane arrived promptly at seventeen thirty. Maryana Jenova had instruction to send them directly through to Marlborough.

'I trust that you're well rested, gentlemen,' Marlborough inquired in greeting them.

'You aren't,' Elliott responded.

'Then I shall rely on you to correct me where I go wrong.' He waved vaguely towards the chairs and continued. 'It's been confirmed that the number redial on the mobile phone recovered from the boatyard is the number of Espachio's villa. The bodies have been identified as expected. So far, neither Espachio nor Mackintosh have given any indication that they may be about to make a move, and *Blue Velvet* still remains static.'

'It looks like I've lost your money,' observed Elliott as he took a seat.

'The money doesn't worry me – besides, we're in profit.' Marlborough smiled. 'I think our next step is to establish why *Blue Velvet* remains static and who has control over her. Also, we need to get a little closer to Espachio. *Blue Velvet* can wait until morning, we'll give her a little longer to move on. In the meantime, Elliott, you'd better collect your passport and fly out to Spain. There's a flight to Madrid at twenty-two hundred hours and there'll be a car waiting at the airport on your arrival, the keys to be collected from the enquiry desk. It's a long drive – that won't present you with any problems?'

Elliott shook his head.

'Good, you can liaise with Observation in the morning. I don't propose to waste my time issuing instructions as, particularly where you're concerned, Elliott, they appear to be superfluous. Take care and stay in touch.'

*

Lyme Regis and *Blue Velvet* had now been static for two days. It was still low season and the marina was quiet. Kane was bored and had been sitting in his car for a couple of hours with nothing worth watching. Had it been high season and hot weather there would no doubt have been some leggy distractions. Elliott seemed to have landed the better deal having been packed off to the Costa Brava to keep an eye on Espachio.

Kane viciously stubbed out his cigarette in the ashtray and climbed out of the car. He slammed the door shut noisily and headed towards the boat. There was no one around, as his eyes roved over the boat and he started up the gangway. No noise, no indication that there was anyone on board, he made his way along the open deck towards the steps and started silently down towards the lower cabins. The corridor into which he emerged was deserted, natural light filtering through the oblong windows. Just for a split second he was surprised at how suddenly it had gone dark – then he forgot about it.

Kane's head throbbed. There was a strong bright light as he opened his eyes, and he groaned and closed them again.

'Switch the light off,' a male voice instructed.

Kane again ventured to open his eyes; this time there was only natural light coming from the cabin window. His sight was a little hazy but he could make out a couple of shadowy figures.

'I really am most terribly sorry, Mr Kane,' came the same male voice, very well spoken, and upper class. 'My sincerest apologies; my man took you to be an opportunist thief. An understandable mistake I think in the circumstances.'

Kane strained to bring the images into focus. The man doing the talking was tall, well built with greying dark hair, and was probably in his late fifties or early sixties. He seemed to be vaguely familiar. Beside him there was a younger man, smaller built and apparently half-caste. Kane started to haul himself up.

'Give Mr Kane a little help, would you, Symmonds?'

The half-caste helped Kane into a sitting position. Kane's hand went to the back of his neck.

'I'm sure you appreciate that Symmonds was merely doing his job. Are you feeling a little tender? A brandy perhaps?' He looked at Symmonds and said, 'Two large brandies if you would be so good. We'll take them in the lounge.'

Symmonds retreated from the cabin.

'How do you feel?'

'Like I've been coshed on the back of the head,' said Kane, rotating his head a little. His neck felt painful.

'You were only unconscious for a short time; there may be a little concussion. I'm sure you've suffered worse.

Should we retire to the lounge or do you require assistance?'

'I'm fine,' Kane said as he winced, 'I just feel a little disadvantaged.'

The man looked at him quizzically.

'I don't have a name to call you,' Kane said.

'How very remiss of me, and bad mannered. Drury – Albert Drury,' he said as he offered his hand.

There was a silence.

'What do you intend to do with me?' Kane asked.

'Do with you?' Drury withdrew his hand and confirmed, 'I don't propose to do anything with you, Mr Kane – other than extend my sincerest apologies and see you safely on your way.'

That was a little difficult to believe as the name had identified the familiarity. Albert Drury was the godfather of the underworld.

'I think you need that brandy,' Drury offered.

Kane figured that he did.

The lounge was comfortable, but Kane wished that he had taken a little more notice of the layout of the boat before he had parted with it. A knowledge of which windows – did boats have windows – opened might have been useful. He took the glass which Symmonds offered.

'If I interest the WIA, Mr Kane, I'm flattered, but I fail to believe that the WIA could prove me to be of interest – which brings us to your reason for being here.'

He was cornered anyway. Kane cast a sidelong glance towards Symmonds who stood by the door. He took a drink and explained. 'The boat interested me. I sold it to a bloke called O'Brien and now he's dead. So is his wife.'

Drury took a sip of his drink, studied Kane openly, and finally he smiled and asked, 'Which has what to do with me?'

Kane's heart pounded against his ribs; he was on dangerous ground with a very dangerous man. Drury was more than capable of disposing of unwanted complications and there was little doubt that he himself qualified as an unwanted complication.

'I intend to retire, Mr Kane, and this boat is a present from me to myself. It was purchased legitimately and I have the receipt and documentation. An examination of Mr O'Brien's bank account should prove it to be in receipt of a draft in the sum of one hundred and fifty-five thousand pounds. I have no interest in Mr O'Brien other than as a party to the transaction,' Drury smiled thinly, 'And you will find nothing to prove otherwise.'

Kane didn't doubt it, and drained his glass.

'Again I must apologise for your headache. If you wish to stay and rest a while a cabin can be placed at your disposal but, if you'll excuse me, I have some telephone calls to make.'

Kane watched as Drury left. Symmonds remained.

'Another brandy?' Symmonds offered.

Kane shook his head and took his cigarettes from his pocket. Symmonds stepped forward with a light.

'Thanks,' Kane acknowledged, drawing on the cigarette, 'I'd better be getting back to London.' He rose to his feet.

'I'll see you to your car,' Symmonds insisted rather than offered.

Kane threw the car into gear and crossed the car park with a screeching of rubber on tarmac, and put five miles between himself and the marina in as many minutes. He pulled in to the side of the road and leaned back in his seat. He lit another cigarette, drew strongly on it and exhaled slowly. Reaching forward he activated the dashboard communicator.

'Put me through to Marlborough.'

There was a short silence.

'Where the hell have you been, Kane, and why is your personal communicator switched off?' Marlborough greeted him.

Kane reached into his pocket and withdrew his personal communicator. It was switched off but undamaged.

'Kane?'

'*Blue Velvet's* changed hands – it's in the possession of Albert Drury.'

'Albert Drury?'

'He claims to have bought it from O'Brien for a hundred and fifty-five thousand pounds, and that he knows nothing about O'Brien's death.'

'You've spoken to him?'

'The boat looked to be deserted – I found out it wasn't.'

'I didn't tell you to go on board!' Marlborough's sigh was audible. 'I want you back here by fifteen hundred hours,' Marlborough demanded.

The communicator went dead.

*

Elliott too had become bored. There was Observation on site and little point so far as he could see in his sitting around watching. Espachio was leading something of a hermit-like existence. He had not been seen for days, and his only communication with the outside world appeared to be the telephone which was being intercepted in any event. Elliott glanced round as the receivers indicated that Espachio was making a telephone call. An Observation operative picked up the headphones and adjusted the dials on the receiver, then switched on the amplifier. The intercepted line crackled a little as the reception quality was affected by humid weather conditions. The Observation base was a neighbouring villa rented out in the summer months to holidaymakers but standing empty over the winter months. It was comfortable enough but Elliott soon became restless with little to do apart from watch television.

'Espachio's asked for his private plane to be made ready,' said the Observation operative as he switched off the amplifier and set down the headphones.

Elliott rose to his feet.

'There's a small aerodrome about twelve miles west; it sounds as though he intends leaving inside the hour.'

Elliott took his communicator from his pocket and opened a channel. 'WHQ Marlborough,' he requested.

'Connecting you.'

A few moments' silence followed.

'Marlborough?'

'How am I fixed for getting a plane?' Elliott asked.

'A plane?'

'Looks like Espachio's on the move. He's ordered his plane at the ready at a local aerodrome. Best way I can watch him's by following him.'

'I was under the impression that man had invented radar,' Marlborough responded.

'So he lands somewhere remote and by the time we get there he's scarpered,' Elliott pointed out.

There was a pause.

'All right, get down to the aerodrome and I'll make the necessary arrangements. I take it I needn't be put to the expense of a full crew?' Marlborough asked.

'I don't like being chauffeured.'

Gonzales, one of the Observation operatives slid behind the wheel of the car as Elliott slipped into the passenger seat. Espachio had not yet emerged from his villa although there was evidence of activity. He was definitely preparing to leave. Elliott was figuring on being ready and waiting at the aerodrome, and the adrenaline was already pumping like somebody had shouted scramble.

★

It was a WIA craft, a small private jet, just landed from DHQ Madrid and being refuelled. Elliott's eyes roved over it as he crossed the tarmac, then moved on to Espachio's private jet waiting outside the hangars. The WIA craft was the same make as Espachio's but a more recent model. It was not a type which he had flown before but as long as it went up and stayed up until he wanted to come down he didn't see any problem, and it appeared that he was to have a co-pilot. The WIA operative who had brought it over was apparently employed purely in the capacity of pilot. He wore a uniform not dissimilar to that of an airline pilot with the appropriate wings on the sleeves.

'Mr Elliott,' he said, and offered his hand as Elliott approached, 'Juan Absteros. I am to introduce you to my plane.'

Elliott shook hands with him, followed him on board and up to the cockpit. Communications were open to control and monitoring Espachio's preparation. Elliott lowered himself into the pilot's seat and scanned the instrument panel.

'You've done the pre-flight visual check?' Elliott asked.

Absteros nodded.

'So we just sit back and wait until Espachio's ready.'

★

Marlborough glanced up as Kane entered his office. Slowly he replaced the cap on his fountain pen and set it down, leaned back in his chair and looked at Kane quizzically.

'The boat looked to be deserted,' Kane offered, trying to explain.

'I told you to watch it,' Marlborough snapped.

'When Elliott doesn't do as you tell him you call it initiative,' Kane objected.

'When Elliott doesn't do as I tell him I also call it stupidity, but Elliott's young and inexperienced. From you I expect more. Tell me what happened.'

Kane hesitated, then lowered himself into the seat opposite Marlborough. 'I watched the boat; I watched it for more than two hours and there was nothing. I was pretty sure that it wasn't occupied. I went on board, and the next thing I remember was coming round in one of the cabins with a splitting headache.'

'Drury wasn't aware of who you were?'

'Drury was well aware of who I was – he called me by name. He must have been through my pockets, I suppose that's how the communicator came to be switched off.' Kane hesitated, then continued, 'I'd been coshed by one of his assistants, bloke by the name of Symmonds. Drury said he'd taken me to be an opportunist thief. He was so cool he might just have come out of the fridge.'

'Drury makes a living out of being cool. You might well have been making a career out of being dead,' Marlborough snapped. 'It appears that things are happening on the Espachio front, he seems to be on the move. Until such time as the results in that quarter are known I'll stand you down. Remain on communications.'

'Sir.' Kane rose to his feet.

Marlborough looked up at him and said, 'This isn't an excuse for a holiday, Kane.'

*

The weather was good; no cloud although it was late into the night. They had been airborne for around an hour and a half and were heading towards the UK on a course which made London a strong possibility. Elliott had Espachio's private jet on radar but was close enough to see its tail-lights, yet not close enough to spook the pilot. The small WIA jet handled well, Elliott thought, another hour to an hour and a half and they would be home free.

'Bloody hell!'

Elliott pulled the jet into a steep climb as a fireball exploded in front of it. The small jet rocked with the force. Elliott looked out of the cockpit window as it levelled out but could see only smoke and shrapnel. He activated communications.

'This is Tango Alpha Brazil to control. Do you read me, control?'

'Control to Tango Alpha Brazil, we read you loud and clear. We have no radar on Zebra Alpha Omega, repeat, we have no radar on Zebra Alpha Omega. Do you have visual contact?'

'Negative, control, there is no Zebra Alpha Omega, do you copy? There is no Zebra Alpha Omega.'

'Repeat Tango Alpha Brazil, there is no Zebra Alpha Omega? Can you clarify?'

'Tango Alpha Brazil to control, repeat there is no Zebra Alpha Omega.' Elliott curled the plane back round in a tight circle whilst descending. 'Mid air explosion, repeat mid air explosion. There is no Zebra Alpha Omega.'

'We copy you, Tango Alpha Brazil, there is no Zebra Alpha Omega. Alerting reconnaissance to last radar position. What is your intention, Tango Alpha Brazil?'

'I don't have water wings. Proceeding to survey area in case of survivors. Gut reaction negative.'

The sea was dark, merged almost with the skyline. There was nothing on the surface save a few smouldering embers.

'See anything?' Elliott asked, glancing across at Absteros.

'Nothing.'

'Tango Alpha Brazil to control.'

'Reading you, Tango Alpha Brazil.'

'Negative, control, no indication of survivors.'

'That is negative on survivors. What is your destination, Tango Alpha Brazil?'

'Returning to flight path; e.t.a. London one hour twenty-seven.'

'We have you on screen, Tango Alpha Brazil. Flight path clear.'

Marlborough had driven down to the small private airport at which the WIA jet would be landing and which belonged to the WIA. He stood in the control tower watching the small specks of light which he had been assured was the WIA jet. There was audio contact, the usual preparations for landing, which meant nothing to Marlborough. His eyes followed the approaching lights, the dark silhouette of the small jet becoming visible. To Marlborough the descent appeared rapid, and he turned away as the wheels of the jet neared the black stretch of runway.

Elliott guided the jet along the tarmac and on to the turning point down to the apron. He closed down the engines.

'Nice piloting,' complimented Absteros as he flicked off the switches on the instrument panel and reached for the clipboard to complete the report sheet.

'Nice plane,' responded Elliott. He took the clipboard, signed the report sheet, and said, 'Maybe I'll get to fly it again some time.' He rose to his feet and headed out into the cabin.

Marlborough waited on the tarmac of the apron and watched as Elliott ran down the steps.

'You weren't hurt?' he asked, concerned.

Elliott shook his head. 'We just hit the turbulence,' he explained as he headed round the plane, 'Maybe a few singe marks.'

'What happened?'

'Espachio took a short cut; he should have gone easy on the rocket fuel.' He followed Marlborough towards the compact terminal buildings.

'There was no warning of trouble?' Marlborough asked.

'No, went straight from being a jet plane to a fireball. No messing.'

Marlborough looked thoughtful. 'You're a qualified pilot – give me your thoughts on what happened. Could it have been an accident?' He stepped into the terminal and held the door open for Elliott to follow.

'Maybe,' Elliott offered finally, 'If the fuel pipe's ruptured.'

'Would the pilot notice if that happened?'

'Unless he was blind or asleep.'

'What makes the greater likelihood?'

'An incendiary on timer.'

Marlborough nodded and said, 'Kane had a run-in with Albert Drury. Does that name mean anything to you?'

'Thought he was dead – but I guess he's only around sixty now. Everybody seems old when you're a kid.' He looked at Marlborough and asked, 'So what's Drury doing now? Still running London?'

'That's a fairly accurate summing up. He claims to have bought *Blue Velvet*.'

'Wanted something to play with in his bath?'

Marlborough smiled grimly.

'What's Mackintosh doing?'

'There's no indication that he has any inclination to make a move – there's been no visual contact and he isn't making or receiving calls.'

'Maybe you should send Kane on a day trip to Warsaw and I'll go and have a talk with Drury.'

There was a pause.

'We'll discuss future moves a little later in the morning, Elliott. Right now we're all tired.'

Chapter Ten

Mornings were getting into the habit of coming around too soon, Elliott thought, as he glanced across at the bedside clock. Two minutes past noon and this was an addition to his already existing list of missed mornings. He scooped up his communicator from the bedside cabinet, activated it and waited for a response.

'Marlborough?'

'What time do you want me in?'

'When I call you, Elliott. I've sent Kane to establish the position in Warsaw.'

'So it's my turn for time off?' Elliott inquired.

'Stay by your communicator.'

Elliott closed communications and tossed the communicator back on to the cabinet. He stared up at the ceiling for a few moments and contemplated the day still stretching ahead. He could go out and find himself a girl, turn over and go back to sleep, or maybe pay Drury a visit if *Blue Velvet* was still down at Lyme Regis. Deciding on the latter he threw back the bedcovers and headed for the bathroom.

Refreshed, and wandering around his apartment, coffee in hand, Elliott entered the seldom-used second bedroom. The computer tucked away in a corner looked pretty basic. Elliott activated it and scanned the options which came up on screen. *Computer* – that seemed as good as any so he highlighted it and pressed *enter*. A few seconds and the screen indicated that the unit had linked up with master computer – *enter query?* it asked. He hesitated, then entered *Blue Velvet*. The screen filled rapidly. He was not too interested in the boat's specifications so he scrolled through the data until he reached confirmation that *Blue Velvet* still remained in Lyme Regis. That was all he needed to know. He gulped down the last mouthful of his coffee, pulled on his jacket and headed out to his car.

Blue Velvet was a good-looking boat. It was the first time he had seen it and he could well imagine that anyone with the right sort of money might view it as a toy. From what little he knew of Drury he did not see him as the type to go pleasure cruising, even less to be considering retirement. Sliding out of his car Elliott locked it and strolled across to the gangway leading up on board. He hesitated. It appeared to be deserted just as it had appeared to Kane, but he had no ambition to be coshed over the head. There was no doorbell, no door if it came to that, so he stepped on to the outer deck and glanced around. The lounge was empty. He made for the steps down to the lower decks and descended them almost silently, then started along the corridor.

He was aware not so much of footsteps as of a light shadow, and he swung round and pinned Symmonds to the wall, his arm across Symmonds's windpipe.

'Just to show that you don't have the monopoly on dishing out the headaches,' he said and grinned. He released the pressure on Symmonds's throat and asked, 'Your boss in?'

'That depends upon whose company I have the pleasure of?' inquired Drury standing at the far end of the corridor.

'Elliott, WIA,' he offered as he reached for his ID card and moved towards Drury.

'I'm honoured,' Drury responded, 'Two visits in as many days. I delight in having guests, Mr Elliott, perhaps I should have bought a boat earlier.'

He headed into the cabin from which he had emerged. Elliott followed into a plush interior lounge which would do justice to a stately home. Clearly Drury was having *Blue Velvet* fitted out to his own tastes. Drury lowered himself on to a soft leather settee and indicated vaguely towards an armchair.

'Have you come for a chat, Mr Elliott, or are you here to arrest me?'

'You've done something I could arrest you for?' Elliott asked as he lowered himself into an armchair.

'Absolutely not,' Drury said, 'Perhaps you've come to arrest the boat?'

'I'm told you bought it fair and square,' Elliott answered.

'Do you require proof?'

'I wouldn't need to ask you for it.' Elliott studied Drury for a few moments. 'During these past few days I've had around six dead bodies on my hands, if I count cabin crew – George Bentley, Steven O'Brien, O'Brien's wife, Miguel Espachio, a pilot, maybe a stewardess or two, and assorted entourage. Now it might be that I've got a reverse Midas complex, like everything I touch turns to dust, but I don't think so.'

'I think I'm going to like you, Elliott.'

'Don't like me too much, I don't like you. So, going back to what I was talking about, if we were just to pick one name let's make it Miguel Espachio.'

Drury nodded and said, 'As you please.'

'And the nominated subject is gun running,' Elliott added.

'Are we playing charades, Mr Elliott?'

'I don't play games, Drury, that's your department.'

'I've never been a game player.'

'No, more a referee. Espachio stepped over the boundary and into your territory, and the underworld polices itself – metes out its own justice.'

'This could be an interesting conversation, Mr Elliott. Would you like a drink?'

'I'd just like to run a few ideas past you.'

Drury shrugged expansively.

'Espachio's running guns from the continent to the UK for sale to the highest bidder. O'Brien provides the transport and Bentley acts as salesman. It's a lucrative business but there's a lack of professionalism and that brings in the likes of Customs and Excise, the police, and eventually the WIA sniffing around. Upsets a lot of people who can't afford to have their affairs looked at too closely, and more particularly it upsets you,' Elliott said.

'Me?'

'Espachio isn't based in this country; he doesn't need to pay you protection or give you a share in his profits. He's going to laugh if you tell him to pay up or get out; he thinks you're just an old man who's living in the past and hasn't realised that crime's become a democracy. That was a hell of a mistake.'

'What was?' Drury asked.

'Underestimating you.'

Drury seemed to be genuinely amused and said, 'Oh, yes, Mr Elliott, I do like you. I have a great appreciation of the fertile imagination.'

'But there's still another body,' Elliott continued.

Drury looked at him quizzically.

'Mackintosh. You weren't too sure whether it was Miguel Espachio or Denver Mackintosh who was running the deals, so Mackintosh was the first to go and I'm glad I'm not going to be the one who finds that body. With Mackintosh out of the way and the dealing still going on that left Espachio.'

'Well – I've been very busy, haven't I?' Drury smiled. 'You're very amusing company,' he said, 'but Mr Elliott,' his smile faded, 'Now prove your allegations.'

'It's all guesswork, Drury, you know that as well as I do. You know I couldn't prove it if I had a million years. That's why you've got the nerve to draw attention to yourself by swanning around in exhibit bloody A, and don't give me that crap about paying a hundred and fifty-five thousand for it – I'd have to prove that whoever did for O'Brien didn't make off with the bloody draft, and nothing's going to lead me back to you, is it?' Elliott rose to his feet, still speaking, 'I hope you were serious about retiring because I'm on your case now, Drury, and if you stick around I'm going to get you. So maybe it's your turn to laugh, but before you do, remember what happened to Espachio when he underestimated you.' He made for the door and threw in a final observation, 'There's a lot to be said for retirement.'

Symmonds looked at Drury and asked, 'What do you want me to do about him?'

'Do about him?' Drury looked across. 'Nothing, Symmonds, absolutely nothing.' He rose to his feet and walked across to the small table on which a decanter stood. He refilled his glass and said, 'I don't think I care much for the new breed of felon. I certainly have no desire to become involved with the new breed of investigator.' He took a drink. 'I like this boat, Symmonds, I feel it to be a just reward for my services to sanity – I don't like guns.'

*

Kane had been under the impression that it was his task to join the observation team and watch. It seemed to be not a particularly strenuous task and he had anticipated that it would leave him with plenty of time to see the sights, particularly the more shapely ones, and so the instruction to break into Mackintosh's motel room had come as something of a surprise, not to mention an inconvenience.

Two Observation operatives accompanied him. They all hesitated outside the door of the apartment: it was usually best to give the opportunity for the door to be opened, particularly on private property. Kane rapped on the wooden panel – maybe he should shout 'room service'. There was no response so he tried again. Stepping back, he drew his gun from his pocket, and indicated to one of the Observation men who carried a heavy mallet to open the door. The mallet crashed into the lock and the door swung open.

'Aw, Jesus,' Kane exclaimed in horror, and recoiled as did the Observation men as a swarm of bloated bluebottles made their escape. The stench was overpowering.

*

'I despair of you, Elliott, I really do.' Marlborough rested his chin on his knuckles and looked at him. 'Do you have a death wish or are you just insane?' he asked.

'Probably,' Elliott said through a smile.

'How the hell you can put allegations like that to Drury and walk away with your life is beyond me. You have no proof, not one scrap of evidence, nothing but the fabrications of your imagination, and what the hell possessed you to put all of that to a man like Drury I can only put down to utter madness!'

'I wanted to be sure,' Elliott said.

'Of what!'

'That I was right. And I know I was right and he knows that he isn't that clever that I won't get him next time – but he's clever enough to know that if he'd killed me you'd have got him this time.'

Marlborough looked at him, stunned and amazed into silence.

'I wasn't unconscious, and nobody switched off my communicator. That gave you a trace; you knew exactly where I was. If I hadn't come back – somewhere between celebrating – you'd have found time to pick him up.

Elliott headed for the door, looked back directly at Marlborough, and added, 'You lose, I'm still number one.'